A LITTLE YELLOW DOG

Walter Mosley was born in Los Angeles in 1952 and now lives in New York. He is the author of four Easy Rawlins novels: *Devil in a Blue Dress*, *A Red Death*, *White Butterfly* and *Black Betty*, and a novel, *R.L.'s Dream*. He has twice been nominated for the Golden Dagger and Edgar awards and, in 1991, was awarded the John Creasey Prize for *Devil in a Blue Dress*.

A LITTLE YELLOW DOG

Walter Mosley

PICADOR

First published 1996 by W. W. Norton & Company, New York

First published in Great Britain 1996 by Serpent's Tail

This edition published 1997 by Picador
an imprint of Macmillan Publishers Ltd
25 Eccleston Place London SW1W 9NF
and Basingstoke

Associated companies throughout the world

ISBN 0 330 35283 0

9 8 7 6 5 4 3 2 1

A CIP catalogue record for this book is available
from the British Library

Typeset by Intype London Ltd
Printed in Great Britain by Mackays of Chatham plc, Chatham, Kent

It was the dog's fault.

CHAPTER 1

When I got to work that Monday morning I knew something was wrong. Mrs. Idabell Turner's car was parked in the external lot and there was a light on in her half of bungalow C.

It was six-thirty. The teachers at Sojourner Truth Junior High school never came in that early. Even the janitors who worked under me didn't show up until seven-fifteen. I was the supervising senior head custodian. It was up to me to see that everything worked right. That's why I was almost always the first one on the scene.

But not that morning.

It was November and the sky hadn't quite given up night yet. I approached the bungalow feeling a hint of dread. Images of bodies I'd stumbled upon in my street life came back to me. But I dismissed them. I was a workingman, versed in floor waxes and bleach—not blood. The only weapon I carried was a pocket knife, and it only pierced flesh when I cut the corns from my baby toe.

I knocked but nobody answered. I tried my key but the door was bolted from the inside. Then that damned dog started barking.

"Who is it?" a woman's voice called.

"It's Mr. Rawlins, Mrs. Turner. Is everything okay?"

Instead of answering she fumbled around with the bolt and then pulled the door open. The little yellow dog was yapping, standing on its spindly back legs as if he was going to attack me. But he wasn't going to do a thing. He was hiding behind her blue woolen skirt, making sure that I couldn't get at him.

"Oh, Mr. Rawlins," Mrs. Turner said in that breathy voice she had.

The adolescent boys of Sojourner Truth took her class just to hear that voice, and to see her figure—Mrs. Turner had curves that even a suit of armor couldn't hide. The male teachers at school, and the boys' vice principal, made it a point to pay their respects at her lunch table in the teachers' cafeteria each day. They didn't say much about her around me, though, because Mrs. Turner was one of the few Negro teachers at the primarily Negro school.

The white men had some dim awareness that it would have been insulting for me if I had to hear lewd comments about her.

I appreciated their reserve, but I understood what they weren't saying. Mrs. Idabell Turner was a knockout for any man—from Cro-Magnon to Jim Crow.

"That your dog?" I asked.

"Pharaoh," she said to the dog. "Quiet now. This is Mr. Rawlins. He's a friend."

When he heard my name the dog snarled and bared his teeth.

"You know dogs aren't allowed on the property, Mrs. Turner," I said. "I'm supposed—"

"Stop that, Pharaoh," Idabell Turner whined at the dog. She bent down and let him jump into her arms. "Shhh, quiet now."

She stood up, caressing her little protector. He was the size, but not the pedigree, of a Chihuahua. He settled his behind down onto the breast of her caramel-colored cashmere sweater and growled out curses in dog.

"Quiet," Mrs. Turner said. "I'm sorry, Mr. Rawlins. I wouldn't have brought him here, but I didn't have any choice. I didn't."

I could tell by the red rims of her eyelids that she'd been crying.

"Well, maybe you could leave him out in the car," I suggested.

Pharaoh growled again.

He was a smart dog.

"Oh no, I couldn't do that. I'd be worried about him suffocating out there."

"You could crack the window."

"He's so small I'd be afraid that he'd wiggle out. You

know he spends all day at home trying to find me. He loves me, Mr. Rawlins."

"I don't know what to say, Mrs.—"

"Call me Idabell," she said.

Call me fool.

Mrs. Turner had big brown eyes with fabulously long lashes. Her skin was like rich milk chocolate—dark, satiny, and smooth.

That snarling mutt started looking cute to me. I thought that it wasn't such a problem to have your dog with you. It wasn't really any kind of health threat. I reached out to make friends with him.

He tested my scent—and then bit my hand.

"Ow!"

"That's it!" Idabell shouted as if she were talking to a wayward child. "Come on!"

She took the dwarf mongrel and shoved him into the storage room that connected C2 to C1. As soon as she closed the door, Pharaoh was scratching to get back in.

"I'm sorry," she said.

"Me too. But you know that dog has got to go." I held out my hand to her. The skin was broken but it wasn't bad. "Has he had his rabies shot?"

"Oh yes, yes. Please, Mr. Rawlins." She took me by my injured hand. "Let me help."

We went to the desk at the front of the class. I sat down on the edge of her blotter while she opened the top drawer and came out with a standard teacher's first-aid box.

"You know, dog bites are comparatively pretty clean," she said. She had a bottle of iodine, a cotton ball, and a flesh-colored bandage—flesh-colored, that is, if you had pink flesh. When she dabbed the iodine on my cut I winced, but it wasn't because of the sting. That woman smelled good; clean and fresh, and sweet like the deep forest is sweet.

"It's not bad, Mr. Rawlins. And Pharaoh didn't mean it. He's just upset. He knows that Holland wants to kill him."

"Kill him? Somebody wants to kill your dog?"

"My husband." She nodded and was mostly successful in

holding back the tears. "I've been, been away for a few days. When I got back home last night, Holly went out, but when he came back he was going to . . . kill Pharaoh."

Mrs. Turner gripped my baby finger.

It's amazing how a man can feel sex anywhere on his body.

"He wants to kill your dog?" I asked in a lame attempt to use my mind, to avoid what my body was thinking.

"I waited till he was gone and then I drove here." Mrs. Turner wept quietly.

My hand decided, all by itself, to comfort her shoulder.

"Why's he so mad?" I shouldn't have asked, but my blood was moving faster than my mind.

"I don't know," she said sadly. "He made me do something, and I did it, but afterwards he was still mad." She put her shoulder against mine while I brought my other hand to rest on her side.

The thirty desks in her classroom all faced us attentively.

"Pharaoh's a smart dog," she whispered in my ear. "He knew what Holly said. He was scared."

Pharaoh whimpered out a sad note from his storage room.

Idabell leaned back against my arm and looked up. We might have been slow dancing—if there had been music and a band.

"I don't know what to do," she said. "I can't ever go back there. I can't. He's going to be in trouble and I'll be in it with him. But Pharaoh's innocent. He hasn't done anything wrong."

As she talked she leaned closer. With me sitting on the desk we were near to the same height. Our faces were almost touching.

I didn't know what she was talking about and I didn't want to know.

I'd been on good behavior for more than two years. I was out of the streets and had my job with the Los Angeles Board of Education. I took care of my kids, cashed my paychecks, stayed away from liquor.

I steered clear of the wrong women too.

Maybe I'd been a little too good. I felt an urge in that classroom, but I wasn't going to make the move.

That's when Idabell Turner kissed me.

Two years of up early and off to work dissolved like a sugar cube under the tap.

"Oh," she whispered as my lips pressed her neck. "Yes."

The tears were all gone. She looked me in the eye and worked her tongue slowly around with mine.

A deep grunt went off in my chest like an underwater explosion. It just came out of me. Her eyes opened wide as she realized how much I was moved. I stood and lifted her up on the desk. She spread her legs and pushed her chest out at me.

She said, "They'll be coming soon," and then gave me three fast kisses that said this was just the beginning.

My pants were down before I could stop myself. As I leaned forward she let out a single syllable that said, "Here I am, I've been waitin' for you, Ezekiel Porterhouse Rawlins. Take my arms, my legs, my breasts. Take everything," and I answered in the same language.

"They'll be coming soon," she said as her tongue pressed my left nipple through thin cotton. "Oh, go slow."

The clock on the wall behind her said that it was seven-oh-two. I'd come to the door at six forty-nine. Less than a quarter of an hour and I was deeply in the throes of passion.

I wanted to thank God—or his least favorite angel.

"They'll be coming soon," she said, the phonograph of her mind on a skip. "Oh, go slow."

The desks all sat at attention. Pharaoh whimpered from his cell.

"Too much," she hissed. I didn't know what she meant.

When the desk started rocking I didn't care who might walk into the room. I would have gladly given up my two years of accrued pension and my two weeks a year vacation for the few moments of ecstasy that teased and tickled about five inches below my navel.

"Mr. Rawlins!" she cried. I lifted her from the desk, not to perform some silly acrobatics but because I needed to hold her tight to my heart. I needed to let her know that this was what I'd wanted and needed for two years without knowing it.

It all came out in a groan that was so loud and long that later on, when I was alone, I got embarrassed remembering it.

I stood there holding her aloft with my eyes closed. The cool air of the room played against the back of my thighs and I felt like laughing.

I felt like sobbing too. What was wrong with me? Standing there half naked in a classroom on a weekday morning. Idabell had her arms around my neck. I didn't even feel her weight. If we were at my house I would have carried her to the bed and started over again.

"Put me down," she whispered.

I squeezed her.

"Please," she said, echoing the word in my own mind.

I put her back on the desk. We looked at each other for what seemed like a long time—slight tremors going through our bodies now and then. I couldn't bear to pull away. She had a kind of stunned look on her face.

When I leaned over to kiss her forehead I experienced a feeling that I'd known many times in my life. It was that feeling of elation before I embarked on some kind of risky venture. In the old days it was about the police and criminals and the streets of Watts and South Central L.A.

But not this time. Not again. I swallowed hard and gritted my teeth with enough force to crack stone. I'd slipped but I would not fall.

Mrs. Turner was shoving her panties into a white patent-leather purse while I zipped my pants. She smiled and went to open the door for Pharaoh.

The dog skulked in with his tail between his legs and his behind dragging on the floor. I felt somehow triumphant over that little rat dog, like I had taken his woman and made him watch it. It was an ugly feeling but, I told myself, he was just a dog.

Mrs. Turner picked Pharaoh up and held him while looking into my eyes.

I didn't want to get involved in her problems, but I could do something for her. "Maybe I can keep the dog in the hopper room in my office," I said.

"Oh," came the breathy voice. "That would be so kind. It's only until this evening. I'm going to my girlfriend's tonight. He won't be any bother. I promise."

She handed Pharaoh to me. He was trembling. At first I thought he was scared from the new environment and a strange pair of hands. But when I looked in his eyes I saw definite canine hatred. He was shaking with rage.

Mrs. Turner scratched the dog's ear and said, "Go on now, honey. Mr. Rawlins'll take care of you."

I took a step away from her and she smiled.

"I don't even know your first name," she said.

"Easy," I said. "Call me Easy."

CHAPTER 2

"Hi, Easy," EttaMae Harris greeted me in our common Texan drawl. She was an old friend who I was almost always happy to see—but not then. Etta worked with me, and the business I had just gotten through was nowhere near my job description.

She was standing outside of bungalow C. Behind her sprawled the nearly empty asphalt yard. The pavement gave off a yellowish glow in the dawn light. There were already two girls playing tetherball and a small group of boys sitting on the ninth-grade lunch court. Beyond them, at the southern end of the school yard, sat the fenced-off gardens. Up on a high grassy hill, behind me, stood the old brick buildings that housed the administration offices, library, and most of the classrooms of the school.

"Hey, Etta. How you doin'?"

She didn't answer me, just turned her gaze down toward the shivering dog in my arms.

"It's Mrs. Turner's dog. They fumigated her house and she had to bring him in with her," I said, happy that my old-time lying reflex was still intact. "I'ma put him back in the hopper room in the main office."

"Uh-huh," she said. "Yeah."

We walked across the playground, past the nine classroom bungalows, to the larger tan structure that was the maintenance building; a building that the custodians and workmen called the main office.

"Nice day," I said.

"Uh-huh," Etta replied.

She rolled back the steel-encased fire door and I followed her in. It was a large room with a long rectangular table down the middle. The cluttered table was strewn with newspapers and magazines that the janitors, carpenters, and electricians read on their union-guaranteed coffee breaks. The walls were lined with shelves that held various cleaning materials.

In the back corner stood a large ash desk where I sat every afternoon administering the laborers who kept the school running.

Behind the desk was a door that led to my personal hopper room.

I unlocked the door to the deep storage closet and tossed Pharaoh in among the steel shelves. He yelped when he hit the chilly cement floor and I felt a coldhearted satisfaction.

"I thought you couldn't have no animals not in a cage around here, Easy?" Etta asked.

"It's just a special thing, Etta. Dog'll be gone tonight."

"Uh-huh," she said for the third time.

"What's wrong wit' you?" I asked.

"All I can say is that you could take a niggah out the street but you sure cain't pull him outta his skin."

"What the hell is that s'posed t'mean?" My language got closer to the street as I got angrier.

"What you doin' moanin' an' groanin' up in that woman's classroom?"

"What you doin' sneakin' at the door?" I asked back.

If we were men it might have come to blows. But Etta-Mae was nobody I wanted to fight. She was a large woman with powerful arms and I'd been in love with her, off and on, for my entire adult life.

Before she could reply the fire door slid open and Jorge Peña walked in.

Peña was a red-colored Mexican-American who was loose-limbed, chubby, and fast with a grin. He had a deadly handsome mustache and dark eyes that laughed silently and often.

"Mr. Rawlins, Miss Harris," Peña greeted us. "How are you?"

"Jorge," Etta said, pronouncing the name in English fashion.

"Hey, Peña." I waved and went to sit down at the head of the table. I lit up the best-tasting cigarette that I'd had in a month and remembered, with a slight shock, what had happened down in bungalow C2.

Over the next fifteen minutes my whole day staff reported in. First came Garland Burns, my daytime senior custodian, a hale vegetarian from Georgia who was the only black Christian Scientist I knew. Helen Plates dragged in moaning about how tired she was. Helen was an obese blond Negro from Iowa who claimed her good health was due to the fact that she ate a whole pie every day of her life. Archie "Ace" Muldoon was right on time; he was the first white man who was ever properly in my employ. And finally, last as usual, Simona Eng appeared. She was an Italian-Chinese girl who was working her way through night school.

They were my work gang, my union brothers, my friends.

I had spent most of my adult years of hanging on by a shoestring among gangsters and gamblers, prostitutes and killers. But I never liked it. I always wanted a well-ordered working life. The Board of Education didn't pay much in the way of salary but my kids had medical insurance and I was living a life that I could be proud of.

After some coffee and laughs I gave out the special jobs from reports and requests left on my desk.

Everybody set out on their daily tasks and the special jobs I gave. The cue for them to leave was me standing up; that meant it was time to go to work.

One of the notes was a request for me to appear in the office of the principal, Hiram T. Newgate. I took the long tier of granite stairs up past the large hill of grass to the older campus. By afternoon any one of us could have taken those steps at a run, but the first time was always hard.

Idabell was coming out of the side door of the administration building when I got there.

"Hi, Easy," she said.

"Mrs. Turner," I said with emphasis.

"Easy."

"What?"

"I've got to go see about something."

"What's that?"

"Nothing important, I just have to leave the campus for a while."

"You wanna get your dog?" I asked.

"No. No, I'll be back a little later," she said. "Easy?"

"Yeah?"

"What if Holly came down here to the school and tried to pull me right out of my classroom?"

"Don't worry about that," I said. A few kind words that I meant to keep her from fretting. But Mrs. Turner heard salvation in my voice.

"Oh, thank you," she warbled.

She reached out for me but I pushed her hands down and looked around to make sure that no one saw.

"I'm sorry," she said. "It's just that I haven't met such a good man in a long time." She stood there for a moment, a kiss offered on her lips. When she saw that I wasn't going to collect right then she smiled and went slowly past.

As I watched her descend the stairs I remembered reading the words "A good man is hard to find." With somebody like Idabell Turner looking for him I could see why.

CHAPTER 3

Hiram Newgate had been principal at Sojourner Truth Junior High School for four months. In that time he had his office laid with thick maroon carpets, moved in a desk constructed from African ebony wood, and had teak shelving installed from ceiling to floor. He took the dictionary and its podium from the library and placed it in the window overlooking the coral tree that branched out over the main entrance of the school.

Principal Newgate, as he preferred to be called, always wore a dark suit with a silk tie of bold and rich colors.

"Come in, Rawlins." Newgate held up the back of his hand and waggled his fingers at me.

"Mr. Newgate," I said.

"Jacobi," he said.

"Say what?"

"That jacket. Gino Jacobi line. Astor's downtown is the only place that sells it."

He knew his clothes. I did too. Ever since I wangled my job at the Board of Ed I decided that I was going to dress like a supervisor. I'd had enough years of shabby jeans and work shirts. That day I was wearing a buff, tending toward brown, jacket that had trails of slender green and red threads wending through it. My fine cotton shirt was open at the neck. The wool of my pants was deep brown.

"Aren't you afraid to get those nice clothes dirty if you ever have to do some real work?" Newgate asked.

"You said you wanted to see me?" I replied.

Newgate had a smile that made you want to slap him.

Haughty and disdainful, the principal hated me because I wouldn't bow down to his position.

"I got a disturbing call this morning," he said.

"Oh? What about?"

Newgate's eyes actually sparkled with anticipation. "The man said that you're the one who's been stealing from the school."

Over the previous year there had been three major thefts at the school. Electric typewriters, audiovisual equipment, and musical instruments. It wasn't kids. The police thought that it was somebody who worked for the schools, because there was never any sign of a break-in—the thieves had keys.

But it wasn't just Sojourner Truth that was hit. Almost every school in the district had been robbed at least once. The police were looking for someone who had access to a set of master keys. It was someone who moved from school to school.

It certainly wasn't someone like me.

"It wasn't just a prank?" I asked.

"He knew what was stolen. He told me about the three IBM Selectrics and the gold watch out of Miranda's desk."

"He said that?"

Newgate was watching me. I was used to it. White people like to keep their eyes peeled on blacks, and vice versa. We lie to each other so much that often the only hope is to see some look or gesture that betrays the truth.

"Why do you think that he would put the blame on you, Ezekiel?" Newgate asked, at once wondering and suspicious.

"I don't know," I said honestly. But I wasn't feeling honest. I had a long history with the police—and it wasn't pleasant. The police would have been happy to investigate my activities on the nights of the crimes. They'd also wonder at how I came upon my responsible position at the school.

"You sure that you don't know anything, Ezekiel?"

"No, Hiram," I replied. I might as well have slapped him; no one called Principal Newgate by his first name.

His jaw set hard and his hands got restless.

"I just want you to know that I'm here, Rawlins. I'm weighing every piece of information. Every piece," he said.

"Okay. Let's call the police right now."

"What?"

"I said, let's call the police. That's what I'd do. When I find out about some crime I call the police. I don't have anything to hide." Bluff was all I had left.

The blood was rising under Newgate's pale skin.

"You're right, of course. It's a police matter. I didn't call you about that anyway," he said. "I wanted to talk to you about Archie Muldoon."

"What about him?" I asked.

I never liked Muldoon. The white teachers and workmen would often take him to the side and confide in him. He was always coming to me with problems that the white staff seemed more comfortable discussing with him.

A short man and balding, he was in his early fifties but wore a faded White Sox baseball cap which made him seem younger; a trick to fool people into not taking him seriously.

"I think he's being wasted down there with you scrubbing out toilets and mopping halls," Newgate was saying. "I mean, I don't understand how you made Burns the head man when you've got an obviously more experienced man like Archie."

"Being young doesn't mean you're not experienced, Mr. Newgate."

"Anyway," he said, dismissing my words, "at least you could cut Archie loose and let him come up here to work with me. You know you're, um, so, uh, busy that you're sometimes slow reacting to my requests."

He said more but I stopped listening. I was thinking about how I'd often catch Muldoon staring at me over the coffee-break table, or from across the yard. It was a piercing stare. A white man's stare that set off an alarm in my southern heart.

Maybe it was Archie who called in blaming me for a thief.

"Mr. Newgate," I said, interrupting whatever it was that

he was saying, "you're the boss of the school. You call the shots. I mean, if you see a problem you come to me and I'm supposed to take care of it. If I don't perform to your expectations, then you call the area office to complain—that's what it says in the rule book. That's how it works."

"It would be better if you tried to work with me, Mr. Rawlins," he said. "I came to this school to straighten things out."

"Oh? I thought it was because Mrs. Jimenez had a stroke and the three people higher than you on the eligible list didn't want the job." I had been a fool with Mrs. Turner and I kept it up with Mr. Newgate.

"Will you let me have Archie?"

"No," I said.

"I want you to reconsider, Mr. Rawlins."

"Mr. Muldoon works for me. Any jobs you need done will come through me. Me or Mr. Burns." It felt good to be standing up for myself. Too good. It's amazing how ten minutes with a woman can turn you silly.

"This isn't over," Newgate said.

"I have to go."

I left the principal to make my rounds of the plant.

The school, like Los Angeles, was a hodgepodge of this and that, old and new. It was once a series of brick buildings at the top of a hill named after President Polk and populated with Irish, Italian, and Jewish kids—all of them working-class or poor. There had been a large empty plot of land down the hill that the school used for a garden. When the population changed, and grew, most of the plot had been paved over. The garden shrank but it was still the size of half a city block. Bungalows were moved in to accommodate the larger student body and the school was renamed. Sojourner Truth; evangelist, suffragette, abolitionist, and—by her own account—a woman who spoke personally with God. By that time the neighborhood was primarily black but there were Mexicans and Asians too. That was still back in the days when all dark people were the same color.

It would have been a fertile ground for a teacher like Miss Truth. But she was dead and her name meant no more to the students, teachers, or parents than did that of President Polk.

My day went on at a natural pace.

A toilet exploded with the help of a quarter stick of dynamite; probably the doing of Brad Parkerhouse, our resident bad boy. Jorge and Simona disappeared for a while but by the time I got to search for them Jorge pretended that he'd been looking for me to ask if we needed to restock the outside johns with toilet paper. There was a pigeon infestation along the gutters of the older buildings and I had to direct the exterminators where it was safe to lay their bait.

Every now and then Idabell crossed my mind. I wondered who might have blamed me for stealing from the school. But mostly I went about my job like half a million other working men and women in the L.A. basin.

There's a routine wherever you find people; even in a condemned man's cell. I missed lunch but made it back to the main office by one-thirty to make sure that my people had finished their midday break and were off at work.

EttaMae was the only one there.

"Hi, Easy," she said.

"You not mad anymore, Etta?"

"I wasn't mad in the first place. Maybe disgusted. Maybe I was worried about you jeopardizin' your job. But I wasn't mad."

"Okay. What you doin' still here?"

"It's Raymond. I got to go get him."

I could live to a hundred and still the mention of that name would send a chill down my spine.

"He sick?"

"Naw. The other car broke down an' he cain't get in here."

"He stuck out there at the house?" I asked.

"Uh-huh. You mind if I go get him?"

"Yeah, I mind. You go back to work, Etta. I'll go an' get Mouse."

Etta smiled. "You always did look after Raymond," she said.

CHAPTER 4

It felt good to be headed down toward Compton. EttaMae lived there with her son, LaMarque, and, sometimes, with his father—Raymond "Mouse" Alexander.

They were together again in the early sixties. Mouse had a change of heart there for a while and wanted to be a family man, a married man.

The change came about late in '61. Sweet William Dokes had moved to L.A. from Jenkins, Texas. Sweet William was a barber and a guitar player, somewhere in his sixties. He was a dapper man who had taught Mouse everything about good dress and conduct with the ladies.

Mouse took his own slant on what William had to say and left broken hearts, broken heads, and more dead bodies than anyone knew throughout Texas and southern California.

Mouse was an old-time gangster. A tough who could work with you or go it alone. He wasn't afraid of prison or death, and that made him the kind of man that people left alone. Even the police didn't come after Raymond unless they were sure they had something on him.

The first man he killed was his stepfather, daddyReese Corn. Some years later he killed his stepbrother, Navrochet, in a back-alley duel.

Over the years many of my friends have asked me how I could be close with a man like Mouse. A man who was a cold-blooded killer.

I never tried to explain. How could I? In the hard life of

the streets you needed somebody like Mouse at your back. I didn't have a mother or father, or close family or church. All I had was my friends. And among them Mouse packed the largest caliber and the hardest of rock-hard wills.

When Sweet William came to town he and Mouse took to the streets together. They plied the pool halls and whorehouses; they gambled and drank deep. William always had his blues guitar with him and because of that they were welcome in almost every door.

People commented on how much they resembled each other. Both had slight builds and long-fingered hands. You would have sworn that they were related and not just good friends.

Raymond treated William like a father and a friend. They lived together and shared the same women. For six months William and Mouse were joined at the hip. And wherever they showed up there was a party going on.

I hadn't seen much of them because I was sick for a while and then I went to work at the school. Mouse and William didn't wake up until the afternoon; by the time they were out on the town I was already in my bed.

So I was a little surprised one day when I got home to find Raymond with my adopted children, Jesus and Feather. Mouse sat solemnly in my favorite sofa chair while Feather offered him a glass of green Kool-Aid. Jesus was sitting at the dining table doing his homework. He was a freshman in high school and, even though he could talk by then, Jesus was still a very quiet boy.

"Raymond, what you doin' here?" I asked.

"Let's take a ride, Easy," he said. He stood up, ignoring the glass that five-year-old Feather proffered. Like all females she was in love with him.

"Okay," I said. I could see that he meant business.

"Don't you want your Kool-Aid, Uncle Raymond?" Feather asked.

I knelt down and kissed my little girl's light brown face. "Put it in the icebox till he comes back, baby," I said. "We got to talk about something right now."

We went out to my Pontiac and we drove off. I took a southeastern route because, like I said, that was the 1960s and black men couldn't take a leisurely drive in white Los Angeles without having the cops wanting to know what was going on.

"It's all 'cause'a my dick, Easy," Mouse said.

It worried me to hear his words because they indicated that Mouse had been thinking—he was always his deadliest when circumstances forced him to use his mind.

"What's that, Raymond?"

"You know I got me a big dick," Mouse answered. "That's a fact. I don't know what the girls think about it but you know I like it just fine."

I was impatient but with Raymond you had to let the story unwind. He couldn't be rushed, so I concentrated on the white line.

"I mean, sometime it might be saggin' a little but I could always get the mothahfuckah hard." He slapped his steely finger against the dashboard. "You know Tisha?"

"Lawrence?"

"Naw, Burnett. Live over in the Russell projects."

"I don't think so."

"She work for John, waitress over there. Sour-faced bitch, but she fine, an' she know it too."

"What about her?"

"I'ont know, Easy. I'ont know what happened. We was drinkin' red wine. Maybe that's it. But my dick was hangin' down just like a goddam water hose. An' you know Tisha didn't like that at all. She say I'm a faggot and a punk. She said to get outta her house 'cause she need a man who could get hard for her."

"An' what you do?" I asked. I asked because he was my friend—but I really didn't want to know.

"I went down to my house and started drinkin'. I was mad. Mad at my own goddam dick. When I got up it was early in the mornin', 'bout four. I don't know what got into me, Easy. I started talkin' to myself like I was crazy. Talkin' 'bout Tisha. And the more I talk the madder

I get. Before you know it I'm out in my car headed for the projects."

We were driving down Hauser. It was a sunny day, I remember. But the shadows seemed darker than usual. The people, out in front of their houses, looked grim.

"I pult up in front'a the projects; I was gonna get that bitch out the bed. You cain't talk to me like that an' get away wit' it. Shit. For all I knew she got on the phone after I was gone an' told ev'rybody." Mouse stopped and stared angrily out at the street.

When we pulled up to a red light I turned and asked, "What did you do?"

"William was comin' outta the courtyard when I drove up. He was walking' across the street to his car but when he see me he smile an' grab on his thing. 'Hey, Raymond,' he say. 'You sure right, man. That Tisha's like satin.' Like satin."

The car behind us honked and I looked up to see that the light was green. I drove across the street and parked at the curb. I couldn't stand the tension of driving and listening to that story at the same time.

"I didn't mean to hit him," Raymond said. "You know that woman didn't mean a damn thing t'me. When William hit the ground I knew I was wrong. I was gonna say I was sorry. I was gonna buy him a drink—but he went for his gun, Easy. I swear he did."

No more had to be said. I knew that Sweet William Dokes's corpse was laid out on a slab somewhere.

"Cops picked me up at the house an' took me down to jail this mornin', but they didn't give fuck. They knew we'd been runnin' together. One of 'em hit me a couple'a times an' when I didn't break down they let me go."

Raymond was crying. Not blubbering or shaking, but there were real tears in his eyes. I had never seen him even sad over anything he'd done. Seeing him cry brought tears uncontrollably to my own eyes.

I didn't know what to say.

Maybe just sitting there is what changed him. Maybe

being in my company, coming from my house, he got the idea to go straight.

We sat there at the curb until sunset. The skies turned a black-tinged orange. We sat silently. I was thinking that my new life as a workingman was a good idea.

As it turned out Mouse was thinking the same thing.

When the streetlamps came on I drove us back to my house. Mouse didn't come in. He got in his car and drove out to EttaMae, his ex-wife and soon to be wife-again.

Etta called me the next day. She wanted jobs for both her and Raymond at the Board of Education. It was easy to get her in. She was a hard worker and had a clean work record.

The only job Raymond had ever held was making license plates at the state prison at Chino while doing five years for manslaughter.

But I was good at making things happen. I got Raymond a job as janitor under my supervision. And, so far, he did it just fine.

Southeast L.A. was palm trees and poverty; neat little lawns tended by the descendants of ex-slaves and massacred Indians. It was beautiful and wild; a place that was almost a nation, populated by lost peoples that were never talked about in the newspapers or seen on the TV. You might have read about freedom marchers; you might have heard about a botched liquor store robbery (if a white man was injured)—but you never heard about Tommy Jones growing the biggest roses in the world or how Fiona Roberts saved her neighbor by facing off three armed men with only the spirit of her God to guide her.

Etta lived in a small house that was by itself on a large lot. She had fruit trees and a large garden. There was a tan Ford parked on the lawn.

Raymond Alexander, wearing a soft gray work shirt and matching pants, was looking under the hood. He didn't get down in it but merely looked from a safe distance. Mouse might have changed but he wasn't ever going to get dirty if he didn't have to.

"Mouse," I said from my open window.

"I think it's the generator, man. Battery spark just fine," he said, not even looking in my direction.

"Jump in," I told him. "I'll take you to work."

We took the long way back. I stopped by my Magnolia Street apartment building, and a smaller place I owned on Denker. I was still in the real estate business in a small way. But I no longer dreamed of making a fortune on speculation.

We didn't even get out of the car. I just wanted to see the places.

Raymond sat next to me, quiet and thoughtful. He drew his right knee up to his chin and smoked a Chesterfield. He reminded me of a man sitting in a solitary cell. There was nothing to complain about because there was no one who could hear him.

"You ever go to church, Easy?" Mouse asked when we were about a mile from Sojourner Truth.

"I been in one or two, even on a Sunday sometimes, but I don't think you could say that I ever properly went to church, not since I've been a man."

"Oh. Uh-huh."

"You thinkin'a goin' to church, Ray?"

"I don't know."

That was a long talk for us at the time.

CHAPTER 5

There were at least sixteen police cars parked around the entrance gate of the new school yard. As I approached the external parking lot a uniformed cop stepped out and put up his hand to stop me.

"You'll have to turn around," the young white cop told me.

"What happened here?"

"You'll have to turn around now." There was no give in his voice.

"I'm the head custodian at the school, officer," I said. "Mr. Rawlins."

"You have keys to the buildings in the garden?"

"Yes I do."

"Then pull around here. Go up to the garden gate and ask for Sergeant Sanchez."

I turned to Raymond and said, "You better head over to the main office."

"Huh?" Mouse seemed unaware of the police activity around us.

"Go on and get ready to start your shift." I didn't want Raymond to be anywhere around the cops if a serious crime had been committed. Ex-convicts make the best suspects.

"Okay, man," Raymond said. He got out of the car and made his way slowly across the asphalt yard. Mouse might have changed, but he certainly wasn't what anybody would call normal. I don't think you would have gotten a rise out of him if the Russians dropped the bomb on New York City.

I drove a little way up the block and parked in front of the school's garden gate.

Two uniforms stopped me there. I identified myself and asked for the sergeant. They pointed out a man standing between two large lemon bushes at the front of the glass-walled garden classroom. He was a tall, weedy man wearing a cheap gray suit with no tie. Mexican definitely, dark Mexican. He was talking to Jorge. I could tell by the way Jorge held his head that they were speaking in Spanish.

When I approached, Sanchez gave me a hard look.

"This is Mr. Rawlins, sergeant," Jorge said. And to me, "Sergeant Sanchez."

"What's goin' on?" I asked.

There was a start of recognition in the policeman's eyes; recognition that was quickly replaced by suspicion. Sanchez twisted his head toward a stand of bamboo that

Wayne Ito, the gardener, kept toward the back of the gardening plots. I followed him and Jorge as they pushed through the long stalks.

On the other side of the bamboo wall stood Hiram Newgate and the gardening teacher, Mr. Glenn. There were also eight cops—in and out of uniform. Laid out on the ground in front of them was the handsomest corpse I'd ever seen. A tall man in brown tweed with curly dark hair that had been oiled. His shoes were fine-crafted snakeskin and his hands were held up over his head in a feminine pose. I didn't think he was a white man; his skin was dark olive and his nose was wider than most Caucasian's. I wasn't claiming him for a Negro either. His racial roots could have been from at least four continents, or a thousand islands around the world.

His left temple was concave and deeply discolored. His eyes were rolled up to the top of his head but, too late, they had seen truth.

"Who is he?" I asked, turning to Sergeant Sanchez. I found him studying me.

"Is the gate here usually locked?" he asked without a trace of an accent. There was an education in his diction; a hard-earned learning that came from the late-night interrogations of used and battered textbooks.

"Always," I said. "Unless there's an afternoon class going on."

"Nobody saw him come in." The sergeant seemed to be challenging me. "He didn't sleep here."

There wasn't anything for me to say.

"Do you recognize him, Mr. Rawlins? Have you ever seen him around here?" Sanchez was taking me in. Maybe he could smell the residue of the street on me.

He'd gag if he ever got a whiff of Mouse.

"Does he look like somebody who'd be here?" Newgate demanded. "He's obviously a thief or a crook who was killed and dropped here. Listen, sergeant, we're going to have to try and keep the children away from here. I have to go organize the teachers. So I hope you don't mind if I leave."

"You can go," Sanchez said. "But I'll need Mr. Rawlins

and Mr. Glenn. I'll need you men to help us look around here. You might see something out of the ordinary that we'd miss."

"I'll get Simona," Jorge said.

"Where is Simona?" I wanted to know.

"We took her in the classroom, Mr. Rawlins. It was me and her found the body. She took it kinda bad, you know."

"Okay." Sergeant Sanchez stuck out his bottom lip and nodded. He was very sure of himself. I've always been afraid of self-confident cops.

"I'd like to see her too," I said.

"Make it fast, Mr. Rawlins. I want to get this investigation going."

The garden course at Sojourner Truth consisted of Mr. Glenn's afternoon lectures on seeds and zygotes and then going out to the garden plot where the students learned to plant and grow radishes. Mr. Glenn, who had majored in botanic biology at UCLA, gave his lectures in a glass-encased room that smelled of earth. There were no desks in the classroom, because the students were graded on a verbal quiz, given one on one, and on the health of their seedlings. The only furniture in the room, other than Mr. Glenn's high metal desk, was four long benches where the students met for roll call before rushing out to the soil.

Miss Eng was sitting, head bowed and alone, on one of those benches. She was crying and holding one finger at the center of her forehead, her eyes still seeing that well-dressed corpse.

Jorge sat down and put his arm around her shoulders. He whispered something, and she rose. She looked at me and smiled, but there was no mirth in her heart.

"I never saw a dead man before," she said.

"I better take her home, Mr. Rawlins. I don't think she should drive." Jorge was looking a little green himself.

"All right. We're not gonna get much work done around here today anyway. You take care of yourself, Simona, you hear?"

She smiled again and let Jorge lead her away. I lingered

a moment after they were gone. The empty room felt safe.
I didn't want to go back out to the police and that corpse; I
was anxious but I had no reason to be. Still, I hung back
checking to see that the floor had been properly swept and
that the trash cans were empty.

Then I took a deep breath and went out to Mr. Glenn
and the cops.

I went with them around the compound while Sanchez
asked questions.

"You get many break-ins?"

"Not too many. Lately somebody got into the music room
and took about a thousand dollars' worth of horns."

"I mean in the gardening compound," he said.

"Oh, yeah." I was offhanded. "The boys like to prove that
they could climb a twelve-foot wire gate now and then.
Once they get in they like to look around a little."

"Why don't you put barbed wire up top?"

"Why should I? They hardly ever break anything and
the only thing they could steal is some vegetables." I was
bothered by the murder but all I wanted was for the
sergeant to take the body away so that I could get back to
work.

"How do you explain this?" he asked.

We'd come upon a slender toolshed that was used by the
children to house the spades, hoes, and pitchforks when
they were hand-weeding or harvesting.

There was a yard-deep hole dug near the shed. Next to
the excavation was a small traveling chest that was caked
with dirt. There was a canvas sack in the chest that seemed
to be full but I couldn't guess at what it held.

"I don't know," I said, answering the sergeant's question.

"Looks like a hole," one of the cops surmised.

"You don't know anything about this?" Sanchez asked
both me and Glenn.

A plainclothes cop was squatting by a shovel that lay
near the mound of mud next to the hole. There was a deep
dent in the scoop.

"I sure don't know," Mr. Glenn said.

I suppressed the "Me neither" that was in my mouth.

"Don't you think you should?" Sanchez asked me just as if I had uttered my denial.

I didn't have an answer for him.

"Do you have keys to the garden gate?" he asked us both.

"Of course I do," said Mr. Glenn. In his brown suit and vest he resembled a limp football, with a hard dome of a forehead under a thatch of unruly brown hair.

"What do you mean?" I asked Sanchez.

"Do you have a key to the garden gate?" He spoke slowly, as if to a small child or an idiot.

"Naw, man," I said. "I mean, why would you think that the killer had a key?"

I sounded smart—too smart. I showed that I knew what the cop was thinking. It was a mistake that I'd never made in the street.

Sanchez gave me an hard look and then said, "The gate was locked when your janitors got here, and there's not a scuff on those fancy shoes. Somebody had a key."

"Lots of people do," I said. "The principal, my janitors, I do, Mr. Glenn does. There's a set of master keys hanging up in my hopper room down in the maintenance office. Even the district gardeners have a set for when they drop by."

Sanchez had his eyes on me.

"Anybody here last night?" he asked. "About four or five in the morning?"

"Not s'posed t'be. Nobody works on Sunday, and nobody works that late anyway." Idabell Turner flitted across my mind but I turned my thoughts back to Sanchez's questions.

"Where were you when the body was found, Mr. Rawlins?"

"I went to pick up one of my men. His car broke down and he needed a ride."

"You always give taxi service to your janitors?"

"He's my night man. If I don't have a night man we won't be ready for the morning. The hour or so gets paid back with a full night's work. Anyway, I took my lunchtime to do it."

Sanchez just stared. He was a living lie detector.

I was a living lie.

"You two can go now," he said. "Mr. Rawlins, tell your people that I'll be around either this afternoon or tomorrow morning. I'll need to talk to each one of them."

"Will do," I said. I wanted to cooperate. I wanted to do my duty. I didn't have anything to do with that man's death. But the way Sanchez looked at me made me feel guilty—maybe he could smell something that I had yet to sense.

CHAPTER 6

"What is it, Easy?" Etta asked me at the main office. She was there with Raymond. It wasn't his shift yet and he was waiting for three o'clock to come. He was smoking another Chesterfield and staring off into space. Maybe he was still thinking about church.

"They found a body out in the garden."

"Murdered?"

"Uh-huh. He had his head caved in out behind Mr. Ito's bamboo."

Raymond looked at me but he didn't say anything.

"Did Simona find'im?" Etta asked.

"Her and Jorge."

"Uh, uh, uh," she grunted, swiveling her head for each syllable. "You shoulda had me out there, Easy. You know that young girl don't know nuthin' about the dead."

I shrugged and went to sit down at my desk. I was worried that an investigation by Sanchez might cause trouble for me. I hadn't gotten my job through the regular channels, and Mouse had come in on my recommendation. If Sanchez suspected either of us he would go to Newgate to ask why he had people like us on the payroll—and

Newgate would have loved nothing better than to see me fired.

There was a foul odor in the air.

"Who was it, Easy?" Etta asked.

"I don't know. Light-colored man. Not white. Maybe Negro, maybe not. Tall, nice suit. His hair was oiled so I don't know what it was like really."

"Colored like a deep tan?" Etta inquired.

"Yeah."

"Kinda thin? With a lean-like face but he got some nose too?"

"You know him, Etta?"

"Sound like your girlfriend's husband to me."

At that moment I identified the scent in the air. "You said what?"

"'Bout two months ago, at the beginnin' of the semester, her car was broke down and he had to pick her up an' let her off. Light-complected guy, tall, straightened hair. He kinda looked like somebody from Hawaii or sumpin' only his eyes was different."

"Damn!" I stood up out of the chair.

"Where you goin', Easy?" Mouse asked me.

"I got to check this shit out," I said.

"Roger! Roger! Return to your seat," Miss Falana was yelling at the McHenry boy. The flat-faced kid grinned and looked around him as if her words were arrows that had missed their mark.

But when I said, "Miss Falana," Roger dove for his chair. He knew me from the yard.

The librarian gave me an exhausted and exasperated smile. "Mr. Rawlins," she sighed.

"Where's Mrs. Turner?"

The little woman wagged her hands in a beckoning gesture that made her look like a chubby chipmunk.

When I came over to her she whispered, "Mrs. Turner's dog got hit by a car this morning. She rushed out to take him to the vet."

"What time was that?" I asked in a regular voice.

She put her hands over her lips to show me, in sign language, that the children shouldn't hear us. It was a conspiracy of most of the teachers to pretend that they didn't have private lives.

"She left before first period. She got a call from her neighbor. It was terrible because we couldn't get a substitute from downtown, so everybody has had to pitch in. You know I can't handle these problem kids, not like her."

Miss Falana didn't like the way men and boys looked at Idabell. She thought that looking like the math teacher did was somehow unprofessional.

I thanked Miss Falana and left.

Before the door closed I heard her shouting, "Roger McHenry, return to your seat!"

I ran into Etta outside of the maintenance office.

"What you gonna do about that dog mess?" she asked, referring to the smell that was coming from my hopper room.

"Etta," I said, "I'm gonna head outta here. Listen. Don't say anything about that dog, all right?"

"I ain't gonna say nuthin'. But what about that mess?"

"Etta . . ."

"No." She shook her head; her face was set and hard.

Mouse had left and the office was empty. I figured cleaning up dog-do wouldn't take over a minute. But when I opened the hopper-room door I thought that Pharaoh must have had prunes for his breakfast.

It took a mop and bucket with ammonia solution to clean up that room. The dog had gone everywhere. Anything that was paper near the floor had to be thrown away. He had crawled up under the steel shelving and made a mess that took over twenty minutes of frantic cleaning.

I wanted to keep the dog a secret, and Pharaoh understood my plight. He sat back on his tail and laughed at me. He had on a dog grin with his pointy tongue lapping up my misery.

I understood why the dead man had wanted to kill

Pharaoh. I was close to it myself. Instead I threw the mutt in a burlap sack that I'd been keeping for rags.

I know it sounds mean to treat a dumb animal like that. And I can't say that I didn't get a certain amount of pleasure out of his discomfort. But I had to do him like that. If somebody saw me in the yard with Idabell's dog it could have caused trouble. That dog was her alibi for something. And I didn't want to cause her any grief if I didn't have to.

CHAPTER 7

Many men would have drowned Pharaoh right then. He was no good to anybody. But I had lived a dog's life and knew what it was to have the big world turn against you.

I drove about ten blocks from the school and then let Pharaoh out of his bag.

At least he wasn't grinning at me anymore.

I took surface streets out of Watts, back toward West Los Angeles and my home. I was trying to live the quiet life with my kids back then, away from the people and problems that I knew during my earlier years in L.A.

It was a nice house. Three small bedrooms and a kitchen that looked out on a bright green lawn. I had rose bushes and dahlias along the back fence and no fence against the southern yard; there I just let my neighbor's wild ferns and bamboo do the job.

"Daddy! Daddy!" Feather yelled as I came through the door.

Pharaoh leaped out of my arms and went straight for her.

"Watch out!" I shouted. But I didn't have to worry. Pharaoh jumped up into Feather's arms and started licking

her face. She laughed and giggled. Pharaoh jumped away
from her and then leapt back into her arms—then he
jumped away again. It was like they had been playmates
for years.

"Daddy, thank you," Feather said. "He's beautiful."

"We're not keepin' him, honey," I said. Feather's instant
frown made me dislike that dog even more. "He's only
gonna stay a day or two. I told my friend that you'd want
to take care of him."

"What's his name?"

"Angina."

"What?"

"Angina. It's a French name," I said. "Means a pain in
my heart. Where's your brother?"

"He went out with Eddie to the store."

Jesus was supposed to stay with Feather until I got
home from work. That was his job.

Feather didn't look anything like me, and Jesus did even
less. They were both pickup children that I'd managed to
save during the years when my employer was the street.
She was seven then with crinkled golden hair and café-
au-lait skin. Her eyes were like topaz at that time but they
had been changing color over the years. Jesus had made
her braids like the horns of a ewe going back and following
the curve of her skull.

She had on a green dress that she'd picked out herself,
with a puffy pink sweater.

"I love you," I said.

When I picked her up the dog started barking. She was
staring down at him, and I kissed her chubby cheek. I felt
something wadded up in her shallow sweater pocket.

"What's this?" I asked, fingering the lump.

Feather's expression said, Uh-oh.

In the floppy open pocket was a fold of six or seven
twenty-dollar bills.

"Where'd you get this money, honey?"

"U'm. I dunno. I fount it."

When I put Feather down, Pharaoh jumped up between
us, barking at me and then turning to lick her fingertips.

"Honey, where did you get this money?"

"In a place."

"What place?"

"In Juice room."

Nobody wanted to use the Lord's name in vain, so Jesus became Juice at Hamilton High School.

Feather led me to a corner in Juice's closet where there was a cardboard chest that used to hold hundreds of little plastic soldiers. But the soldiers had all died or gone AWOL and in their place were neat stacks of different denominations of bills from one to twenty. Four hundred and eighty-nine dollars in all.

"It's Juice treasure chest," Feather said. "But it's a secret, okay?"

I sat down on the floor. Pharaoh was growling at my elbow. There was too much money there to hope that he would get away from court with a warning.

"Daddy?"

"Yeah, honey?"

"Can I go downstairs and feed Frenchie?"

She'd already given the damn dog her own name.

I went outside to have a cigarette and wait for my boy. He was lucky that he stayed away. In the mood I was in I might have struck him—and that was something I swore I'd never do.

My next-door neighbor, Mrs. Horn, came home before Jesus did. She was a skinny and nervous woman from white Christian California stock. Still, I never found any reason to distrust or dislike her.

"Hi, Mr. Rawlins," she said.

I went over to help her with her bag of groceries.

"Jesus is out, Mrs. Horn," I said. "And I got an appointment to keep."

"That's okay. You go on. I'll come over and look after Feather. You know she's just a darling little girl. I really love her."

I'm sure she did.

Before I went down to my car I said, "U'm, when Jesus

gets here, please tell him not to go anywhere and wait for me."

Mrs. Horn gave me a second look; she could hear the threat in my words.

The ride back to Sojourner Truth was quick. I got there just a little before six. Everyone from the administration building had gone home. I used my keys to get into the office. There I opened the key closet where they kept the keys to the personnel files drawer.

Turner was her maiden name even though she called herself "Mrs." Her husband's name was Holland Gasteau.

She was thirty-two years old and had been born in French Guiana but had immigrated to America when she was four years old. I unlocked the phone plug on the rotary and dialed the Turner-Gasteau residence. I let it ring fifteen times before hanging up. I redialed but still no one answered.

I wrote down her Butler Place address, a street above Hollywood Boulevard, and also the address and phone number of a Miss B. Shay who was given as someone to get in touch with in case of an emergency.

I didn't know for a fact that the handsome dead man was Idabell's husband, but I knew that she was in trouble and that she'd lied about the dog.

Coming out of the administration building I ran into Sergeant Sanchez. A lock of his longish black hair had trailed down onto his forehead.

"Working late, aren't you, Mr. Rawlins?"

"How's the investigation going?" I replied.

He didn't like my answer. He didn't like my clothes or the way I walked. If we'd worked side by side on a road gang, swinging sixteen-pound hammers, he wouldn't have liked the way that I smelled.

"You find out his name yet?" I was actually sweating under his gaze.

"Where's your night man?" Sanchez asked.

"I don't know. Mr. Alexander follows his own schedule.

All I care about is that the work is done when I come in
in the morning."

"And is it always done?"

"He's a good worker."

"Mr. Newgate says that there's been some property missing from the school over the last year. TVs, musical instruments." Sanchez the fisherman.

The only thing I was sure of about the thefts was that
Mouse hadn't been involved. Mouse would never have
wasted his time with petty theft. But I couldn't tell Sanchez that.

"You have a little time to walk me around the grounds
to find your night man?" Sanchez asked.

"No. I got to make dinner for my kids."

A frown knitted itself into the policeman's brow. "You
married?"

Of course, I thought, he'd read my files.

"No," I said. "I mean, I was. But things didn't work out."

"And she left you with the kids?"

I could feel my heart swell in fear. Neither Jesus nor
Feather was legally mine. I had gotten Jesus the papers
of a child that had died in infancy, but his real story was
worse than most orphans. He'd been sold as a child prosti-
tute when he was about two and had probably come from
Mexico, or maybe even from further down south.

There was no birth certificate for Feather at all. If the
sergeant started looking into my private life everything
could have fallen apart.

"Any more questions?" I asked him.

He shook his head but it was more disapproval than an
answer to my question.

"Don't you find it strange that someone would come into
the school to hide something, Mr. Rawlins?" Sanchez asked.
"I mean, why, how would they even know to do it?"

I wanted Sanchez to see me as an honest and hard
worker. So I asked, "What was it they were hiding?" not
because I cared or wanted to know but because I thought
that that was the kind of question an honest man would
ask.

"That's police business," he said. "Why don't you answer my question?"

"No," I said. "I don't understand it. But I figure that if you want to do some late-night larceny the garden is the perfect place for it. You can't see the lights on in the garden building because it's surrounded by trees and bushes."

"Oh?" he said speculatively. "And how would somebody know that?"

"Well," I said, still the stuttering honest man, "I mean, the custodians know 'cause you can't just look over there and see. You got to walk over there, open the gate, and go down behind the trees to tell."

"I see," he said.

I was beginning to dislike Sanchez as much as I did Mrs. Turner's dog.

"Why don't we take a walk and look for your night man?" Sanchez asked again.

"I told you. I got to get home to my kids."

"It'll just take a little while. We could answer some important questions."

"That's your job, sergeant," I said. "My job is at home."

He shook his head again.

"Excuse me," I said. And then I turned my back on him.

CHAPTER 8

Night had come by the time I reached 1646 Butler Place. Butler was on a hill so steep that I had to turn my front wheel into the curb to help the parking brake.

The small house basked in the dim glow of a granite post streetlamp. It was surfaced in corroding light-colored plaster and surrounded by stands of bird-of-paradise plants. There was a small tree that took up what little yard there was; it had dark berrylike fruit hanging from it. I didn't know what kind of tree it was, but that was no surprise. There was almost every kind of plant in the world growing on the city streets. L.A. is a desert pumped full of water. A haven for plant life, but if anybody ever turns off the tap, ninety-nine percent of the life down here would wither.

There was a light on in the house and a dark '58 Thunderbird in the driveway. The porch was unlighted and I stood there in front of the door for a good minute before ringing the bell.

I stood waiting on that cool step because I wanted to control my temper. I should have told Sanchez about the dog; if he had been friendly I probably would have. But that cop could have looked into my business; my job history, my kids. And just by looking he could have destroyed all that I had built. I blamed Idabell for that. Leaving her damn dog with me and then lying about his accident. I was an accomplice to something and I wasn't even sure what.

Nobody answered on the first ring, or the second. I put my ear to the door after five tries; not a sound. The doorknob didn't turn. The window, hidden by the secret berry tree, was locked.

I could have gone home then—I should have. But the street had been calling me all day long. I had been seduced, hoodwinked, and blamed for a thief; I'd been bullied and looked at like a crook instead of an honest man. I could have gone home but I knew that I wouldn't be able to sleep.

The side driveway consisted of two slender paths of concrete laid to accommodate the wheels of a car. Spare grass sprouted here and there in the trail of dirt that passed in between the cement tracks.

The backyard was dark and overgrown with shrubs and vines. Anything could have happened back there in the dark. I was no longer in the law-abiding workaday world. I was alone, hanging by a thread again.

The back door wasn't open but the sliding window was. I slipped my hand in and twisted the knob.

The back porch housed an old-time washing machine. A

big barrel-shaped thing that had a chrome arch over the top. There were clothes that had been left in the washer for days; they had begun to mildew.

I went from there into an unlit kitchen. Even in the dark I could see the mess. Dirty dishes piled everywhere, the stench of garbage. I could feel grit on the floor through the soles of my shoes.

The dining room held a faint glow from the light of the room beyond it.

I froze there next to the maple table when I saw two shod feet in the next room. They were the feet of a man reclining on his sofa chair.

I don't know how long I stood there; thinking about walking backwards, thinking about calling out or maybe just walking in on him. I looked around for a bludgeon to use if he came at me but there were only fragile teacups on the table.

Finally, without thinking about it, I walked right in.

I wasn't thinking but my fists were tight and my hips could have taken me in any direction I chose.

I thought I was ready for anything, but the dead man lying on the plaid chair almost took me out of my skin. How could it be? Somebody took him from behind the stand of bamboo at Sojourner Truth? No. From the police morgue? No. Sanchez?

The body laid out on the chair was the same one I had seen earlier. Same tweed suit, same snakeskin shoes, same olive skin and oily hair.

"Damn!" I said loudly. "Damn!" I had a sinking feeling in my groin and there was sweat at the back of my neck. It was a fear from way back in my boyhood days in Louisiana. I remember thinking that if he got up from that chair I would have run all the way to the ocean.

But then my rational mind kicked in. This man had blood down his chest. He was stabbed or, more probably, shot in the heart. His temple was unmarked. And this man's eyes were closed.

Also he bore a big, dark red kiss on his cheek.

A goodbye kiss.

*

I wanted to run but instead I forced myself to stay and look around. The blood was dry. The man laid out in the chilly room had been dead for many hours. He could spare a few minutes more.

I scanned the disheveled room but nothing registered. My breath was coming in gasps and, for the second time that day, my heart was playing the drums.

I forced myself to stare at the low coffee table that was off to the corpse's left. There lay a crumpled pack of Salems, a plate completely filled with the red shells of pistachio nuts, a nearly empty fifth of Gilbey's gin, a single glass, and a black-bladed knife. The knife was curved like a boomerang, the inner curve sharpened for hacking away thick vegetation.

The glass was hand-blown and had a thick green base.

He hadn't finished his last drink.

The bedroom was a mess too. I remembered that Idabell said she'd been away. Holland, I supposed, was one of those men who expected women to clean up after them. There was a week's worth of socks, underwear, and trousers on the floor. The bedclothes were piled up at the head of the bed. Four squashed down pillows had been stacked in the middle of the mattress. There were also a few drops of dried blood near the foot of the bed, near the pillows.

There had been two suitcases in the corner of the large walk-in closet. But one had been removed, leaving a suitcase-sized gap between its brother and the wall. There was also about an eighteen-inch space on the hangar rod. Only the man's clothes remained. On top of his shoes sat three large shopping bags filled with thin blue rubber bands.

I don't like handling the dead but there was no way out of it. There was no clue to the dead man's murder in the house. Nobody broke in. Everything was out of place. Maybe Idabell had done it. But she'd said that they were in trouble. Maybe somebody wanted to kill her.

I had come that far. I could have left without looking, but who knew what would come back to me later on? Better make sure I knew all I could before I left. The most likely place to look was in the dead man's pockets.

All he had was a wallet. But what a wallet it was. It was thick with pieces of paper: receipts, notes, addresses, ads, even a letter. He had six hundred-dollar bills and a wad of various other smaller denominations.

I was about to sit down and sift through the papers and cards when a light played across the window shade. It was only a passing car but I took it as a sign that I should go.

I reclaimed my fingerprints from the back door and window, then opened the front door and rubbed those surfaces down.

"Mr. Gasteau?" An elderly white woman was standing at the gate. I didn't think that she saw my face because I was still partly hidden by the night and the berry tree.

I'm proud to say that homicide never crossed my mind. Instead I splayed my left hand in front of my face, using the spaces for my eyes. My right hand I held above my head, dangling the car keys. I crouched down low enough to be five foot six and walked at a sway as I strutted toward the woman like a fleshy and belled crab.

She fell back. "Oh."

I went right to my car, turned the wheel out, and released the handbrake. When I hit the ignition I was already coasting down the hill. With any luck the old lady had bad vision or didn't think to take down my plates.

With any luck.

Miss B. Shay lived on the second floor of a two-story stucco apartment building in Culver City. There was a bright talisman hanging from the protruding peephole of her front door; a small shield of brightly colored glass beads that came from somewhere in the lower Americas. I would have liked it, and the eye that placed it there, at any other time.

"Yes?" came a voice from behind the closed door.

"Miss Shay?"

"Who is it?"

"My name is Rawlins, ma'am. I came to ask you about your friend Idabell Turner."

"What about her?" I didn't blame her for wanting to keep the door closed against a big man who came knocking unannounced.

"It's about her dog," I said. "She left him with me today at work but then she took off and now I don't know what to do."

I guess the desperation in my voice convinced her. She opened the door to the length of the safety chain and filled that opening with her body.

B. Shay was tallish, about five eight, with thick hair that was tied back into a lace cloth. She was a deep brown with naturally smiling lips. Her face was full of feelings and memories that I thought I might know. She had on a big loose gold sweater that came down below her knees. Her legs from there were bare. Even though the sweater was supposed to be shapeless there was definitely form underneath. I didn't care. A beautiful face wasn't going to save my job and my kids from Sanchez.

"Ida left Pharaoh with you?" she asked me.

"Yeah."

"And how did you know to come here?"

"U'm, I work at school with her like I said, and so I asked for her emergency card when I realized that she was gone. You see, she was having some problem at home. As a matter of fact she said that she wasn't gonna go home and that she was staying with a friend. I hoped it was you."

"No," B. Shay said. It was when she looked me in the eyes that my sleeping mind started making poetry out of her face. "Ida and I haven't seen too much of each other in the last year or so. We used to be close but I haven't even talked to her in months."

"Uh-huh." There really wasn't anything else for me to say.

"Have you tried her home?"

"I called but nobody answered, and if she was havin'

trouble with her husband I didn't wanna go by there. Maybe I could give you my number and if you talk to her . . . "

A frown flitted across her face. "What is it?"

"You got a pencil?"

"Just tell me. I'll remember long enough to write it down after you go."

She frowned again while I was reciting my number, at least giving the feeling that she was trying to remember it.

"Okay," she said when I was through.

There seemed to be something else on her mind, but she wasn't opening up to me. Maybe she knew where Idabell was; maybe she'd give her my number. I didn't know.

I left with a plan in mind. I'd given Idabell Turner/ Gasteau every chance that I could. Now I was going to take care of myself. If Sanchez questioned me the next day I'd answer every question with complete honesty. If he mentioned the dog I'd tell him what I knew. I wasn't guilty of anything—he'd have to see that.

At least I hoped he'd have to.

But the more I thought about it the more I feared that Sanchez would suspect me for some reason. What if he looked into the Seventy-seventh Street station's records? I was all over those papers; suspected of everything from conspiracy to murder.

The closer I got to home the more I thought that I should get rid of the dog. Idabell wouldn't claim that I had him, because he, or his "accident," was her excuse for leaving school that morning. Sanchez was bound to get on the math teacher's trail. There was a corpse in her house. The dead man in the garden had to be related to her in some way.

Get rid of the dog. That's what I was thinking. After all, it was only a dog. And a damn mean and worthless dog at that.

CHAPTER 9

Jesus was sitting at the dining table doing his homework when I got home. Feather was playing with the soon-to-be-gone dog.

"Hi, Daddy," she said happily. "Frenchie could do tricks. I taught him to jump. Can't we keep him?"

"No, honey. I have to take him back tomorrow. But we can get you another dog."

"I don't want another dog! I want Frenchie!"

Feather ran out of our main room through to the back hall. Pharaoh went after her but he stopped at the doorway and turned around to give me a hard stare.

Maybe he understood English.

"Jesus," I said.

The dog darted off after Feather.

"Yeah, Dad?"

"Did you two eat?"

"Uh-huh. I made meat loaf sandwiches and chicken soup." Jesus had a lot of Indian blood in him; he was slight and dark-haired. He was also Hamilton High School's best long-distance man in track; he might have been the best in the city at that time.

"You put tomatoes and lettuce in the sandwiches?" I was trying to teach them to eat their vegetables.

"Uh-huh."

"You wanna tell me about that money up in your closet?"

"What?" He looked up from his notepaper.

"Don't mess with me now, Juice. I saw it. Now tell me where it came from."

"I don't know," he said.

That was the first time I didn't hit him.

"Listen, I'm upset. I've had a really hard day. You got hundreds of dollars in your closet and I got to know if you're going to jail or not. So tell me where it came from or I might get mad." I said that all in a calm voice but anyone with half an ear could have heard the violence underneath.

"It's ours."

"And where did we get money like that?"

"You know," Jesus said. I almost smiled because it was so rare to hear the boy flustered. "I saved it."

"Where'd you get it from?" I asked.

It was during the boy's long silence that I didn't hit him for the second time.

"Well?"

"I got it from you," Jesus said simply.

"From me?"

I realized that the palms of my hands had gotten hot because suddenly they cooled.

Jesus squinted at me, looking like a sailor trying to peer through a high wind. He nodded.

"You stole from me?"

He didn't have an answer.

"Juice, I'm talking to you. This ain't nuthin' like takin' twenty-five cents from my change drawer."

"I took it," he said. "I took it . . . "

"Where? Where'd you take it from?" I was thinking about the cash box that I kept hidden under a sloppy pile of bricks at the back of the garage. The garage was locked, and there was a lot of brick. No burglar would find it, but a healthy inquisitive boy might.

"I took it from the grocery money," Jesus said.

"Don't lie to me now, boy. I don't give you that kinda money for groceries."

"Uh-huh."

"What're you talkin' 'bout?" I took a violent step toward the table. Jesus was up and around the other side with all the speed and graceful awkwardness of a young deer.

"If you give me ten dollars for stuff and if I save some coupons and stuff, then I took the money I saved and put it in my money box."

"That's some shit, boy."

"No," he said, shaking his head. "I did too take it out of the shopping money."

"If you did that, then where'd all these big bills come from? You didn't get any twenty-dollar bills in change from Safeway."

"But if I saved up enough change and dollars then I'd use them and keep the big bills." Jesus was almost pleading. I knew that every word was true.

"You been stealin' from me for years?" The rage in my chest was beyond any anger I could have felt at my son. It was Principal Newgate, Idabell Turner, and Sergeant Sanchez that made me rage. I knew it but I just couldn't help myself.

"You know, Jesus," I said, "the only reason I don't kick the shit outta you is 'cause I want to. We gonna talk about this later, but in the meantime I don't want you spendin' one goddam dime'a that money. Do you understand me?"

He started to say something but then nodded instead.

"Go on then." I wanted to talk more to him but I was just too angry.

By two a.m. I'd gone through every scrap of paper in Holland Gasteau's fat wallet. I supposed that the man was Holland Gasteau because his driver's license said so. I also figured that there was something wrong with him. He had over seven hundred dollars in his pocket. An everyday workingman only carried around what he needed for a day or two—all the rest of an honest man's money was out paying bills or stacked in the bank for a rainy day. So Mr. Gasteau was either a fool, trying to be a big man on the street flashing his money roll, or he was a crook. Seeing the condition I found him in I figured that he was both.

But he was a workingman too.

There were fourteen check stubs from the *Los Angeles Examiner* shoved in his wallet. He'd received seventy-four dollars and nineteen cents a week up until mid-April of that year. There were six or seven racing tickets—two-dollar bets.

But the most interesting thing in his wallet was a note, a letter actually, scratched in peacock blue in the smallest print that I have ever seen. It was written on a sheet of paper that was half the size of a standard typewriting leaf.

Idabell you know that I love you and that I need you too. It's only me and you in this world and I would never NEVER hurt you unless it was the best for both of us. I only took your peepee dog because that was the only way to make you do what's going to make us rich and happy and you won't have to work anymore unless you want it and people won't believe that they can walk on me because they know that they got more money in their pockets while I'm down at the paper shack on my knees on the dirt floor.

I'm too classy for all that Idabell. You know I am. I know you're out there right now taking a chance but that can't be helped. Only you could do it and so I had to make the decision for what was the best for the both of us. Don't worry. If you get in trouble I will take the blame. If you do it all fine then you could have Peepee and a house that's paid for and a man you could be proud of. But because you know you got to trust me and then everything will work out fine.

I didn't understand all of it. I wasn't even sure what it was. A note to himself? A letter he intended to send? He was very careful not to say what it was that Idabell was doing. But he couldn't hide how nutty and childish he was. His note reminded me of a twelve-year-old pretending with adult words and ideas. Not a mature child like Jesus but some kind of crazy unloved boy who pulled the tails off lizards and threw rocks at girls he liked.

There were scraps of papers with notes and numbers written on them but nothing that made any sense. When I'd finished I took the wallet and buried it under the pile of bricks in the garage.

The whole time I had the feeling that someone close by was searching for me. It was my imagination I knew, but it took that kind of fancy for poor men to survive where

I'd come up. My imagination was urging me to hurry up and finish the game before I lost it all.

I wasn't afraid, exactly. I rarely got frightened unless I was faced with immediate danger. But there was anxiety rooting around in my gut. It's the kind of feeling I'm sure birds get when it's time for them to fly south.

Whatever it was, worry or instinct, I wasn't sleepy. I was so tired that it was hard for me to rise up out of my chair, but my mind was running like a hound that just caught the scent of blood.

I couldn't sleep, so I sat down to read the papers.

Maybe it was just my mood but the news seemed especially bad. Volcanoes erupting in Alaska. A military coup in Iraq. Thirty people dead in a retirement-home fire in Atlantic City. The only thing I learned worthwhile was that it was supposed to rain the next day.

I was wondering where I'd put my umbrella when I saw something moving from the corner of my eye. Over near the hallway door Pharaoh was hunkered down with his snout pushing forward. He was giving me the evil eye.

"An' you know when a animal hate ya," Momma Jo, Mouse's swampland voodoo godmother, once told me. "You need a counterspell a'cause that mean the whole world have turnt against ya."

It was a memory from so long before that it seemed like I had made it up. But real or fancy, those words struck me. It was late and a good time to take Pharaoh from my house. I couldn't have killed him. But I could take him out somewhere and let him go. At least he'd have some chance to survive on the streets. I'd survived when I was just a boy.

I moved to rise from my chair. Pharaoh growled and took half a step back. I halted, preparing for my lunge.

My big toe was digging into the carpet and I was ready to leap when the doorbell rang.

The doorbell at three a.m. had only meant one thing in my L.A. experience—the police. Pharaoh and I both looked at the door and then at each other. Then he started yelping for his life. I don't think he actually knew that there was a cop out there, but he smelled the fear on me.

There was no help for it. No hand in front of my face was going to save me from Sanchez. The Horns could take care of the kids while I was in jail. Maybe my old friend Primo or Etta could take them after that.

The bell rang two times more before I had the heart to answer. By that time Pharaoh was howling.

I opened the door and he walked in, right past me, and sat down in the sofa chair. He sat heavily like a man at the end of an especially hard job.

"Mouse!"

"You got a drink, Easy?"

"Naw, man. I gave it up. You know that." I was so relieved that I didn't complain. All I felt was a sense of relief that was laced with exhaustion.

"That's all right," he sighed. "That's all right. You know I got my spot right here." He took a flat bottle of scotch from his back pocket.

As he tilted the liquor to his lips I had the strange feeling that it was me knocking back a drink.

Pharaoh crawled up beside him and nuzzled his hand for a caress. Mouse scratched him behind the ear. I sat down opposite them realizing that I had been up for almost twenty-four hours.

After a while I said, "Raymond, it's after three."

He turned his stony gray eyes at me.

"What do you want?" I asked.

"You know, Easy," he began, "I done some terrible things."

The silence that followed his declaration was such that we could have been on a stage or in a courtroom, the performance just begun.

"You remember Agnes Varel?" he asked. "An' her boy-friend, what was his name?"

"You mean back in Houston?"

"Yeah, uh-huh." He took another sip. The smell of alcohol caught in the back of my throat and made me cough.

"Cecil," I said. "Her boyfriend was Cecil."

"Mmm." He nodded, not really remembering. "Etta was

down Galveston an' he was at work. Agnes told me to come on upstairs. You know I hardly got on my shoes 'fore I was there. I got inta that stuff." For a moment the old Mouse rose out of the sad man. "She was walkin' on the moon, an', baby, I was right up there wit'er. I mean that woman had five hands, two mouths, an' on top'a that she could fly. You know we go at it for a while an' then lay back an' she be lookin' at me like a wildcat be lookin' up a tree. An' then we was prowlin' again.

"We been goin' at it for half the night when her boyfriend walk in. He all mad an' yellin' high like a girl. I jump up offa Agnes hard as a motherfuckin' rock. I say, 'What?' An' 'fore he could do anything I grabbed a bottle an' th'ew it upside his head."

Mouse stared at my wall, seeing that long-ago scene there. Pharaoh leapt up into his lap. Mouse's eyes blinked slowly and I felt the fumes of his whiskey swimming around my head.

"I wanted to finish wit' Agnes but she's all scared that he's hurt. But you know when he was laid up in bed she come on down an' finished our li'l job. Hm. An' you know sumpin', Easy?"

"No, Raymond. What?"

"I don't feel a damn thing about it. Not a damn thing. I mean, I know it's wrong but I don't care. I don't feel good about it neither. It just happened. I just did what I did. That's all. Ain't no more to it. I coulda killed the mother-fuckah. If I had a gun in reach I probably would have. Just like with William. But you know it's just water off my back." He paused for a second. I remember thinking, half dreaming, that it was more likely blood than water that he shook off so casually.

"You met William down in Pariah, right, Ease?"

"Yeah," I said.

"He was sumpin', right? Make that guitar sing like it was a bird. A gottdamned bird."

"It ain't your fault, Raymond," I said.

"What?" His voice was so light that it could have been a child asking.

"It's not your fault. You wouldn'ta been up there wit' Agnes if she didn't ask you. And Cecil still married her after all that. William knew the company he kept. Shit. He died livin' more than most men ever even dream about."

Mouse heard my voice but the words didn't seem to register. He frowned when I mentioned William.

"I got to thinkin' 'bout Agnes up in the manual arts building; got to thinkin' that it was the same shit that put William down in his grave," Mouse said.

"How come you thinkin' 'bout that?"

"That policeman come up to me on the third flo'a the manual arts buildin'. I was doin' the windahs an' he come up an' ask if I wasn't Alexander."

"What he want?"

"He said that he knew who I was, that they were aware'a me down at the station. Then he look at me like I'ma fall apart right there. But you know, man, I ain't scared'a him. He couldn't take a damn thing from me. But then he showed me a Polaroid picture of that man they found. He asked me if I knew him."

"Did you?"

"Not that I told him, I didn't. But you know that picture stayed in my mind. It was in my mind all night. I kept on seein' him an' then all the other people I seen dead, daddy Reese, that sheriff in Texas . . . William . . . " Mouse trailed off for a few seconds. Pharaoh stood at attention in his lap, his jaundiced ears perked up. "You ever think that William looked like me?"

"I'ont know. You light-complected an' light-eyed. He wasn't all that light."

"My momma was part Indian, part Negro, an' then there was some white in there too. I don't know what exactly but I could be a mix of her and William."

It was strange that Momma Jo came to my mind a second time that night. I hadn't thought about her in years. She had as much as told me that William was Raymond's father. That's why he came around from Jenkins every now and then when Mouse was growing up.

"I can't see that," I lied. "If he was your father why wouldn't he have said so?"

"Maybe 'cause he had a problem wit' my momma. Maybe . . . I don't know."

"What you sayin', Raymond?"

"That maybe I killed my own blood." There was a dangerous look in Mouse's eye. A look that said someone had done him wrong.

When Mouse reached for his bottle, Pharaoh cringed down between his knees.

I took one deep breath, then another. I felt sleep coming on but I was afraid to let go. Raymond was nodding too.

"I come here to ask you what you think, Easy. You good about feelin's and all."

"You wanna know what I think?"

"Yeah."

We were both battling the sandman.

"I think you should wait for a while. Wait and see. Right now it's just too soon. You don't have no kinda handle on it. You an' Etta an' LaMarque just startin' out again. I think one day real soon you'll wake up and be happy with your family and so these things you thinkin' will be far off like. Far off." The words seemed to call to me.

"You mean like I'll get a sign tell me which way to go?" Mouse asked.

My eyes were closed. I was drifting on the way to a dream. "Yeah," I remember saying. "Like a sign."

CHAPTER 10

Feather was squealing on the floor next to the couch. She squirmed on her back with Pharaoh switching his rat tail back and forth across her stomach like a windshield wiper. Mouse was coming awake on the chair across from me.

"Hi, Dad," Jesus said from the dining table. And then to Feather, "Come on, little sister. Breakfast."

"No," she said playfully.

But she got up.

Mouse groaned and leaned forward. "Easy, you goin' in?" he asked.

"Yeah, I guess." All the problems from the day before were quickly settling back into my mind.

"Mind if I sleep in your bed awhile?"

"Go on."

He got up and staggered toward the hallway.

Before he was gone I called after him, "Raymond."

"Yeah?"

"You told Sanchez that you didn't know that man, right?"

"Uh-huh."

"But did you know'im?"

"I seen'im. Up at the school."

"Beginnin' of the semester?"

"Uh-huh, yeah. He was wit' Mr. Langdon down in the wood shop."

"What they do there?"

"'Ont know, man. Wasn't none'a my business."

He went off toward the toilet. While he was there I got clean clothes out of my bedroom closet. When Mouse sacked out I took a shower and shaved. It was almost eight o'clock by the time I was finished. It would be the first time that I'd ever been late for work.

Pharaoh had to stay with us for at least one more day. I wouldn't have been able to bear my daughter's tears that morning. I left the house with them romping around the living room, having the time of their lives.

I went to the external lot of the lower campus first. Her car wasn't there. I looked into C2. A tall white man, a substitute teacher, was guiding the students through their algebra.

I drove around to the main campus then, wondering how much longer I'd be able to hold on to my job.

The oleander bushes along the front of the old school were

decorated with white flags. T-shirts, handkerchiefs, corners torn from old sheets. They were hung from branches and spread out over the grass.

Glue sniffers' rags. Boys, and some girls, crawled behind the bushes in the middle of the night with airplane model glue. They emptied the metal tubes into cloth and breathed deeply, almost eating the poison. Afterwards they staggered out into the streets, grinning like idiots. A few months of glue and half their brains were eaten away.

Every morning Mr. Burns came out and collected the rags for the trash. It was all we could do.

I came into the main hall of the administration building. Students were moving around, heading toward their first-period classes.

"Mr. Langdon," I called down the crowded corridor. "Mr. Langdon."

Casper Langdon turned around quickly, as if my voice had grabbed his shoulder and yanked. A teenager bounced off of his great paunch and went crashing into a bank of lockers.

Langdon ignored the boy and called, a little too loudly, "Mr. Rawlins?"

He was a man who was used to people running away, not calling out to him.

Small-headed and bald, he had an enormous body that was almost perfectly round. He had no nose to speak of and hardly any lips. He breathed through his open mouth and resembled a great albino turtle in overalls.

"Hi, Mr. Langdon. How are you today?"

"Oh, okay I guess." He opened his eyes very wide and then squinted. Mr. Langdon was nearsighted but he was too vain to wear his glasses. "You know, with all this stuff about people getting killed, right here on the school grounds. What's this world coming to?"

"Yeah, well," I said. "You don't get any guarantees in this life."

Langdon gasped twice and worked his eyes at me. "Did the police talk to you yet?"

"Not yet. I expect that Sanchez'll get to me today."

"Sanchez? Is that his name? I hope he doesn't want to talk to me."

"Why not?" I tried to make the question as pointed as possible without seeming to know anything.

"I'm no good around authority figures. They make me so nervous."

"Well, do you know anything? I mean, something about what happened?"

"No, I don't."

Like hell.

"Then you don't have a thing to worry about, Mr. Langdon. Not a thing." I slapped him on his shoulder. He winced and winked and tried to laugh.

"Did you want something, Mr. Rawlins?"

"No. Why?" I asked innocently.

"Why did you call me?"

"No reason." I smiled. "I just haven't said good morning to you in a long time." Lying is mainly achieved by the tone in your voice. If you sound like you mean what you say, most people will believe you.

Mr. Langdon believed me.

I watched him go down the hall, pillow-punching children and adults alike with his girth.

The administration office was a big room of oak and cream. A yard-high wooden wall separated the outside world from the secretaries that ran Sojourner Truth. The seven secretaries had four desks behind which stood a row of shallow offices. Between each office and the next sat two large filing cabinets. The women moved from desk to desk and cabinet to cabinet like bees in a hive. Every now and then one of them would duck into a door and make a call or type a letter. Trudy Van Dial puffed cigarettes behind a closed door now and then because she was addicted to both work and nicotine and couldn't bear to take the time to go down to the teachers' lounge.

Gladys Martinez, a fifth-generation Mexican-American Los Angelena, was office head. Gladys was a good-natured woman. She usually had a smile and a story whenever we talked, but that day she didn't even answer my question.

I asked her if Mrs. Turner was coming in that morning. She just turned her back to me and said, "Joanna, I need some staples up here." She kept her back to the front desk for a while. When she turned around and saw me still standing there she smiled, raised her shoulders to indicate her helplessness, and then hurried into a back office.

I didn't run out of the front door. I didn't get into my car and drive out of the state with my children. I didn't, but I should have.

The main office was clear of custodians when I got there. The painters were sitting around waiting for their tarps and rollers to be delivered. The plumbers were there with a final plea for me to sign off on tearing out the boiler-room floor—I refused them and they left to figure out another way to change the pipes under the school.

"What's happening with that killing, Rawlins?" Conrad Hopkins, a watery-eyed painter from Detroit, asked me. Some of the craftsmen liked to feel important. A few had annoying habits, like not calling me mister. Hopkins was especially obnoxious because of the high-handed tone he took. He was an older man, more washed out than white.

"I don't know a thing about it." I lied to him because keeping in practice keeps you alive.

"They're all óver the garden, and I hear that they took over Teale's office for questioning people," Hopkins said.

Mrs. Teale was the girls' vice principal; she had an office on the second floor of the administration building.

"It was probably drugs," one of the younger painters said. He put a cigarette to his lips and held his hand out with authority. "Cases like this it usually is."

"You don't know shit, Hank," Hopkins said.

The other men laughed while the painter named Hank looked around trying to hide his humiliation. In the crowds I'd once run in, Hopkins would have had to back up his words with fists; sometimes the street has it over the office.

I sat down at my desk to go over the quarterly vacation

requests. That's when I noticed the pink slip from up the hill informing me that Simona Eng had called in sick.

The workmen hung around talking and drinking coffee. They took longer breaks, but at the end of the day their work had to be done, so I didn't try to push them. I just filled out my progress reports and made recommendations to the area supervisor, Bertrand Stowe.

Soon after the nine-forty class bell rang, the door to the main office was flung open. Sanchez came in with two uniformed white cops. The plumbers and painters were struck dumb. Maybe they thought that they'd be arrested for slacking off on the job.

"Excuse us, sirs," Sanchez said to the men. "But Mr. Rawlins and I have some police matters to talk about."

They cleared the room in seconds.

It took Sanchez half a minute to come sit at my desk. He and his goons knew their script by heart. Policeman number one started looking around the shelves and at the papers on the table while policeman number two positioned himself close to me, just in case I got the notion to run. Sanchez in the meanwhile chose a chair, shook it for no reason that I could tell, and then dragged it over to my desk. Before he sat down he took out a new pack of Kools and tamped it hard against the heel of his palm. He pulled the red strip on the cellophane wrapper and tore the aluminum paper from one side of the pack. He gestured the cigarettes toward me as an offer. I declined and so he put the pack away without taking out a cigarette for himself.

I don't remember being frightened. I was so concentrated on him and what he did that there was no room for feeling.

He hadn't shaved that morning and his brown suit was rumpled. His breath was coming quicker than mine and there was dirt under his chipped nails. He had on a violet tie with a knot that even Jesus would have done over. All of that made the sergeant look vulnerable, like he was human. But his eyes were none of that. I've been told that there's no such thing as truly black eyes but Sergeant Sanchez's small orbs were no other color. They were animal eyes. And I was lost in the woods.

"You know Lieutenant Lewis?" he asked. He straddled the chair backwards, leaning his chest against the backrest.

I didn't trust my voice not to crack.

"Arno Lewis," he said. "From the Seventy-seventh Street station."

"What about'im?"

"I thought I recognized you in the garden yesterday, Rawlins. I've been at the Seventy-seventh for eight years. A long time ago I saw you, but I didn't remember what you were there for. I talked to Lieutenant Lewis this morning." Sanchez proved that he could smile and scrutinize at the same time. "He likes you."

It almost sounded like a proposition.

"But," Sanchez sighed, "with friends like him your enemies would see you hung up by the balls."

It was a simple trick. He knew about the times I had been in jail and the kinds of people that I'd been involved with. What he wanted was for me to confess to that history without him actually mentioning anything. That way I would be in the position of confessing to him, telling him things without him having to ask.

"We take our friends where we can," I said. He was going to have to do better than that if he wanted to hogtie me.

"You were looking for Idabell Turner this morning."

"I what?"

"Mrs. Turner," Sanchez said. "You asked about her in the main office this morning. Mrs. Martinez mentioned it."

"I did?"

"You were asking for the victim's name yesterday."

"No," I said.

"Well, you asked if I'd found out the victim's name."

I didn't have to answer that.

"His name was Roman Gasteau," Sanchez continued. "Twin brother of Holland Gasteau."

Sanchez's eyes were saying, loud and clear, that I knew what he was talking about. They were inviting me to enter into the conversation.

But I refused.

"Why'd you ask about Mrs. Turner this morning, Mr. Rawlins?"

"She's a friend'a mines. I heard her dog got killed or somethin'."

"If she's such a good friend, why didn't you call her house?"

"I did. She wasn't home," I said. "What's this all about?"

"Where were you last night, Mr. Rawlins?"

"At home mostly. For a while I was out lookin' at my property."

"And where's that?" he asked. He'd been leaning forward but now he sat up straight; it wasn't going to be as easy to break me down as he'd thought.

"I got a buildin' on Denker and one on Magnolia Street. I went out to see how they was lookin'." My language became completely comfortable. I didn't need to pretend about who I was with Sanchez. "You could ask my manager—Mofass."

He wanted Mofass's number, and I obliged him with the answering-service line. Any call Mofass got from the LAPD, he'd talk to me first.

"Now what's this all about, sergeant?" I asked. "You got some kinda problem with me?"

He shrugged his shoulders. "Has Mrs. Turner been having any problems lately?"

There are moments in your life when you can tell what's right and wrong about yourself—your nature. I wanted my job and my everyday kind of life. I wanted to see Jesus get his track scholarship at UCLA and Feather to become the artist I knew she could be.

All I had to do was say, "Yeah, she said she'd been fightin' with her husband. He threatened to kill her dog. I know 'cause she gave the dog to me yesterday morning." I didn't have to talk about our good time on the desktop. I didn't have to confess about breaking into her house.

Instead I said, "Not that I know of. But you know, she's kinda private about anything at home. I mean, I got her number but last night was the first time I ever called it."

I was a fool; but I was my own fool.

Sanchez sniffed at the lie and then stood up suddenly.

Before turning to leave he pointed at me. "We'll be talking again soon, I think, Mr. Rawlins."

They left and I went back to my vacation charts.

CHAPTER 11

I spent a while going over other papers and requests that had piled up. I started filling out an order form for central supply, but no matter what I tried to concentrate on I ended up thinking about Simona on that bench and Jorge taking her off.

"Hey, Peña!" I found him an hour later on the lower campus. He was hosing down the handball wall out beyond bungalow I.

"Hey, Mr. Rawlins." Jorge twisted the nozzle on his hose until the water stopped spouting. "How you doing?"

"Okay. All right. I wanted to ask you something."

"What's that?"

"What's wrong with Simona?"

"What do you mean?"

"I mean, why is she home sick today?"

"I don't know. Why don't you ask her?"

"Listen, the cops came out to the main office to see me a little while ago—"

"Yeah, I heard that. One of the painters said."

"They wanted to know about Simona."

"Really? What they want to know?"

"What I knew about her. If she had some reason to lie to them."

Jorge and I were close enough. He knew that I had his best interests at heart. And I did, too. I was only lying to get the story; not to get him or his girl into trouble.

"We didn't wanna say nuthin' to the cops, Mr. Rawlins, you know."

I waited.

"Simona knew that man. She used to go out with him."

"Yeah?"

"Uh-huh. His brother was married to Mrs. Turner. They would get together sometimes after school and go out to some place and have reefer parties. You know, Mrs. Turner liked Simona because she was going to college, so she would ask her out with some of the other teachers sometimes." Peña's usually cheerful eyes had the dull luster of dread in them. "But they got kinda weird and she stopped goin' around with them."

"Did she tell the cops?"

"No. I told her she better not. 'Cause you know if they found out about her and the reefer then she'd get in trouble. Maybe it would be a mark on her record." Jorge was nervous. He was afraid of trouble himself. He had a good job with his sister and her children covered under his medical insurance.

"Don't worry, Jorge," I said. "Just keep it quiet. Everything's gonna be fine." I clapped the young man on the shoulder and left him with the illusion of security.

EttaMae was mopping up some girl's thrown-up lunch on the top floor of the language arts building. She was looking almost mean enough to dissuade me from approaching her. You learned where we were reared to avoid tough customers with sticks in their hands.

"Hey, Etta."

She kept pushing her mop. Yesterday she'd been mad at me for acting like a man does. Now she was mad at all men.

"Don't go droppin' your jaw on the floor now, honey," I said. "Mouse stayed with me last night."

"Says what?"

"Listen, Etta, the cops showed Raymond a picture of the dead man and he went off a little. He started drinkin' and worryin' that William was his father. He didn't wanna bring that kinda sadness home to his own boy."

It took her a minute to let her anger go. There had been hatred stirring in her heart for Mouse. And, you know, hatred has deep roots in a black woman's heart.

"Let's go up on the roof," I said. "Take a break."

Up on top of the language arts building you could see for miles. L.A. down around Watts was mostly flat to the sea. The blacktop roads were wide and green sprouted up everywhere. Little houses ran in rows between the avenues. They seemed frail in comparison with the streets. It was almost as if the houses were just resting points on a forever roadway to somewhere else.

I lit up a Camel. Etta took one too. She leaned over the brick wall to look down on the new yard.

"He still crazy, Easy." She exhaled deeply.

"He loves you and LaMarque."

"Yeah. I know. But he so strange now. Two nights ago he was sittin' on the sofa, not sayin' a thing, an' then all of a sudden he sit up straight an' call out, 'LaMarque! LaMarque!' I tole'im to be quiet, that the boy's sleepin', but he just kept on shoutin' till finally LaMarque come outta his bedroom rubbin' his tears 'cause he's asleep an' afraid at the same time."

I heard what she was saying but my gaze lay on a giant cloud that was passing. Etta's words were painful for her but she had to say them. And while she talked I was comforted by her voice and the familiarity of our lives.

"You know what he said?" Etta asked.

"What?"

" 'LaMarque, don't you never kill a man don't deserve to die.' Then he sat there an' look for a long time and then he say, 'An' don't you never kill your father or your mother either.'

"Can you beat that?"

Instead of saying anything I took her in my arms. It wasn't sex. I just needed to be held and she did too. She smelled of cleaning wax and bread, of the sweat from hard work.

Our embrace would have hurt most people. It was strong and straining.

Two double bells sounded in the yard.

Etta's arm moved up to caress my head in its padded vice. I felt that explosion go off in my chest again. The wind kicked up, fanning the tiny ember left years before.

Again, two double bells.

"That's for you, Easy," Etta said in a voice that had no sympathy with the words.

"I know."

We kissed and then kissed again. But the ember didn't have anything to catch on. My right hand laced itself together with her left.

Our smiles were sorry grins.

By the time the bells sounded again I was off down the stairs.

CHAPTER 12

"Mr. Rawlins," Gladys Martinez, the snitch, said shyly, "Mr. Preston wants you to meet him in the aud."

"Okay." I turned to go. I wasn't really mad at Gladys. The way I figured it, Sergeant Sanchez had told her to report on anyone who asked about Mrs. Turner. People in the working world went by the rules. That's how they knew to survive.

"Mr. Rawlins," Gladys called when I was half the way out of the door.

"Yes?"

"Mr. Stowe called from the central office. He said that he'd like you to come down there."

Any other time I would have gone to meet Mr. Preston

with no qualms. He was the boys' vice principal at
Sojourner Truth, and he was okay, in an aloof way. He was
a squat, muscular man, in his late forties. Bill had come
up the hard way, working as a gym teacher for twenty
years before they promoted him.

I was a workingman just like him. But as I made my
way to the eastern side of the administration building, I
remembered the last time Preston wanted to see me in
Truth Auditorium . . .

" . . . mothahfuckah!" was the first word I had heard when
I came through the back door. After that came the low
murmur of another voice. It was the kind of man talk that
sent sensible people going in the opposite direction.

The auditorium was mostly dark. From the elevated
aisle I could see the two men standing in the glow of the
floor lighting in the space down between the last row of
seats and the stage.

"I don't give a goddam 'bout all that shit! I want my boy
and I want him right this mothahfuckin' minute." The man
talking was big, really big. Taller than I was and younger
too. From the look of those bulging short sleeves he was
stronger than I had ever been.

The folding knife went limp in my pocket.

"He's in good hands, Mr. Brown," Bill Preston was saying.
"Your son has been badly injured repeatedly over a long
period of time. He has broken bones that have never been
set right and maybe some internal damage . . . "

I hugged the shadows and moved down toward the men.

"I don't know what the fuck you talkin' about, man!"
Brown screamed. "Eric's just accident-prone. It's in his
feet."

"Many of his injuries just couldn't happen—"

Mr. Brown used both hands to push Preston backwards.
I flowed quickly through darkness.

I was next to the last tier of chairs, behind the brutal
father—unseen by either man.

Preston righted himself and held up his hands.

"Hold on, Mr. Brown," he said. "There's enough trouble

here already. When I saw what was wrong with Eric I had to call the nurse. She had to call the police. That's the law. They took him to a hospital."

"He my boy," Brown said. "And I say what happens to him. If I say he goes to a hospital, well then okay. If I say he stay home with a broke arm, you better believe that that's where he gonna be."

Andrew Brown—I'd later found out his name from the police forms I signed—was six foot four if he was an inch. Bill Preston might have grazed five eight on a good day in his twenties. But despite the height difference, Bill Preston had a hidden advantage—he had steel springs in his legs. He pointed his right fist at Andy's jaw and took off like a jet-powered pogo stick.

You could have heard the bones cracking from the back row. Andy Brown sagged backwards but he couldn't fall down because Preston's fists came on like mother birds protecting their nest. When the larger man finally slumped to the floor I was actually relieved for him.

The vice principal jumped up on the stage and ran back behind the curtains. I came over and kneeled down next to the unconscious man, to make sure that he was still breathing.

The jaw was definitely broken, his face was already swelling from the blows.

I heard something and looked up to see Bill Preston coming toward us with a black metal platform extender rod in his hands. He held the thing like a club. I stood up in front of Brown, expecting Bill to come to his senses. But he didn't even see me. He raised the rod high and I tackled his midsection. Preston dropped his weapon, which fell on Brown's foot, and started tussling with me.

"Bill! Bill! It's me, man!" I yelled. "Stop! Stop!"

He struggled with great strength but no intent. When he said, "You can get off me now," I knew that he'd regained self-control.

We sat there on the floor breathing hard. Preston rubbed his face. He was pressing so hard that I thought he might get crazy again.

"Let's get our stories straight," I said.

"What?"

"He pushed you," I went on. "And then he was gonna hit you again. You threw your lucky punch and then fought until he was out of it. I was coming down the aisle and saw it all."

"I wouldn't have hit him if he hadn't talked about the boy like that," Preston said, remembering. "They shouldn't let people like that have kids. They shouldn't even let them live."

"Hey, hey, hey, hey . . . hey." I had my hands up in front of his face to keep his eyes off of Brown. "Let's get down to the office and call the cops."

"We can't leave him here," Preston said. "We have to tie him up or something."

"Ain't no niggahs gonna be tied up anywhere around here today." I don't know where the words in my mouth came from. But they were angry words and they weren't to be toyed with. "We ain't the police, and even though we got a story we both know what really happened."

"But you should see what he did to his son."

"You took the man's child and broke his jaw. If he wants to get up and go before the cops get here, then we're gonna let him."

The cops found Andrew Brown trying to limp away from the school. He was the definition of a loser in L.A.: a man without a car.

Eric was in the nurse's office the whole time. They tried to call his mother after the fight but she had to go down and get Andrew out of jail and into the hospital.

It took the courts to finally remove Eric from his home. Andrew had put him in the hospital that time. The police didn't like that, and so they worked Mr. Brown over so bad that the judge took Eric away to keep his own police from someday being charged with murder.

Preston had been friendly with me since that day. Friendly in that superior-feeling white man kind of way. He'd do things like slap me on the shoulder and give me advice that I didn't need.

*

The lights were on in the auditorium this time. Preston was down toward the front seated in one of the hard ash tiers. He was gazing up at the drawn curtains as if there was a play going on.

"Mr. Preston," I called from the high ground.

He stood and waved. He didn't look crazy so I strolled down to meet him. We walked out into the same space where he'd broken Andrew Brown's jaw.

"Mr. Rawlins," he said lamely. "How, um, how are you?"

"Fine," I replied, smooth and cool as glass.

"The kids?"

"I got to get down to the area office by one, Mr. Preston."

"Oh?" he said, pretending to sympathize. "Some problems?"

"What do you want, Bill?"

He took a deep breath and then looked back over his shoulder at the curtain. I wondered briefly if he was going to throw a roundhouse right.

He didn't.

"You talk to the police?" he asked.

"Some."

"I heard that they had you down at the gardens."

I nodded and looked at my watch.

"What did they say?"

"I don't know." Easy, the honest man, was reluctant. "I mean, they said that it was all hush-hush, confidential. You know, police business."

"Did they say anything about me?" he asked innocently.

"I don't know what you mean," I said, as doe-eyed as I could be. "Why would you think I know any more than anybody else?"

"Because of Gladys Martinez."

"What about her?"

"She was telling Newgate about how Sanchez suckered you. He told her to report anybody who asked about Idabell."

"So? I heard that she was sick or something."

"I don't care, Mr. Rawlins." Preston put up his hand to

assure me. But instead of relaxing I put up my forearm to block anything he might have thrown.

"What's wrong with you?" he asked, surprised at my reaction.

"Forget about me. What is it that you're asking, and what do you have to do with Mrs. Turner and that dead man in the garden?"

"The police said that?" There was real fear in Preston's voice.

"No. You did."

Suddenly Preston was confused.

"Didn't you just ask me about what the cops knew about you?" I asked him. "And then you said that it had something to do with Mrs. Turner. I don't need a Ph.D. in PE to figure that one out."

Preston was guilty of something—I was sure of that. All of his military certainty and gym-class tough-guy pose went out of the window when I caught him in his words. His breathing got shallow and his hands began to wander as if he were trying to ward off what I had said in sign.

"Well?" I asked.

"Forget it. Just forget I asked you anything. Just go on down to the area office. I, uh, I was out of line."

Preston had fallen into another trap. It's the way many people, then and now, fall under the spell of their own superiority. There he was a white man with a college education who dictated the rules to children, their parents, and their teachers. No waitress or gardener or janitor—certainly no colored man—was going to disobey his rules. I was supposed to erase all of his questions from my mind and go on about my life.

"I'm sorry, Mr. Preston, but I can't forget what you said."

"What?"

"I mean, what if Sergeant Sanchez wants to question me again? If I lie and then he finds out that I knew you were askin' questions, then he could see me as a whatyamacallit—an accomplice."

"Are you crazy, Rawlins? I didn't do anything."

"How do I know that? Here you callin' me in here all

secret-like. And you know the last time I saw you in here you almost killed that man Brown."

"What does that have to do with anything?"

"That man in the garden was hit. Somebody hit him with something like that rod you tried to hit Brown with."

That really opened Preston's eyes. He saw for the first time how much trouble he'd opened himself up for with me.

"Sit down, Mr. Rawlins," he said. "Please, sit down."

"After you."

Preston jumped up to a seated position on the apron of the stage. I followed his lead.

"What can I do to keep you from being worried, Mr. Rawlins?" he asked.

"I just wanna know why you all secretive," the worried and honest janitor asked.

"Well, let's just say that I didn't have anything to do with what happened but I know something about the people and I don't want it getting around that I do."

"You knew that dead man?"

"Now listen . . . " He was trying to be reasonable.

"Did you know him?" I said with emphasis. I was looking down at his hands as if I were afraid of the answer; as if I were just a poor peasant afraid of a world that I could barely comprehend.

"Yes," he said. "His name, well, his name is Roman Gasteau, and he's Idabell's brother-in-law."

"But her name is Turner."

"It's really her maiden name. She kept it because she was a teacher before she got married."

"What was he doing in the garden?" I asked, pretending nervous impatience.

"I don't know. I swear I don't."

I just looked at him.

"Listen, Mr. Rawlins. A lot of people around here knew Idabell and her husband, and brother-in-law. For years she's been giving faculty teas at her house. Maybe five or six a year. And when her brother-in-law moved into town . . . "

"That's the dead man, what you call him, Roman?"

"Yes, Roman Gasteau. When he moved in some of the men teachers would go to some, uh, parties a little bit wilder than a tea. If you know what I mean?"

"No, Mr. Preston, I don't know what you mean at all. If half the school knows this, this Roman, then why are you scared that somebody might put you with him?" Or with Idabell Turner, I thought.

"Well, you see," he said, "Idabell's husband is a real jerk. He was okay at first, she said. But then he went off the deep end. She blamed it on Roman, because he had a wild lifestyle. But Roman was a nice guy. Holland was abusive. He had girlfriends, he quit his job and used Idabell's money. He even hit her once. She didn't know what to do."

Bill Preston took a deep breath as if he had gotten some big problem off his chest.

After his second gasp I said, "So? What if she told you all that? That doesn't make you a crook to be hidin' from the cops."

Another sigh.

Another silence.

"She used to come up to my office, Mr. Rawlins. She'd come because I was the only one . . . " He paused for a second. " . . . the only one that she could talk to. You know what I mean. I couldn't do anything but console her. We got close. I think we fell in love."

"You fell in love right up there in your office?" At least I wasn't the only fool at school.

"When he hit her that time . . . "

"When was that?"

"Two weeks ago. When he did that I begged her to leave him. I told her that I'd go tell him that she was gone and take her clothes and everything. At first she said no, but then she said that she'd think about it while she was away with a friend who could get cheap tickets to France. She wanted to clear her mind.

"I was glad that she was gone, because if she had stayed in that house with that man I don't know what I might have done. The night before she left I went by there with some state aptitude tests that I said she had to have graded by the time she got back. I just wanted to know that she was all right."

"And was she?"

"She walked me out to the car and said that she was fine, that she'd see me when she got back."

"And she saw you?"

"Only for a moment. Yesterday. The day they found Roman. She told me that you had her dog and that Holland was going to beat her for something. She didn't say what. Just that she was going to leave right then."

"So you think that Sanchez is going to point at you for Roman?" I asked.

"No. He was killed in the early morning. I was in bed with my wife out in the valley. That's what I'm afraid of, that Sanchez might find out about me and Ida. Maybe she told somebody, maybe somebody saw us somewhere."

Or maybe somebody saw him drive out to her house to shoot her husband. He might have done it. Maybe. I didn't care, though. Not unless it brought me grief.

"Well," I said, "they didn't ask me anything about you, Mr. Preston. They did ask me about Mrs. Turner, though, and they mentioned her husband too."

"But nothing about me?"

"Nope. Not a word about you."

"Will you tell me if you hear anything?"

"From the cops?"

"Or from Idabell. If she calls about Pharaoh, tell me, and tell her that I really need to see her."

"Tell me somethin', Mr. Preston."

"What?"

"Did the police show you a picture of Roman?"

"Yes. Yes they did."

"And did you tell them that you knew him?"

"Of course. I just didn't say about Idabell. You know it doesn't really have anything to do with it. I'm sure it doesn't."

He looked the part of an honest and ignorant man, but, then again, so did I.

"Do you have any idea who could have killed Roman?"
I asked.

"No. He was a great guy. Not like his brother at all."

Except, I thought, that they were both dead.

CHAPTER 13

I drove down to the district office of the Board of Ed.

Bertrand Stowe was short and gray-haired, with a nose
that thrust straight forward. He had eyes that were absol-
utely sure about things and a voice that his mother must
have pulled out of a well.

He stood up, as far as he went, and put out his hand.
"Easy."

The fact that he used my street name meant that
Bertrand had known me before I became a respectable
workingman.

We met in the fall of '61. I'd just recently gotten out of the
hospital. I'd been recovering from a wound inflicted upon
me by an old friend. While convalescing I reflected on my
life, wondering how it could be that I was in danger even
from my friends. I had decided, upon coming home, to
concentrate on getting honest work.

I was reading the want ads when a woman called me at
home one afternoon.

"Easy? Easy Rawlins?"

"Yeah? Who's this?"

"It's Grace Phillips. You remember me? I'm John's friend.
We met down at his bar."

"Oh," I said, thinking, Oh no. "Yeah, yeah."

I didn't ask what she wanted.

"John told me to call you, Easy. He said that maybe you
could help me."

"Oh?"

"Uh-huh. Could I come over your house?"

"What you want, Grace?"

"Well, um, okay . . . you know Sallie Monroe?"

"Sure." Sallie was the toughest gangster, next to Mouse, in Watts.

"Well, Sallie think he own me."

"He your pimp?"

"It ain't like that really, Easy. Sallie just give some parties, that's all. If I wanna go an' have some fun, well, that was up to me. But he never owned me."

I knew the kind of parties she was talking about. Sallie, or some other gangster, would rent somebody's apartment for the night and sell tickets for a hundred dollars or so to his customers. He'd bring booze and reefer and sometimes something stronger. He'd also bring the girls. He'd give them twenty dollars or so to come and then they'd work a tip out of the man they danced with.

"So," I said. "If you don't wanna go, don't go." I was ready to hang up. I would have hung up if it wasn't John that had given her my number.

John was my friend, one of my best and oldest friends, solid and stronger than rock. I knew John from the old days back in the Fifth Ward, Houston, Texas. He was a hard man. He had to be in his line of work. He'd run a speakeasy down in Watts in the forties. Now he owned a restaurant-bar.

"You ain't heard me yet," Grace complained. "I don't go no more. I only ever went in the first place 'cause I thought it was fun. But I got me a boyfriend now."

"So?"

"Well." She hesitated a moment. "Well, I met my boyfriend at Sallie's and now Sallie wanna mess it up."

It took a long time to get the story out of her. She was embarrassed, and I didn't blame her. The head custodian at Sojourner Truth before me was named Bill Bartlett. Bill had taken his boss, Bertrand Stowe, to one of Sallie's parties, and Sallie had paid Grace to be extra nice to Bert. He told her not to ask for tips and to do everything that

Bert wanted. She said that she didn't mind because Bert was sweet. He didn't really know what the party was all about. He thought that she just liked him.

"You know," she said. "Bill Bartlett got Bertie all excited about goin' out an' havin' a good time. He told'im that he should go out an' see how his workin' staff relaxed. Bertie didn't think he was gonna meet no girl—not an' like her too."

The next day he sent roses and chocolate. That weekend he told his wife that he had to do work at Sojourner Truth with Mr. Bartlett but instead he spent long afternoons of love with Grace.

Soon he was helping her with her rent and had agreed to help her get into Los Angeles City College to get a degree in office management. If she passed her courses, he told her, he'd get her a job working in the central office with him.

He even talked about getting a divorce.

"But now Sallie wanna mess up all that," she said.

"How?"

"He got pictures."

"Of you two?"

I could almost hear her nodding over the phone.

"Where'd he get that?"

"He had somebody take'em on the sly at the party when we was, when we was in one'a the back bedrooms. The door didn't have no catch on it. I didn't even see'em take it. He showed'em t'me an' said if I didn't get Bertie to help'im he gonna make sure that he's fired from his job."

"Help him what?" I asked.

"I don't know."

"Come on, Grace, I don't have time t'be messin' on the phone."

"I don't!" she whined. "It's sumpin' about the inventory for his district. They want to make Bill Bartlett his assistant an' then say that things is used an' things is broke. I don't know."

But she did know. So did I.

We met with John at his restaurant and discussed the

matter. John liked Grace. I could see why. Her skin was blackberry and her lips had never lost a thing from her African forebears. She was the kind of small that every man wanted to help. I asked what she thought Stowe would do.

"He's a good man, Easy. He'd either turn us in or kill hisself."

"Then why don't you go someplace else?" I asked. "Get outta L.A. an' let Sallie dig his own hole."

Grace pouted with those beautiful full lips.

"She don't wanna run, Easy," John said. "If that was all she wanted I could help her to do that."

"How come you say that this man Stowe is so good an' he's goin' to one'a Sallie's reefer parties?" I asked.

"It wasn't no reefer that night," she said. "It was only liquor an' Sallie made it seem like it was just a party. You know Bertie just ain't got no experience with that kinda stuff."

Grace wasn't in love, I thought, but it was something. I couldn't figure it out at that time. But I could see that I had some possibilities.

"Okay," I said.

"Okay what?" asked John.

"I know what to do."

"Really?" That was Grace.

"Yeah. I do. You go tell your boyfriend everything."

"Everything?"

"Well . . . you don't have to say that you was at a whole lotta Sallie's parties. But just say what Sallie and Bill Bartlett wanna do. Tell'im about the pictures, tell'im all that, an' then tell'im about me. Say that if he wanna get out of it he should give me a call."

I had already been to the main personnel office for the Board of Education to see what I could see. Grace Phillips offered me some possibilities—that much was for sure.

Three days later I got the call. I had been taking a nap because I was still recuperating from the deep infection that settled in after my wound. Stowe told me that he'd talked to Grace, and then Bill Bartlett. He wanted to know what I could do. I made an appointment to meet him at his office. At first he balked, but I held firm.

I liked the man. He was straightforward and nervous. I guess I'm always a little gleeful when I'm in the seat of power with a white man.

"Grace says I should trust you, Mr. Rawlins," he said. "What can you do for me?"

"It's easy, Mr. Stowe. You just sit at your desk and wait till I come to you. I'll have the photographs, whatever they are, and a promise that Sallie will leave you be."

"How can you do that?"

"I cain't give ya all my secrets now," I said. I smiled and so did Stowe.

"And how much do you charge, Mr. Rawlins?"

"I want Bartlett's job."

"You what?"

From my jacket pocket I took out an application form that I had filled in for the job of supervising senior head custodian. I handed the sheet to Stowe.

"I've managed apartment buildings with the Mofass real estate agency for over fifteen years. And I know how to work with people. It says in the handbook I got with the application that someone can be hired at a higher position at the discretion of the area supervisor. I figure if I can make all this happen smoothly then you might wanna recommend me."

Stowe was amazed at first and then he began to laugh. He laughed very hard and for a long time.

When he was through laughing we had a deal.

Sallie Monroe was a life-taker; a man who had a good mind and great strength of will and body—but nowhere legal to use them. He took up a lot of space, dominating almost every situation with his girth. Sallie hated white people because, on the whole, they didn't respect his mind. He was a buck to them, suited only to tote and break under the weight of unrelenting labor.

Like most black men Sallie took out his anger on other Negroes. But he was always looking to have sway over a

white man, or woman. Usually it was a woman. A prosti-
tute or drug addict. White women or white trash men were
an easy target for Sallie, but he didn't indulge his hate
much, because, first and foremost, he was a businessman—
he never did a thing unless there was a profit to be made.

I knew all that going into Petey's Rib Hut on the corner
of Central and Eighty-third Place.

The Rib Hut had started out as a stand, a patio in front
of a small enclosure where Petey and his wife smoked the
ribs that they sold through the window. As the years went
by Petey made enough money to surround the patio with
a high wooden fence. After a few more years the fence
turned into walls covered by an aluminum roof. The floor
was the same painted cement and the furniture was still
redwood benches but Petey had himself a restaurant all
the same.

Sallie spent every afternoon sitting at the back of the
Rib Hut. He liked sucking ribs and doing business at
the same time.

Sitting with him was Charles Moody, his driver and
bodyguard, and Foxx, a small dandy-looking man who was
always whispering into Sallie's ear.

Little Richard was shouting "Good Golly, Miss Molly" on
the jukebox.

When Sallie saw me coming his eyes went over my
shoulder. He was looking for Mouse, I knew. Mouse was
my friend, and that meant something on streets from Galveston, Texas, to the San Francisco Bay.

"Easy." Sallie grinned at me.

"Hey, Sal. S'appenin'?"

"They say I'ma be free if I just get offa my fat ass an'
walk down the streets of Selma wit' my hands in my
pockets." Sallie slapped Charles on the back and laughed
loud enough to drown out the song. His henchmen
laughed, and looked really pleased, but I don't think they
got the joke.

I didn't have to laugh because Sallie didn't pay my bills.

"What you want, Easy Rawlins?"

"Talk," I said.

"Then talk."

"Just you'n me, Sal."

Charles and Foxx both gave me a who-is-this-fool? look—but I ignored them. I had a strong reputation in the streets and Sallie knew it.

He also knew Mouse.

"Give us a minute," he said to his men. After they moved away he whispered, "This better be good."

I sat down and pulled my jacket closed, hoping that no one saw the weight of the .38 in my right pocket.

"I'm here for a friend'a mines," I said.

Sallie gestured for Petey to bring over more food.

"Bertrand Stowe," I continued.

That got Sallie's attention. "Don't get yo' nose caught up in my business now, Easy."

"I ain't messin' wit' you, Sal," I said. "Stowe called me when he heard that you was gonna mess wit' him. He told me that he wasn't gonna do what you say an' that he was gonna go down to the police."

"Say what?"

I gave a small but definite nod. "You got to understand, Sal. Bert's from a straight white family. He cross at the crosswalk an' leave a dime in the cigar box when the paper boy ain't around."

"He gone leave his liver under my back tire he call cop on me," Sallie said. I knew he meant it. Sallie was a hard case. He didn't play.

But I was serious that day too. I had shared the same sour air with men like Sal and his lackeys for my whole life. One day one of them was bound to kill me—unless I could make the break.

I could have gotten a job as a dishwasher or stone buster, I could have become a regular janitor for the city or state. But I was like Sallie when it came to the disrespect shown to blacks by white men. I needed a job with responsibility and, at least, some pride.

"That's what I told him," I said. "I told'im that you cain't play wit' Sallie. Sallie will fuck you up."

The gangster eyed me. He didn't know what where I was coming from—yet.

"What you want, Easy Rawlins?" he asked again.

"Bert's gonna go to the cops you push'im," I said. "That's a fact. He's a straight arrow an' only go one way. I know that you'll go after him. All that is cut in stone. But it don't have to be."

Sallie stared at me.

I let my hand drift toward my pocket.

"So I got another choice," I said.

"What's that?" Sallie mouthed the words with no voice.

"I give you seventeen hundred and sixty-two dollars and you give me the snapshots—and the negatives."

I was a shorebird crying at the sea.

Sallie gauged me for a moment. The record on the jukebox switched and "Stagger Lee" came on. It played down to the sax solo before Sallie spoke again.

"Tell me why I don't reach over there an' break yo' neck, Easy Rawlins."

He wanted me to say Mouse. He wanted me to run for cover under the protection of my friend. All I had to do was call out Raymond's name and Sallie would have slapped me silly and then gone to have a sit-down with Mouse.

Maybe I would have been smarter to say his name.

But not that day.

No.

"Because if you reach at me," I said, dead serious, "I got a little something right here in my pocket for you. I got it right here."

I've run across quite a few white men who have bragged to me about how they worked their way through college; about how they worked hard to get where they're at. Shit. I'd like to see any one of them working like I did with Sallie that day. I had my hand on the trigger and my eye in his. There was going to be blood or money on the table before long because neither one of us was walking away until the issue was settled.

If it had been Mouse sitting across from me I would have shot without any words. If it had been Mouse I wouldn't have even made it into the room. Mouse would have seen trouble coming and shot me for luck.

But Sallie wasn't on Mouse's level. He was a bully, a pimp; an angry man—but not a courageous one.

"Twenty-five hundred dollars," he said.

I stuck to my number because it was all the money I could get. I decided that I would pay for Mr. Stowe's freedom and he would pay me back with a job.

The trade happened the next morning.

I went alone to Petey's to meet with Sallie and his thugs. I was a fool, I know, not to have brought Raymond with me. But it was my own move. It was a chance at a new life and I was willing to gamble everything for that chance.

Mouse was in the room anyway. Sallie had to be thinking that he wanted me dead. Seventeen hundred dollars was nothing compared to what he could steal out of the Board of Education warehouses. But if he killed me it was only a matter of time before Mouse got to him.

I was playing a card that was still in the deck.

Sallie folded.

He gave me the photograph and negative. It was a blurred image of Grace half-naked, sneering happily down on Bertrand—who was on his knees.

I guess we all have to submit sometimes.

I told myself that that was the last favor in a lifetime of doing favors. From that day on I planned to work for my living; to put in my eight hours and take home my paycheck.

Stowe demanded Bill Bartlett's resignation, got it, and then hired me. There was a lot of red tape but we got through it. Bertrand and I became good friends. I was his confidant.

He'd broken up with Grace after the whole thing was over. But almost every week he'd call me in, or come to my office, and talk about her. He'd tell me about her calling him at work and at home. I knew she did because she called me too, trying to find out how to get to him.

Finally, more than a year later, he broke down and went

back to her after she'd gotten pregnant by some other
man. That's the way Bert was, he wanted to take care of
somebody—Grace needed a whole lot of care.

"Bertrand." I took his hand and shook it.

"Sit down, sit down," he told me. "How's it going?"
Bertrand wore thick glasses that magnified his already
intense eyes. His black-and-gray mustache stuck out like
a bristle brush.

"Oh, I don't know," I said. "I guess it could be better."

"The police were here," he said.

"Oh?"

"They told me that you were suspected for crimes at the
Seventy-seventh Street station." Stowe angled his lenses
at me.

"I see," I said. Each passing minute brought me closer
to the tight-lipped attitude of my earlier years in the street.

"I never knew that you were suspected of murder." Stowe
looked at me for some kind of reply.

He wanted a declaration.

"Is that what they said?" All he got was another
question.

"Is that all you have to say?" asked my boss.

"You didn't ask me about what my record might be when
you had problems with Sallie Monroe and Billy B. All you
cared about then was your wife—and your girlfriend too."

"Is that a threat, Easy?" Stowe was turning whiter, in
more ways than one.

"You the one threatenin', Bert," I said. "The cops come
in here an' scare you an' you ready to give me up. You
already got your story all set about how you didn't know
anything."

Bert took off his glasses and wiped them clean. He looked
up at me with an indecipherable expression.

"Did you have anything to do with that man getting
killed?" he asked.

"What do you think?" I asked back.

"I don't know what to think. The police say that you've
been involved in this kind of thing before."

"And you believe that?"

Bertrand Stowe was confused. He didn't see anything wrong with asking a man if he was implicated in murder. He didn't see anything wrong in believing a stranger in uniform over a friend. It wasn't a rude question—for him to ask.

"Don't you understand me, Easy?"

"I understand you. It's you who don't get me."

Bert sat down and I did too. He put his glasses back on. I crossed my right leg over my left.

"What do you want?" he asked me at last.

"You called me, Mr. Stowe. You wanted me to come here."

"I told you," he said. "The police called. They said that you were a suspect in the killing. They said that you knew something about the people involved and that you were involved in similar crimes in the past."

"They said all that?"

"Yes they did."

"And what did you say?"

"I didn't say anything," Bertrand said. "What was I supposed to say?"

"You could have said that you knew me, that I wasn't the kinda man who went around killin' folks. You could have said that I was an excellent worker who came in on time every day and who bent over backwards to make sure that my plant worked smoothly for the kids and teachers. You could have said that I got a hard principal but that, to your knowledge, I never lost my temper or spoke a word in anger." I sat up straight in my chair. "You could have said I was a good friend to you who never asked you for nuthin' without givin' you something in return. It wouldn't have cost you a dime to tell that man that you backed me up. Not a goddam dime."

Bertrand Stowe had his strong stubby fingers splayed out in front of him on the desk.

"What do you want?" he asked me.

"Just don't count me out unless I'm on the canvas. That's all I ask you for. That, and I might be out of work a couple'a days. You could tell Newgate that you needed me for somethin'. Give him a call and tell him that I'll be needed for a few days at the area office. Tell him that I'll check in at the school but I'll be out a lot too."

Stowe gazed at me like some dumb animal mesmerized by a snake. He nodded after a while and took off his glasses—then put them back on again.

He'd do what I asked him to.

I'd do what I had to.

CHAPTER 14

Simona Eng lived in the San Fernando Valley with her father, Conrad Eng.

During our lunchtime talks in the maintenance office Simona had told us about her father. Mr. Eng was a tall Chinese gentleman who had come to the United States from Hong Kong when he was only five. His father was already dead from weak lungs and a hard life of labor; his mother was dying. Conrad was raised by Hilda Coke, daughter of a prosperous orange farmer from Pomona. Hilda had met the Engs on board the liner *Sea Carnation*, a Dutch ship that had a route across the Pacific early in the century. Hilda had found a great deal of pleasure in the playful boy and was heartbroken when, the night before they landed in San Francisco, his mother succumbed to pneumonia in her cramped quarters in the lower decks of the *Carnation*.

After leaving the home of the Coke family in his late teens Conrad had become a butler. His wife, Irene, was an Italian cook. Conrad only worked until his middle years, when chronic weakness and a mild confusion set in. Early on, Simona's mother died, leaving her daughter and slightly doddering husband to fend for themselves in the San Fernando Valley.

Their house was small but impeccably well kept. The mums and honeysuckle made me jealous. The oranges were the pride of their race.

"Hello," Mr. Eng said. He'd come to the door in a full butler's tux with vest and bow tie. He was two inches taller than I but a full forty pounds lighter. He wavered a little on his feet, reminding me of a reed or a tall stalk of wheat.

"Mr. Eng?"

"Yes," he said through a bright smile. The question in his eyes found no words.

"Is Simona in, sir? My name is Mr. Rawlins. We work together."

"She's very sad today," he confided in me. "You know children shouldn't stay in. Old people have to stay out of the sun. But children need it." His smile was wonderful.

"May I see Simona?"

"Just a moment," he said. He turned and wandered into the small house.

He left the door open and I came in. I wasn't spying on Simona but if I happened to see something you couldn't blame me for that.

All that I saw was beauty. The pale violet walls and sunny green-and-yellow carpets. The furniture was constructed from cherry. There was silver and glass here and there and light coming from every window. Passing a framed mirror on the wall I saw my own smiling face.

"Mr. Rawlins." Her voice broke the smile.

I turned and said, "Hey, Simona. How are you?"

She was wearing a gray sweatshirt with tight exercise pants and red tennis shoes.

"What are you doing here?" Her father had kept all of the manners to himself.

"The police came to see me this morning." I decided to keep the lie in place, not knowing whether Jorge had called or not.

"About the killing?"

"About you."

Simona looked around to see if her father was anywhere near. "Can we go outside, Mr. Rawlins?"

"Sure."

We cut across the front lawn to an old wooden gate that had a doorway but no door. Ivylike vines made a roof for the corridor that led toward the back of the low house.

The yard was a large plot. It was surrounded by three high walls from the neighbors but was still sunny. The lawn bulged toward the middle; a fake well built from weatherod pine was placed at the highest point. Simona sat on the grass near the well and motioned for me to join her.

"Nice place," I said.

"My dad works around the house all day," she said. "He likes . . . doing things more than talking or looking at the TV."

"Did he decorate from memory?"

"What do you mean?"

"From China?"

"I don't know really," she answered, a little perplexed. "He left before he was five. He always says that he doesn't remember anything, but then . . . " She looked around her.

I yanked a blade of grass from the lawn.

"What did they say?" she asked. "The police, I mean."

"That they thought you knew more about that man they found than you said."

"Why?"

"They didn't say," I said. "You know that cop Sanchez has a hard eye."

Simona shivered and nodded. "I know, but . . . I don't see what he could want with me."

"You don't have to lie to me, Simona. I already told Jorge that the cops had been asking about you. He told me that you knew that man," I said. "I told him that I didn't think you had anything to do with anything anywhere near somebody gettin' killed. I don't, but I figured I better come out here and warn you about what they were saying."

Simona was biting her lip. She shifted her position and I noticed how shapely her legs looked in those close-fitting pants.

She noticed me noticing and shifted into a more modest pose.

"You're right, Mr. Rawlins," she said. Maybe it was just to get my eyes back on her face. "I wouldn't be involved. I hadn't seen Roman in over a year."

"Roman?"

"That was his name. He was Mrs. Turner's brother-in-law."

"So you really knew him?" I was amazed that a young coed, from this manicured little house, would actually lie to the police.

"He came to one of these parties that Mrs. Turner used to give—more like teas actually."

"Who would go to those parties?" I asked. "I mean, were there other people from the school there?"

"Mr. Langdon went," she said and then she frowned. "Miss Charford and Miss Hollings too—Mr. Preston came once. She used to have them every six weeks or so, but that was a long time ago."

"How come she stopped?"

Simona let the lids of her eyes get heavy, so they almost closed—that was her way of getting dramatic.

"It was after Roman came," she said. "Idabell's husband brought him to that first tea but pretty soon Roman was having parties of his own. Holland didn't want to have the teas anymore, he wanted to go to Roman's parties."

"I guess Roman didn't have finger sandwiches, huh?"

"No," she said softly. "They would smoke marijuana sometimes. I mean, I never did, I only had some wine, but some of them would. And Roman . . . well, Roman . . . "

"How well did you know him?" It was the right question at the right moment.

"He spoke French," she said as if that should have explained everything. "He was very sweet. At least he was at first. But then, when I couldn't help him, he just dropped me. If it wasn't for Jorge I don't know what I would have done. I couldn't eat or work . . . "

"What did he want?" I heard my voice. It was softer than chamois cloth.

"Huh?"

"Roman. What did he want from you?"

"I don't know. He liked it that I spoke French. At first I thought he was lonely for that. His parents spoke French in the house when he was a boy. But then he wanted me to go to Paris with him. He said that I could study at the Sorbonne. I told him that I couldn't go. He said that if I wanted to be a teacher it would help a lot if I studied in Europe. But I told him that I couldn't leave my father alone for even a week. And that we needed my salary."

"So what'd he say to that?"

"He said that he'd come up with the money I needed. That scared me and I said no. We went out a few times after that but then he just never called again."

"Where did Roman have his parties?" I asked.

That was one question too many. Simona looked in my eyes wondering if I might not have a reason for being out there; a reason of my own.

"I don't remember," she said. "I never drove. Different places, you know."

A large jay landed on the ground near us. She cocked her head in our direction and then proceeded to gouge an earthworm from the lawn.

"Can I get you something, Mr. Rawlins?" Simona asked.

I could see her father, in his butler's suit, standing inside the back door of the house. He was watching us. Suddenly I got the impression that the simple-headed old man had an antique pistol in his pocket. All I had to do was grab Simona trying to make her tell me where the parties were held. I'd grab her and he'd squeeze off a lucky shot that would lodge in my brain. It would be ruled self-defense; a father saving his daughter from rape out by the old fake well.

"When will you be coming back in to work?" I asked.

"Tomorrow," she said. "Mr. Rawlins?"

"Yeah." I stood up.

"Do you think that the police knew that I was at those pot parties?"

"No. But if there were other teachers from the school

around there, then you better tell the sergeant that you were there. Tell him that you were in shock when you saw your old boyfriend and that you couldn't bring yourself to say that you knew'im. Sanchez won't like it but in the long run it'll be better for you."

"You really think so?" the young woman asked.

"Uh-huh. And, Simona?"

"Yes, Mr. Rawlins?"

"The cops'd be mad if they knew I came down here to warn you. Maybe you shouldn't mention it."

She looked at me and nodded. But who knew what she thought?

CHAPTER 15

I'm a book reader. There's always a book on my nightstand; sometimes more than one. At that time I was reading *Dr. No* by Ian Fleming and *The Earth* by Emile Zola.

I love literature but the phone book was still my favorite reading. It was the ledger of my world. Holland and Roman Gasteau were right next to each other in the Gs. They were born one after the other, in school they were seated in the same row. Their mother probably dressed them the same and they died on the same day.

Roman lived in an apartment building down on La Brea; not too far from my house. I drove by in the late afternoon. It was a great block of a building with two police cars parked out front. I even saw the back of Sanchez's head in the open arcade that led to the atrium.

I drove on trying to think of a way into Roman's life.

Jesus and Feather weren't at the house when I got there. Usually he'd go to her school after practice and bring her home. Sometimes I'd pick her up. Feather loved it when I came by the school. I liked meeting her. But I had to pass that day. I sat down and tried to think out the problem. Did Holland really threaten to kill Pharaoh? If he did, was that why his brother came to the school? Why did Idabell leave? And why lie about the dog?

The dog?

Where was that damned dog? I still planned to get rid of him. I had softened up a little, though. My new plan was to take him out to my old friend Primo. Primo would know somebody who wanted a dog.

I got up and looked around the house. There was no sign of him anywhere except for a small gift he'd left on my slipper. It was a dry turd so I figured that he'd done it in the morning.

He wasn't in the yard. Or, if he had been, he'd slipped out through the bushes into the Horns' property.

I was about to go next door when it struck me—why was I looking for that damn dog? He didn't know anything, and if he did know, and he could talk, he wouldn't have told me. That dog hated me more than any other solitary being ever had.

An hour later I had a plan.

Feather came running in the front door.

"Daddy, Daddy, Daddy!"

Pharaoh dashed in at her heels. He was yelping happily until he saw me. Then he crouched down and growled. Jesus walked in over him.

"Hi, Dad," my son said.

"Where'd that dog come from?" I asked Feather. I could tell that my voice had a sharp edge because a scared look came over her face.

"We left him over with Mr. Horn," Jesus said. "He was crying so much this morning when we were leaving that Feather wanted to take him to school. But then I said that maybe Mr. Horn wouldn't mind."

"That's an awful lot to ask of your neighbor," I said.

"Uh-uh," Feather whined. "Mr. Horn like Frenchie. He said so, huh, Juice?"

Jesus nodded. He looked at me and then looked away.

There was still that money in the box upstairs to talk
about. But Jesus was too afraid to bring it up—so was I.

I let them settle in. Pharaoh followed me around the
house staying at the corners and watching my every move.
That dog got under my skin.

After a while I said to Jesus, "Take that ole wagon'a
Feather's and go on down to Mr. Hong's shop. Get me a
box of steaks. Two-pound porterhouse steaks. The aged
stuff. Tell'im t'put'em on my bill."

Jesus nodded and went to get the wagon from the garage.

"Honey," I said to Feather.

"Yeah?" She was watching Pharaoh watch me. "Frenchie
like you, Daddy."

"Oh? Why you say that?"

"Cause he always wanna look at you."

That devil dog had everybody fooled but me.

"Honey," I said again.

"Uh-huh."

"You know I would keep little heartache here if I could.
But he belongs to somebody else who loves him even more
than you do."

"I'll feed him, Daddy. I'll build him a house in the
backyard."

"But honey, it's not that. I know that you'd take care of
him. But he's not ours. Do you understand that?"

"Yeah," she said through pouting lips. "Can I go play
now?"

"Don't you want to tell me what happened in school
today?"

"No. I wanna go play with Frenchie."

Mr. Hong sent a few bottles of barbecue sauce along with
the steaks. He had no idea of how devious my mind was
at that time.

The police cars were gone from in front of Roman Gasteau's
building by the time I returned. I took the white carton of
steaks from the trunk of my car and went in the external
entranceway through a corridor of coral-colored plaster.

Once inside I went from door to door. The inner walls of the atrium were also coral. They shone from electric lights and doors that opened on evening TVs. There was talking and music and shows playing. In the courtyard children darted and screamed among the rubber plants and dwarf palms.

My plan was simple. I was Brad Koogan, a name borrowed from a friend who died at the Battle of the Bulge. Brad was going from one apartment to another trying to sell two-pound porterhouse steaks for a dollar each. He got the steaks from a truck driver friend of his. My reasoning ran like this: If somebody thought that I stole those steaks but they were still willing to do business with me, then they might know something about Roman and the circles he ran in.

Nobody answered the first door I knocked on. Maybe they weren't home or maybe they got a peep of me and decided that I was bad news.

The next door was answered by an elderly black woman in a red-and-black-checkered robe. Thick bifocals dangled from her neck on a fake pearl necklace. She was small and almost bald.

"Yes, mistah?" Her nearly toothless smile was down-home friendly.

I hesitated a moment because she was so old and frail. But the street is a wild place and compassion there is more dear than gold. I had to ask myself was this woman worth that much to me.

My answer went like this:

"Hi. My name is Brad Koogan. I'm sellin' porterhouse steaks, two pounds each at a dollar apiece."

"Hi. My name's Celia," she said. "But, Mr. Koogan, I ain't tackled a steak in over ten years."

"Celia," a man's voice called from the back of the apartment.

When he came into view I saw that he was the male version of her, checkered robe and all.

"Celia," he said again.

"Yes, Carl," she answered, slightly perturbed. "I hear ya."

"Who is it?" he asked, looking right at me.

"Brad Koogan, sir," I said. "I'm sellin' steaks."

"I don't buy my meat offa the street, mistah," he said.

He was gruff but I liked him anyway. Celia was smiling at her man. I lost heart then.

"I'm sorry, sir," I said. "I'll move on."

"What's your name again?" Celia asked.

"Koogan," I said. "Brad Koogan."

"We're the Blanders," she told me.

It was an apology for her husband's rude behavior. I thought that when I'd gone they'd spend a good two hours enjoying themselves arguing back and forth about how she shouldn't have opened the door to a stranger and how he should learn to be more courteous to people.

I steeled myself to be more ruthless from then on.

The next few doors were closed politely in my face. I was happy to know that there were so many honest people in the world but at the same time it cut into my ability to exploit the situation. I knew that some of the people who closed their doors would call the landlord and ask him to keep hustlers away from them and their kids. If he was a good landlord, like I hoped that I was, he would come down to see what was going on—or he would call the cops.

I had no desire to talk to the police, so I hurried on my way.

Cassandra Vincent wanted three steaks but she didn't know anyone who lived in the apartment building.

Butch Mayhew wanted me to give him a sampler before he'd agreed to buy. When I told him no he tried to convince me by saying, "I'll buy all of 'em if the one I taste ain't tough."

I wasn't fooled by Butch. He'd try to get me to leave him a steak to taste. If I refused he'd offer to cook it up right then and there. At least he'd get a few bites in.

"You wanna taste, huh?" I asked.

"Yeah." Butch had something wrong with his back. His chest jutted forward and his stomach hollowed back toward his spine as if someone were trying to tickle him. He wore a tattered T-shirt and striped boxer shorts.

"You could leave me a small one and go on," he said. "An' when you come back around I'll buy what you got left—if the one I et is tender."

"That's okay," I said. "I'll cook it for ya. Just show me the stove an' I'll burn it right now."

Butch had a two-burner Phillips-Regent gas stove. It was so crusty and greasy I was surprised that the jet caught the flame from my match. I had to fry the steak because the oven was beyond repair.

"Smells good," Butch said as he inhaled fumes of burning flesh.

"You live here long?" I asked.

"'Bout six months. But I'll be gone two weeks after the first."

"Eviction day?"

Butch grinned and cocked his head.

"Say," I said. "Tell me, did Roman Gasteau live here?"

"Still do. Or maybe so. I ain't seen'im in a few days."

"You know'im?"

"To say hi. Hey, hey, why'ont you flip it ovah, you know I likes my meat bloody."

"Uh-huh. You got some garlic powder?"

"Naw, man."

I followed the crippled man's gaze over to the kitchen shelf. There I saw a crumpled-up handkerchief, a can of Barbasol shaving cream, an uncovered jar of Skippy peanut butter, and a loaf of Wonder Bread.

"I used to run with Roman a while back," I said. "He give some bad parties."

"Yeah?" Butch wondered. "He ain't never asked me. But he live down in one-B if you wanna run down there an' see 'im."

"Uh-huh. But if he ain't there you think anybody 'round here might know how I could get in touch wit' him? You know I could use a party after pullin' all'a this meat around after me."

"Ridley an' them know'im."

"He live here?"

"Up in three-A."

I could tell by the way Butch was looking at me that he was suspicious of my questions. But the main thing on his mind was steak.

I put the pan of fried and bloody meat down in front of him. It smelled good.

I was impressed at the way Butch made Mr. Hong's tender aged steak seem tough. He chewed and chewed, frowned and grimaced.

"Hey, brother," he said through a mouthful of meat. "This shit here ain't prime."

He wanted to play, and so I gave him a show. I banged on his tile counter and swore at him and all his relations. After I got through yelling I stormed out of his apartment leaving the partially eaten steak in his frying pan.

He'd earned the tip.

Ridley McCoy was a nondescript man. His hair was wavy and his eyes tended toward brown. He had a small nose and dark skin. His pants could have fit with a sports jacket but he could have also worn them to work; they went perfectly with his thin-strapped undershirt. Ridley wouldn't look me in the eye but I knew that he was interested in cheap steak.

"Where you get'em?" he asked my chin.

"From a guy I know."

"Could you get some more?" Here he hadn't even tasted one steak and he already wanted a dozen.

"Maybe I could. Why? You wanna be a regular customer?"

Ridley looked from side to side and then said, "Why'ont you come on in outta earshot."

His furniture, I was sure, was stolen from a motel. The console TV still had the markings from where a coin box had been attached. There was a small Formica-topped table that stood on a single chrome stalk in the corner. The battered Venetian blinds were levered shut and there was only one lamp, leaving the room uncomfortably dark.

One half-open door led from the room. Maybe that was a bedroom, or maybe he slept on the couch.

"How many steaks could you get?" he asked in a whispery little voice. It was the kind of voice that got you mad because you had to strain to hear it.

"I cain't hear you, man," I said loudly. "Somebody sleep in there?"

Ridley looked at the door and then back at my chin.

"Girlfriend," he said.

"Well, maybe I better come back later."

"Naw, man. That's okay. She could wake up," he said. Then he shouted, "Penny! Penny, come in here!"

I heard a rustling and then a thump; a few seconds passed and then came a groan. Soon after that the door opened. A young brown woman wearing only a man's dress shirt came in the room. When she saw that Ridley wasn't alone she brought two fingers to the base of her throat—I guess that was all the modesty she had left.

"Wha?"

"This is Brad, Penny. He got some steaks he wanna sell."

"So? I was sleep."

Ridley went to his roommate and gave her a big unfriendly hug. The tussle pulled the shirt far up enough for me to see that she didn't have anything on underneath. Neither of them seemed to care what I saw.

"Why'ont you bring out some wine, baby," Ridley said to her.

Penny went back into the bedroom and turned on a light. I could see her, through the now open door, go into another room. She returned with a quart of Black Wren red wine and a small stack of Dixie cups. She set the cups and wine on a small motel coffee table and sat down on the couch, pulling her bare feet up under her thighs.

There was a time I would have walked across fire for a woman like that. I could still feel the heat.

"Come on, girl," Ridley complained. "Cain't you pour it?"

"Pour it your damn self," she replied. "I was sleep."

Ridley did the honors and said to me, "Sit'own."

I perched myself across from the man and his mate.

Penny had a broad face and hair that would never let you know where it was going. Her lips were there to curse, kiss, or complain. And her widely spaced eyes saw a spectrum of light that most men never suspected existed.

"Mr. Koogan here is sellin' steaks," Ridley said to Penny. Then to me, "How many more steaks can you get?"

"How many can you eat?"

"I was thinkin' that I could sell some. I know just about ev'rybody in this buildin'. The one across the street too. Maybe I could go partners wit' you if you could get enough steak."

That was business in L.A. An opportunity comes and you make a grab for it. Ridley didn't know a thing about me, or my steaks, but he was willing to cement a partnership anyway. He was on me faster than I got to Idabell.

"Well, that sounds good," I said tentatively. "How many you want?"

Ridley's eyes almost met mine, he was that excited. Penny yawned and I wondered if there were any black dentists in L.A.

"I bet I could sell fifty'a them, if they really prime, in two, three days."

"Fifty?" I was impressed.

"Yeah," Ridley said.

Penny's gaze rolled across me. She had no idea what we were talking about but she was still an important part of the negotiations.

"Well," I said, doing the numbers in my head. "You gimme thirty-five dollars an' we got a deal."

"Thirty-five dollars!"

I was surprised that he could shout.

"Yep," I said. "That give you a profit of fifteen when you sell'em."

"Uh-uh, man. I'm the one gonna be doin' all the work. I should get at least half."

I tried to look like I was upset but at the same time greedy to have a man out there doing my sales.

"Okay," I said. "Fifty-fifty."

"When could you bring'em by?"

"I could get'em by tomorrow. But I'ma need my money."

"What money?"

"Twenty-fi'e dollars for fifty steaks."

"You get that when I sell'em."

I shook my head, a somber man of experience. "No, brother. Uh-uh. I tried that once. Actually that's why I'm here at your buildin'." I held my breath.

"What's that?" he asked.

"Dude name'a Roman owe me some money. Right after I unload these steaks I'ma go down to Roman's place an' have me a talk wit' that man." I stroked my chin and looked menacing.

"Roman gone." That was Penny. The mention of the Gasteau brother had gotten her to sit up.

"Moved?"

"I'ont know," Penny said. "Cops come here today askin' 'bout him. They took everything outta his place in bags."

I slammed my hand down on the table so hard that both of my hosts jumped. "Goddam!"

After he settled a little Ridley asked, "He owe you a lotta money?"

"Fi'e hunnert dollars. Is that a lot?" I asked.

"Yeah."

"You know where I could find him?" I asked Penny.

She cut a glance at Ridley and said, "No."

I could see that Ridley was torn between greed and jealousy. He wasn't a bad-looking man but he wasn't tall and handsome, he didn't wear snakeskin shoes. I was sure that Penny had given Roman the eye, and maybe even a little bit more of her anatomy. Ridley didn't want to bring that man into their motel-decorated home. But one thing I was certain of—Ridley would have dropped Penny in a minute if there was a dollar to be made.

"What about that place?" he asked her.

"What place?"

"That place I told you not to go to no mo'."

"I thought you didn't even wanna talk about that," she said, sneering at her man, moving her head from side to side in a disdainful rhythm. "I thought you said that you

was gonna tear my head off if I ever even said somethin'
about it."

"And now I'm sayin' t'tell the man here!" Ridley was
asserting himself.

Penny turned to me. "There's a club up in the Hollywood
Hills," she said. "The Chantilly. It's a white club but the
man who run it got a place around back for black—
the Black Chantilly. It's a big house and a private club
like. They got a room for dancin' an' one for gamblin'. They
got private rooms too—"

"An' what the hell was you doin' up there?"

Ridley was up on his feet. He swung at her with an open
hand and missed, on purpose it seemed to me, over the top
of her head. Penny screamed and went down on the floor,
ducking under the low coffee table.

"You said you wanted me t'tell'im where Roman was!"
Penny shouted. "I didn't say nuthin'!"

"You the one said he was gone!" Ridley swung at the air
again. "Maybe you know where he went to!"

"Noooo!"

"Hey! Hey, Ridley," I said, using his name for the first
time since he'd given it. "Hey, man. You wanna talk about
them steaks?"

Ridley took a deep breath. Penny looked up at him and
he jerked his hand like he meant to swing again, but he
just wanted to see her flinch one more time.

"Hey, man," he said to me. "Sorry, but you know this
here bitch just don't ack right. She gonna lay up on her
ass wit' me payin' the rent, an' then got the nerve t'be
winkin' at some fancy-assed mothahfuckah upstairs. She
lucky I don't kill both they ass!"

Penny crouched down further.

"Get the hell outta here, bitch!" Ridley screamed at her.
"Why the fuck you come out here near naked in front'a
some strange man?"

Penny moved quickly, staying close to the floor as she
went. She made it to the bedroom, slamming the door
behind her.

Ridley was staring at the closed door.

"Women like to drive a man crazy," he said.

"Don't you know it," I agreed, hoping to calm him down. "I'll tell you what I'll do, brother."

"What?"

"I'll leave these nine steaks here wit' you tonight and then I'll come back tomorrow with fifty more. You gimme the four dollars and fifty cent an' then I'll come back for the balance in two more days."

I handed the box over to him and he took it. He let his gaze ride high for a moment to catch a glimpse of my eyes.

"What you doin' here, man?" he asked.

"Sellin' steaks an' lookin' for a man wear snakeskin shoes."

"You gonna hurt him?"

"If I can," I said. "If I can."

CHAPTER 16

It was a little after nine when I got home. I was soaking from the rain that had started while I asked questions. It was that blanket type of L.A. rain and I'd left the umbrella a block away in my car.

Feather was asleep on the couch with the damn dog nestled in her arms. Jesus was watching a western on channel thirteen. He was nodding. Jesus spent two to three hours every day practicing for track and field. He ate large meals and went to bed early but he always tried to stay up until I got home. In the earlier years it was because he felt bad for me after my wife, Regina, had left. But now it was just habit. I was used to my kiss good night and he was used to giving it to me.

"You better go to bed, Juice."

He nodded and then reached over to shake Feather but I said, "Leave her. I'll get her to bed."

He came over to hug me and I kissed him on the top of his head. Then he stumbled down to the hallway toward his bed.

I went to the bathroom and then to the kitchen. There was ice water in an old-fashioned milk bottle in the refrigerator.

I took the phone on its long tangled cord into the living room and sat down on the couch next to my girl. When Pharaoh growled I battled his nose with my finger. He moved away from me, down to the other end of the sofa, and considered dog curses to lay upon my soul.

I placed the phone in my lap and was about to dial a number when the thing rang. I picked it up quickly. Feather moved her head up and opened her eyes, but when she saw me she closed them again.

The first thing I heard was the racket of a crowded room or maybe a public space. There were people talking and things being moved and slammed down. There was laughter too.

"Easy?" Her voice was loud to get over the din and also hoarse because she wanted to whisper. But as strained as the words were I still knew who it was.

"Idabell?"

"Oh, it is you. Thank God."

"Where are you?" I asked.

"A little place on Santa Barbara. I have to talk to somebody here. Oh, I'm in a lot of trouble, honey. A lot of trouble."

Somebody laughed in the background, a good joke being told in some other part of town. There was music but its words and melody were lost in the static of the telephone wire.

"What is it?" I asked.

"Somebody killed my husband," she whispered. "And, and . . ."

"And what?"

"And his twin brother . . . Roman."

"Who killed them?"

When she said, "Easy?" I knew that she wasn't going to give up any information right away.

"What?"

"How's Pharaoh?"

The cur raised his head from his corner of the couch. Maybe his dog ears picked up the name on her lips.

"He's fine," I said.

"Can I talk to him?"

"Talk to him? No. The kids're sleep. But don't worry, he's fine."

"I have to get away, Easy."

"Idabell, what happened? What happened to your husband?"

"I don't know," she whimpered.

Pharaoh raised his head a half an inch more.

"I left home just like I told you. Holland was high, I guess I didn't tell you that. He'd been drinking, drinking." She repeated the word as if she were trying to convince me of its accuracy. "And then he went out."

"Where'd he go?"

"I don't know," she said. "But as soon as he was gone I left with Pharaoh."

"Why were you so scared, Idabell?"

"He'd gone crazy."

"Crazy from what?"

"I don't know, Easy," she whined. "I don't know."

"And did he call you at school?"

"Yes."

"And you went to meet him?"

There was an explosion of laughter somewhere in the restaurant.

"No," she said. "He said that he was going to come down to the school to get me and Pharaoh. He said that he would pull me right out of the classroom if I didn't come. You know he would have done it. So I ran. I'm sorry that I left Pharaoh with you but I was scared that if Holly found me with him he would have done what he said."

"And so then you went to go'n tell Mr. Preston about this?"

"How did . . . I mean, yes. I went to tell Bill, because I was scared. You had already helped me with Pharaoh. I couldn't ask for any more than that."

"Uh-huh." I was thinking that Holland wasn't the only one to ever hate that dog. "So why are you callin' me if you got so much trouble? We don't even know each other."

"Don't be like that, Easy. I meant yesterday. You're the first person in a long time that I feel safe with."

"What about Mr. Preston?" I asked.

She paused a moment and then said, very softly, "I called you, not him."

"Because you feel safe with me?"

"Yes."

"But what about me?" I asked.

"What do you mean?"

"I mean, am I safe? The cops are on me already. I asked where you were gone to and now the cops wanna talk to me."

"You didn't tell them about Pharaoh, did you?"

"No, I didn't. But I woulda told'em if I didn't think that they'd throw me together with you. For all I know you'd tell'em that I killed your husband 'cause we had a roll on the desktop."

She had no answer to that.

"Don't you have anything to say?" I asked her.

"I don't know what to say, except that if you don't help me I don't know what I'll do."

"Hold up, Mrs. Turner. I don't even know you. I don't give a damn about you or your husband an' I surely don't care 'bout that damn dog—"

Pharaoh jumped to his feet and yelped once. I swatted him off the couch and he went running, probably to look for my other slipper.

"Was that him?" Idabell asked. "Was that Pharaoh?"

"Yeah, but I can't put him on right now. He had to go to the bathroom."

Feather shifted peacefully, putting her arm up on my lap.

"I know you're angry, Easy," she said. I was sorry that

I'd told her my name. "It's not your problem, you're right. But I still need you to do one thing for me."

"What's that?"

"Could you bring me my dog? I'm going to leave L.A. I'm going to leave the country. All I need is Pharaoh."

"That dog'll mark you," I said. "You'd be better off leavin' him somewhere and having him sent on later."

And I didn't feel guilty either. If Ida was running that meant she thought the police could get her on something. If she ran their attention would concentrate on her. But if they got frustrated and wanted to give me heat, and if I knew where she was—well then . . .

"I couldn't live without my little man, Easy. He's all I have. Bring him to me. Please."

"If I was going to give'im to you when would you want him?"

"Tonight. Late though. I can't get to the place I'm staying until late."

"How late?"

"Not before eleven."

"Where?"

She gave me an address on Hoagland Street, off of Adams Boulevard. It was a house and not an apartment. She promised that she'd be there by twelve.

So did I.

"Daddy, where's Frenchie?" Feather had been sleeping with the top of her head nuzzled up against my thigh for nearly half an hour. I didn't have anywhere to go and no place that I'd rather be.

"He ran off in the back somewhere," I said. "But the woman who owns him called. She wants him back. You know she really loves him."

I wanted to be able to say the next day that I'd told her about returning Pharaoh to Idabell. She might get upset but at least she wouldn't think that I was doing things behind her back.

She sat up pushing her little hands against my chest and asked, "What was my momma like, Daddy?"

"Oh," I crooned in a low voice. I lifted her and held her in my lap. "She was light-skinned and a very beautiful dancer. I only ever met her once," I lied. "That's when she asked me to take care of you. She was flying away to Europe somewhere to dance for somebody really important but the plane crashed and she was lost out there in the ocean."

It was a story that we'd made up together over the years. Most of it was true. Her mother was actually white. And she was a dancer, of the exotic variety. I never knew who Feather's father was; her mother might not have known either. As a matter of fact I had never even met her mother. I found Feather after the police had forced me to help them catch her mother's killer.

"Was my real daddy on that plane too?"

"Uh-huh."

Feather nestled her head against my chest.

"Did they love me a whole lot?"

"More than anything, honey. More than anybody. That's why they asked me to take care of you forever if anything happened, because they loved you so much."

Feather went to sleep with the declaration of love burrowing down into her dreams. I took her to her room and undressed her. I placed her in the high bed that she wanted so much and hung all of her clothes in the stand-up closet that I'd built for her.

A girl's voice answered my call to Mofass. "Hello?"

"Jewelle?"

She hesitated a second and then said, "Hi, Mr. Rawlins. How are you?"

"Fine, JJ. Just fine. Mofass there?"

"Uncle Willy up in the bed. He's sick."

My real estate agent, Mofass, had emphysema and surprised the doctors with every breath he drew.

"I got to talk to him, honey."

"Sorry, Mr. Rawlins, but I can't get him outta the bed at this time of night."

Jewelle was a distant cousin of Mofass's ex-girlfriend,

Clovis MacDonald. She was only sixteen two years before when she helped Mofass contact me to get away from her auntie. Clovis was trying to bleed away everything that Mofass had, but we put a stop to that.

After that Jewelle worked for Mofass and lived with EttaMae. But as soon as she turned eighteen she moved in with Mofass.

Jewelle had one of the toughest minds I had ever encountered in man or woman. She was a straight-A student all through Crenshaw High School but she decided against college because Uncle Willy, her pet name for Mofass, needed her. Clovis and her brothers had it in for them, so Jewelle moved them to an isolated little home in Laurel Canyon. She got a place there through a man who owned property down in Watts that Mofass represented. Then she hired Buford D. Howell, a UAW man from Detroit, to collect the rent and maintain the properties.

On the night of her eighteenth birthday she moved in with Mofass. She said that he was sick, she still called him Uncle Willy, but we all knew that there was more to that relationship than good friends.

If you wanted to get a letter to Mofass you had to send it to his PO box. If you wanted to call him you had to use his answering service—unless you were one of the three people who had his private number. He and Jewelle stayed in their posh little house perched up over Sunset Boulevard living like two young lovers; him hacking from emphysema and her holding camphor and menthol under his nose.

"I got to talk to him, Jewelle," I said.

"What about?"

"Did the cops call your service?"

"Yeah, but you cain't talk to Uncle Willy 'bout that. He didn't even get the message."

"Okay," I said. "All right. But listen, I told the cops I was out lookin' at the apartments night before last. I said I was with Mofass. Could you get him to back me up on that?"

"Sure can. I'll tell'im first thing when he get up." She

thought for a moment and then said, "At breakfast, I mean."

"Do you wanna know why I'm askin'?" I wondered if she understood what she was getting into.

"It don't matter, Mr. Rawlins. Uncle Willy owe you his life and I owe you too. It don't matter what you want. Anything we got is yours."

"Is that true?" I asked, no longer thinking that I was talking to a child.

"You could drink it," she answered in a phrase formed in north Texas.

Never in my long years of knowing Mofass could I trust him completely. He was small-minded and cowardly. All he ever thought about was the money roll in his pocket. But when Jewelle came along he became as constant as the tide.

"Thanks, honey," I said, ready to get on with the rest of my troubles.

"Mr. Rawlins?"

"Yeah?"

"Um, well . . . "

"Come on, JJ, spit it out. I got to go now."

"Uncle Willy an' me was just wonderin' if maybe you wanna come work for him. I mean, you'd be making more money from us than they pay at the schools. You know all about how buildin's work and stuff. Mr. Howell have people he trust to do work but you know they won't even talk to a girl. I figure, I mean me an' Uncle Willy, that you could show me how stuff works and then I could make better decisions on the spot."

She was right. Men didn't like women who wanted to be independent. I could have taught her everything she needed to know about real estate maintenance and value. But that's not why she wanted me to work for them. She loved Mofass but she was lonely too. She needed somebody who read books to talk to sometimes. Buford Howell read the racing forms on Saturdays and the hymnal on Sundays—that was it.

Jewelle needed someone to talk to her about the paper and the big world out beyond a paycheck or a dirty joke.

"I can't just up and quit my job, honey. It's not so much the salary but the benefits and the future."

Her silence told me how sad I'd made her.

"But maybe I could work with you on the weekends. Maybe every other one, you know, like a consultant."

"That would be great," she said. And I was happy because she sounded young again.

I cleaned up and put on my good brown woolen suit. My shirt was buff silk and the cufflinks were yellow gold and onyx. My shoes were a soft, light brown leather, and the socks matched my shirt in fabric and in color.

I looked at myself in the mirror and smiled. Then I thought about the Gasteau brothers; they were dressed fine too. It hadn't helped them.

I left a note on the kitchen table for Jesus. If Feather woke up he would take care of her.

I walked out of the house exhilarated that I could still get out, and scared that it felt so good.

CHAPTER 17

Pharaoh didn't want me picking him up and told me so. But when I bared my teeth and snarled the yellow dog backed down.

I drove toward Hoagland Street while he sat in the back-seat planning guerrilla tactics that I couldn't even imagine.

The wide boulevards shone brightly and black under a glassy sheen of rain and streetlights.

The address on Hoagland was another small house. There was another light on and another car parked on the side. There was no berry tree, no recessed porch in which to hide. The walkway was a series of cement disks that were laid out in a meandering trail up to the front door.

The rest of the street was empty. Nothing stirred except the splattering rain.

After five minutes I hadn't seen anything. No matches struck in darkness; no black cats hissing at their own wet fur.

Pharaoh gave out a little yelp and for the first time I agreed with him—it was time to go out and ring the doorbell.

The bell was disconnected or maybe it was broken. I knocked lightly but no one stirred. I was afraid to knock loudly or call out, so I tried the doorknob. If it was locked I would go to Primo's the next morning and give him the dog; then I'd forget Idabell and her dead relations.

But the door was not locked.

"Hello?" I called into the dark entrance. "Idabell?"

I closed my umbrella and shook the loose water from it.

To the right was a dark doorway and to my left a turn into a lighted room. On the wall facing the door was a mirror that reflected my own shadowy silhouette and the blurry lamp from the street behind me.

I went toward the light thinking of how many times I'd called moths fools.

She was sprawled on her back in the center of the floor, one hand flung out over her head and her mouth agape.

"Naw," I said in the smallest whisper.

At the sound of my voice her eyes opened and a soft smile came to her lips. She reached toward me with both arms like my daughter did almost every morning. Out of habit I extended my hands.

"What you doin' on the floor?" I asked as she rose.

"My back hurt," she said. "I must've fallen asleep like that."

"But . . . "

"Hold me." Her body thrust forward as if some invisible force were pulling her to my chest. "Hold me."

I didn't love her, I didn't care about her—I didn't even like her since she tricked me into taking her dog. But the warmth of her body through our clothes couldn't be denied. All of those proper ideas and good women couldn't hold my wild heart like she did.

"I've been so lonely," she whispered.

It might have been a sweet lie but her words were true to my heart. I was lonely. I was cold inside. Idabell spoke to a deep hunger that grew in me back when there was only hunger and need. She'd pulled me out into the street and now I wanted to play.

Her hands moved down between us and showed me what magic they could do.

"Your suit's going to get wrinkled," she told me.

My pants fell down around my ankles again. She shoved me backwards into the chair using her shoulder to push because her hands were busy making me mumble. When I was seated I leaned forward to pull off my pants, but she grabbed both my hands by the fingers and pulled them away.

"Leave them," she said. "You can't run if your ankles are tied."

I tried to push past her hands but when she took my erection in her mouth I faltered. And then, when she kissed my lips with that salty brew, I relented.

She moved her head half a foot back from mine and gave me a serious look as if she were searching for defects in my character. Then she kissed me again, moving her tongue deeply inside my mouth. She went back and forth between my hard-on and my lips a few times, each time stopping to gauge her effect.

When she saw that there was no fight left in me she stood up and opened her blouse, showing me with a coy smile that she had no bra on. She hiked her skirt way up on her waist.

When she moved to come astride me I put up my arms to steady her but she said, "Put your hands down," just like she must have said every day in her classroom.

I was used to being in charge with women, at least I was used to playing that role in love. But Idabell ruled that night. I grabbed on to the wooden arms of the chair obeying her command and she rocked me further and further down into the cushion. When I tried to pull back up she told me to be still.

Every now and then she'd arch back telling me with her body, and a turn of her eye, to kiss her breast.

I was getting more and more excited, and so was she. We were going at it hard and loud when all of a sudden we both just stopped. We were very excited and neither one of us had come, but we had to stop and be still for a little while; like small birds who have risen too high on a hot breeze, we had to coast back down toward the earth.

Her face was wet. The look in her eyes would have been called insane at any other time.

"Easy?"

"Yeah?"

"Oh. Uh, I want to ask you."

"Wha'?"

"Do you believe me?"

I did. I really did and I told her so.

"I'd never lie to you," she said. "I mean . . . " She laughed a little. "I mean I would lie but I'm not. I need you."

Those three words shot a tremor through me.

"Hold it, Easy," she said, feeling my mood. "Wait a second. I didn't do anything wrong. I want you to believe that."

"Yeah," I said.

"Really?" she asked.

I didn't answer. Neither of us said anything for the next while. I fell out from the chair and we wrestled across the floor more like snakes than humans, or birds.

In the dream there was an orange-hot sunset at the horizon of a dense German forest. I was a dogface again, separated from my troop and deep behind enemy lines.

The forest was beautiful and rich with the scents of things living. I wanted to take off my uniform and get down on my belly. I wanted to grow fur and scurry off between the thick branches that bristled at the road.

There were men coming up through the woods. They

moved cautiously and abreast. I could see snatches of them but they were mainly hidden by the foliage, and I was nearly blinded by that orange sun.

Were they GIs like me? Or Nazi soldiers? My heart thumped in my throat and I tried one last time to become a beast and run.

A rifle swung up and aimed at me. Was it a GI who saw a bear or a German shooting down an American invader? Maybe it was just a white man shooting at shadows.

Whatever it was, I jumped, gasping my last breath.

"Easy, what is it?" Idabell was lying next to me, her hot skin against my back.

The lamp in the living room had an orange shade.

My pants were down around my ankles and my shirt and jacket were pulled up to my chest. I was in a strange house in the middle of the night sleeping next to a woman who might have been a murderer.

My nightmares were no more threatening than my waking life.

"Nothin's wrong," I said. "I got your dog out in the car."

She jumped up with a wide grin on her face.

"I was so happy to see you that I forgot. Where is he?"

"Out in the car," I said again. I was sitting there pulling up my shorts and pants. Then I stood trying to straighten out my clothes.

"Can we go see him?" she begged.

Pharaoh leapt high into the air on our walk back to the house—splashing in the puddles and putting paw marks on Idabell's skirt. Inside he licked her face and wagged his whole backside along with his tail while Idabell cooed and giggled and scratched.

After a long reunion I pointed out that it was nearing two o'clock in the morning.

"I have a bus ticket for five." She yawned deeply and smiled at me. When she reached out to stroke my face Pharaoh growled.

"Oh shush," she said. "You silly dog you."

"You wanna ride to the bus station?"

"Yes. I just need to drop something off."

"What's that?"

"Just a note to my friend Bonnie," she said sleepily.

"Is that Bonnie Shay?"

"Yes."

"Did you get my number from her?"

"She called me here after you came by. We've had our differences but Bonnie's still my friend."

"So you just wanna drop this note off and then go to the bus station?"

"Yes." She had very white teeth. "When I get somewhere I'll write you. Maybe you could come visit—after a while."

"Uh-huh, sure." I was as sincere as a boxer putting up his guard. "Well, let's go."

"I just have to bring a couple of things," she said.

She ran somewhere in the house and came back with a child's croquet set that consisted of two wooden mallets and six large wooden balls held together in a wire frame that had a handle at the top. She also had a carrying case for Pharaoh. It was a little doghouse with a screened door and a handle at the top.

I took the child's game and dog cage, she took Pharaoh and held the umbrella over all of us out to the car. The croquet set was very light. I remember thinking that it must have been made from balsa wood.

Maybe Idabell thought my head was made from the same material.

She might have thought it, but she was wrong.

CHAPTER 18

"All this ain't over no dog," I said.

We were driving south and west toward B. Shay's apartment house. Pharaoh was so excited to be with Idabell that he was leaping around the car and barking. I had to stop the car and make her put him in his cage.

"All what, Easy?" she asked.

"Your husband, your brother-in-law."

"I don't know what happened," she said, rising a little from her dozing posture. "For about three weeks Holland was really upset. He was mad and said terrible things to me. You know I'm from a good family, I'm not used to men using language the way he did. And then he was mad at Pharaoh. It's true. I left because he wanted to kill my little baby."

"What was he mad about?" I asked.

"I don't know. Maybe it was something with a business deal he had with Roman."

"What kind of business were they in?"

"Roman was a gambler. He didn't have a real job. He did business ventures now and then but mainly he gambled. He played in Gardena and Reno and Vegas."

"And what about Holland?" I asked.

"I loved him," she said. "I mean he was kind and sweet. We'd go out to a movie and then walk back to his house speaking to each other in French. My parents are Guianese but I learned French in school because I came here so young. Holly came when he was a child too but he learned French at home. Sometimes we'd talk all night long. He loved it that I was a teacher. He was proud of me. He'd take me everywhere and say to everybody that I was an educator and that I worked among black children to educate them."

A police car moved up alongside of us as we went. The cop in the passenger's seat shone a powerful flashlight on me and then on Idabell. He turned to his partner, they said a few words, and the car turned off onto the next cross street.

"He sounds nice," I said. "What did he do for a living?"

"He managed paper routes in Hollywood."

"What?"

"He used to get up early in the morning and go down to his paper shack on Olympic and prepare the paper boys for their bicycle routes. He had six boys doing morning routes, seven in the afternoon, and three who did street sales. He did the whole Sunday route on his own with two helpers."

"Used to? He give it up?"

"Then Roman came," Idabell said. "Holly quit after he saw how flashy Roman was with his deals and his gambling."

"Holland get into that line'a work?"

"He didn't know what he wanted to do. One day he was going to trade the T-bird in for a Cadillac and go into the limousine business; the next day he was going to be a musician. Roman killed Holland."

"He did?"

"I don't know if he actually did it, but when Roman came to town Holly went crazy. He would have done anything to outdo his brother."

"That's how come they were dressed like each other?"

"It was only since Roman came," the schoolteacher said again. "Roman always wore snakeskin shoes and one of three tweed coats, or a black jacket. After Holly saw how he lived he bought the same things, he even spent four hundred dollars on shoes. I told him that he shouldn't try to copy his brother. But he just told me that the same clothes looked better on him. They were identical twins but Holly was always saying that he was taller and more handsome."

"Sounds crazy," I said.

Idabell didn't deny it.

"Roman really wasn't a bad guy. He was full of himself

though—Holly hated that. He wanted everybody to look at him the way they looked at Roman."

"But you said that they worked together."

Ida's face flashed hard for a moment but then turned soft and tired again. She shook her head and blinked twice before saying, "I don't know anything about that."

"Were they close as kids?"

She nodded lazily. "Roman was two minutes older than Holland. Their parents came to Philadelphia from Guiana. When I met Holland, Roman was in the army, stationed in Europe.

"The first time I ever met Roman was here in L.A. That's when Holly got all crazy. He wanted to go to parties all the time. There'd be drugs, people were having sex in the bedrooms right on top of our coats." She was waking up with the memory. "Holly said that there was nothing wrong with it. I wanted him to stay at home but he went anyway. And if I didn't go with him he'd come home smelling of women's perfume. Either that or he smelled like soap because he'd taken a shower somewhere."

"Did Simona Eng and Mr. Langdon come to any of these parties?"

"Simona came to protect me." Idabell smiled. "I had her come to a couple of teas I gave for the teachers. We became friends. I told her how upset I was about going out with Roman and Holly and she tried to come along. I think that she was kinda stuck on Roman for a little while there. But after a couple of parties she convinced me that I should keep away."

I had just turned onto B. Shay's street. The architects who planned the apartment buildings that dominated the block didn't seem to think that their future tenants would be driving cars. There were very few buildings that even had garages and those that did certainly didn't have enough space. The curbs were packed with cars all down the street. I had to park almost a full block away.

"What about Langdon?" I asked before moving to open the door. "What's his story?"

"I don't know," she said, her tone begging me to stop

asking questions. "Roman met him at the same tea that Simona came to. Roman liked talking to people. He started taking Casper to a private black club that they went to behind the Chantilly Club."

I had cajoled and lulled enough. The time had come to get serious.

"All right now, I've heard you out, Idabell. I can see that there was something wrong with your old man and that he pushed you—hard."

The schoolteacher was fully awake now.

"And I'm willing to help you," I continued. "But I need to know some things first."

"Anything," she said.

"Did you kill Holland or Roman? And if you didn't, do you know who did?"

"No," she said with certainty.

"No to all of it?"

"Yes," she said. "I know nothing about them getting killed."

"All right," I said. "All right. What about this thing Holland made you do? What about that?"

"I can't say anything about that, Easy. Don't ask me."

"That's okay too, but if you can't help me then I'm gonna have to help myself."

"What do you mean?"

"That I will drive you down to the police station if I don't get some kind of satisfaction that you aren't tied up in a murder."

"But I told you . . . "

"What you say doesn't make any sense, Mrs. Turner. You're so upset that you're crying, you're willing to throw away your whole profession by bein' with me in your classroom, and then the next thing anybody knows your brother-in-law is dead in the garden, your husband has been murdered, and you're on the run. All that an' you don't know nuthin'?"

"There's nothing to say," she said. "Nothing that has to do with the murders."

"If that's all you have to say then I'm gonna drive us down to the police station."

"Why? It's not your problem. You haven't done anything."

"But that's what an honest man is supposed to do," I said. "If there's something wrong he's supposed to stand up and say, 'Look here,' and tell what he knows. If he can't do that then his whole life falls apart, it just falls apart. Now I've given you a chance. I took your dog and I came out here to meet you. You're a beautiful woman, Idabell, but that don't mean I got to go to war for you."

"I thought you liked me," she said. It was her last attempt.

"I do like you. I wanna help. It's no good for you to get on a bus and run. The cops will find you. And if you run they'll prove you guilty. That's what cops do best. If they think you're guilty then makin' up evidence is just cuttin' corners for them. Believe me." I paused to let my arguments settle in. Then I said, "What did your husband have you do?"

"He had me bring something from Paris."

"Bring what?"

"I don't know."

"What do you mean? How can you get something and not know what it is?"

"It was in a box. He didn't tell me what was in it. He said that it was better if I didn't know. I just picked it up at a place that he told me to go to and then I brought it back. If I hadn't done it he would have killed Pharaoh."

"Why you? Why Paris?"

Idabell turned her head and motioned up the block. "Bonnie's a flight attendant. She got me a ticket. I told her that I wanted to go shopping in Paris with her. That's what Holly told me to do. And then one day, when she was off with her friends, I went to the address that Holly said to go to."

"She didn't know?"

"No. Not until we got back. I told her then because I knew it was wrong. I wouldn't have done it for anyone but Pharaoh."

"So if you did everything he wanted, why did you run?"

"He was wrong," she blurted. The tears came freely. "I never wanted to see him again."

I put my arms around her. I needed to hold on to someone.

"It's okay," I said. "It's okay. What we need to do is get you a lawyer."

"A lawyer? Why?"

"Because," I said, "you need to tell the police this story. A good lawyer can make you look like his victim. Really you were. And then, if they can figure out what it was that you brought back, they can solve the murders." I didn't add that I would be out of it and that Sanchez would have another trail to follow.

"Will you help?" she asked in my ear.

"I sure will." I pulled away from her then. Her whisper reminded me of other things; things I knew I should leave behind.

She smiled at me. "Thank you."

"No problem."

"Will you take this note up to Bonnie's? She's not there. She won't be back from her flight until later in the morning. But at least she'll find this."

"Maybe you better keep it," I suggested. "You know this thing with the cops could be kinda tricky. You don't want to incriminate yourself."

"I can trust Bonnie. Anyway, the letter says that I'm sorry, that's all."

She kissed my lips. Her lipstick tasted like chemicals.

I took the note in hand. She smiled and then leaned toward the window, huddling against the damp chill that had settled in the car. I walked down the street angling my umbrella against the wind and rain. I went up the stairs and down the hall to Miss Shay's apartment. But I didn't shove the letter under the door; I put it in my pocket instead. Idabell didn't understand that you had no friends once you'd gone across the line from the law. But I'd help her.

I was happy walking alone and making my own

decisions. I knew a lawyer. She didn't care for me much but she knew her job better than most. I was free for the first time since I'd met the little yellow dog.

As I walked back down the block to my car I saw a man walking in the opposite direction across the street. He wasn't wearing a raincoat or even a hat; that's why, I figured, he was moving so fast through the rain.

Idabell was still resting against the passenger's window. "I left it," I said.

She didn't answer me. Pharaoh began whimpering. He wasn't hungry for company but truly sad in his cage.

I remembered the man running down the street.

That was when I knew Idabell was dead.

She'd been shot twice in the temple, right through the window. No pulse, no breath. Her eyes were open. There was very little blood.

I don't know how long I sat there looking at her. Pharaoh whimpered and I tried to get myself moving. But where was I going to go? I wanted something to happen: Idabell to rise as she had before from her friend's floor; a shot to punctuate her death; anything but the pelting rain and the dog's cries.

I drove off in a kind of daze. At first I looked for the man who'd been running. He'd disappeared though. He might have turned left or right at the corner but I was in no condition, or position, to execute a thorough search.

There were thoughts in my head; things that I had to do. But anything I had to think about fled when I tried to catch it. Fragments of final words and prayers went through. The address of a hospital on Santa Monica Boulevard was there.

She was dead. I knew dead from World War Two. I knew dead. What I should have done was to pull into an alley and throw her in the street. That's what I needed to do. If I reported the crime the cops would have me up on charges with the first waking judge.

I drove on while Pharaoh sang his dirge.

Finally we came to a small park that was partially

secluded by a hedge. I drove up into an alley behind the park and turned to Idabell.

I tried to think of anything she might have carried that pointed to me. In her purse I found my phone number on a piece of paper. I rummaged through the bag and took out all the papers I found and her pocket phone book. Then I looked through her clothes.

The whole time I kept breathing slowly to keep my mind clear. There were no pockets on her, no identifying tags that I could see.

It was almost four. I had to act. I got out of my side and went to open her door. A gentleman, I took her out as gently as I could and lifted her as if we were dancing. She was heavy, not like in room C2.

I walked her to the park bench and laid her out there in the dark and leafy alcove. The rain muffled Pharaoh's cries.

When I got back into the car I lowered her window so that nobody would see the bullet holes. I didn't care if the seat got wet. Three blocks away, across the street from the hospital, I called them and reported the body in the park. My voice caught as I repeated the words to the dispatcher. Then I hung up and hurried away.

All the way back down Pico Boulevard, Pharaoh was yowling; Idabell's death was alive in his senses and my mind.

I stopped at a closed gas station past La Cienega and busted out the passenger's window. There was a large trash bin, almost filled with refuse, near the toilets. I tore up her driver's license and Board of Ed ID and sprinkled the confetti around. I rubbed off the purse as well as I could, leaving three hundred and some odd dollars. I figured that even if anyone found the purse they'd think twice before turning it in with no ID and a three-hundred-dollar windfall.

I buried the purse and tattered IDs as far as I could.

It was when I was getting back into the car that I noticed the croquet set was missing from the backseat.

I parked in front of my house and let Pharaoh out of his

cage. He sniffed and sniffed at Idabell's seat, whining and begging to be reunited with her. After a few minutes I picked him up and carried him into the house.

It was the only time we didn't express hatred or disdain for each other.

That's because we were both in mourning and on the verge of seeking our own separate brands of revenge.

CHAPTER 19

"Daddy, Frenchie's sick."

She was standing there in her orange dress, the one that had four big white buttons down the front. Bleary light reflected on the mirror of my dresser. That meant it was late in the morning.

"Feather, what are you doing here? Why aren't you at school?"

"Frenchie's sick," she said patiently. "I stayed home to take care of him."

"Where's Juice?"

"He gone to school. He said that I was gonna be in trouble." She looked at me with slightly enlarged eyes. "But I told him that Frenchie was sick an' he needed me to pat him and take his tempachur."

I was seeing the woman in the child just beginning to flex her muscles. I was sick at heart but I could still smile at the beauty of Feather and her power to love.

"I'll take care'a the dog, honey," I said. "You go put together your lunch and I'll take you to school."

Pharaoh was moping by the front door. His tiny rat chin rested on slender yellow paws. He looked up at me and tried to growl but the snarl turned into a whimper and he put his head back down.

I had on my painter's pants, a cross-hatched-red-and-blue flannel shirt, and thick work shoes. I would be unshaven and unbathed that day. I was coming back to the old ways and feeling mean.

It wasn't far to Burnside Elementary School.

"What happened to the window, Daddy?"

I walked Feather into school and explained, vaguely, that I'd had to keep her home that morning. Nobody seemed to mind.

I went back home and called Trudy Van Dial at Sojourner Truth. She rang for Garland Burns. When he got on I told him that I was working out of the area office for Mr. Stowe for the day.

"You tell Newgate about it," I said. "He can call up Stowe if he has any problems with it. And make sure that Archie is getting to his assignments."

"Sure thing, Mr. Rawlins," Burns said.

"Anything else, Garland?"

"That policeman, Sergeant Sanchez, talked to me and Mrs. Plates yesterday," the clean-shaven young Christian Scientist said in his schoolboy way.

"Yeah?"

"What he mostly asked about was you."

"Really?" I said in my most perplexed tone. "Oh, well. See you tomorrow, Mr. Burns."

"Okay. Bye now, Mr. Rawlins."

I drove the long ride out to Watts but I wasn't going to work that day. I went all the way down to 116th Street and the first home I ever owned.

Primo was sitting on the front porch of my house, protected by the overhang from the light drizzle. When I got out of the car he stood up and waved. He yelled something in Spanish into the front door and then limped his way out toward me.

It was in the past couple of years that Primo developed his limp. I didn't know what had happened and I never asked.

The fence around the yard had been torn down and there were three cars parked on the lawn. One hulk had the engine next to it while another jalopy was up on boxes instead of wheels. The house could have used a touch-up but I knew that it would have been an insult for me to offer to have it painted so I let it ride.

"Easy," Primo hailed. "How are you, my friend?"

"Well . . ."

"You don't have to say it." Primo smiled, showing me a pitted silver tooth. "I can see that you're in bad trouble."

"How can you see that?"

"Because when you're okay, or maybe just a little bad, you always got a present for us and the kids. You feel like a guest and the guest always brings a gift so everybody knows how happy he is to come there." Primo raised his hand like a country teacher. "But when you got a problem bringing a gift is like, like a snake making with pretty eyes."

As he grew older Primo studied philosophy by considering all of the things he knew in Spanish, English, and life. His thoughts were always powerful because the pictures he used to describe them stayed with you over time.

I managed a chuckle and clapped his back. He was still a strong man.

Big black Panamanian Flower came out of the front door. She gave me her wide grin and a big kiss.

"Easy," she said loudly. "You don't come out here enough."

"Working, you know," my mouth said. But Flower could hear my heart. Her welcoming smile turned sad. She kissed me again and then cupped the back of my neck with her big hand.

"You take care of him now," she said to her husband.

"Window on my passenger's side is busted out, Primo," I said, looking after Flower as she went back into the house. Two little brown kids came running from around the screen door. They had dark and almond-shaped faces and slanting eyes, from the oldest American stock, like Jesus. They were stalking up to us with silly grins on perfectly balanced feet.

"Oh," Primo said. "You have a accident?"

"Somebody shot my girlfriend through the window while

I was droppin' somethin' off down the street. She's dead." I said it all at once; partly just to say it, to know that it was true, and partly because I didn't want to get Primo mixed up in anything that he didn't know about from the beginning.

"What?" he asked.

"I'm just tryin' t'stay outta trouble, man."

Primo nodded his head and said, "So clean it up and put in a new window, huh?"

"If you wouldn't mind. I'll pay ya for it."

"You need a car. I got a nice Chevy right out here."

It was a late model, fierce metallic blue with balloon tires in back.

"Don't you have somethin' a li'l quieter?" I asked.

"Sometimes a loud noise is the best way to hide what you don't want somebody to hear."

"Do you have another car?" I asked the philosopher again.

"Not that'll drive."

"So then this one is just fine. Fine. Fine."

Primo laughed and I managed to shake my head. The two boys made roaring noises and leapt at us.

"My grandchildren," Primo told me proudly. "They are jaguars from the deep forest. Killers of great birds."

The rain had stopped by the time I made it home. I had just pulled Primo's souped-up Chevy into the driveway and gotten out to go in my house.

"Mr. Rawlins." I didn't need to turn around to know Sergeant Sanchez.

He was getting out of a parked car.

I cursed under my breath for not checking out the street before parking. For some reason I felt safe at my own home—a mistake that a poor man should never make.

"Sergeant." I smiled, trying to read in his bearing whether or not he knew about Idabell Turner's demise.

I was pretty sure that he didn't intend to arrest me. He'd come alone, and policemen never arrest a man single-handed if they can help it.

"You're not at work today," he said as he approached.

I remained silent.

"Do you have some time for a few questions?" he asked.

"Sure," I said. "Whatever you wanna know."

"Can we go in your house?"

Remembering Pharaoh moping around the front door I said, "House is a mess, officer, we better stay out here."

"Oh." His eyes were looking for an opening through my defense. "That's a wild car you got there."

"It takes me from place to place. That's all you could ask for."

"Is it yours?" he asked.

"No."

"Where's your car?"

"I lent it to my friend Guillermo to ride out to Las Vegas. My car's better than his and he wanted to trade just for his vacation."

"Where does this Guillermo live?"

"Out past Compton."

Sanchez winced, just a hair. It was intuition about my car. He could smell something about it. But he didn't want to push me, and that was a surprise.

Cops didn't mind pushing around men like me. That kind of pushing was part of their job. It didn't matter that he wasn't a white man. Cops is a race all its own. Its members have their own language and their own creed.

I realized then that Sanchez was on the trail of something bigger than me, and bigger than the death of mulatto twins. Something that Idabell Turner had brought to America in a box.

"The man we found at your school was Roman Gasteau," Sanchez said. "Idabell Turner is his sister-in-law."

Is.

"His twin brother Holland," Sanchez continued, "was found dead at his own house night before last and now Mrs. Turner is missing."

"That's a lotta happenin'," I said to Sanchez. "Damn."

"You don't know anything about this, Rawlins?"

"Idabell is a kinda friend'a mines, sergeant, but I never

had her confidence. I didn't know her husband or her brother-in-law."

"She never said anything to you about what her brother-in-law did for a living?" Sanchez was almost human in his need for an answer.

"No sir," I said. The regret in my lying mouth was real.

"You busy right now?" he asked me. It was a simple question that one friend might ask another on a street corner in May. Maybe he'd met a woman who wanted a date for her girlfriend.

"Well, I got some work to do around the house."

"This wouldn't take long. Why don't you come on up to the Hollywood station with me?" He didn't sound urgent. "I think you could help."

"Well . . . "

"Drive your own car. You're not under arrest or anything. You don't have to come if you don't want to."

"What's this all about?"

"Nothing. Just a few questions about Idabell Turner. Captain Fogherty asked me if I'd ask you to drop by. It's not far, you know. Just up here in Hollywood."

"Okay," I said. "If it'll be short."

"You can follow me."

"Uh-huh."

At that moment Pharaoh started barking. He yipped and whined and barked again. Maybe he wanted to tell Sanchez the truth.

The sergeant heard the dog. He even looked at the house but there wasn't enough there for him to grab on to and so he turned around and went back to his car.

CHAPTER 20

I knew a shorter route to the Hollywood station but I trailed behind Sanchez's unmarked car anyway. I wanted to know what he was thinking. I didn't have faith that anyone would care for me. The only chance I had, I believed, was to make sure that nobody could bring me down.

Sanchez parked at a blue curb painted with big white letters that read for OFFICIAL POLICE BUSINESS only! When I passed by he tooted his horn and pointed that I should park in front of him. I made a U-turn and nosed up in front of his black Chevrolet. He was waiting for me with a blue-and-red cardboard sign that had a long code number printed on it.

"Here, put this on your dashboard," he said. "They'll leave it alone then."

The number reminded me of an arrest ID. When I put it down I was hoping that I wouldn't meet its brother inside

We went in through the large garage doors; a black man and a brown one strolling through a cavern full of white cops.

"Can I do something for you?" the first cop we ran into asked.

"Sergeant Sanchez," my escort replied. He had his ID out and ready.

"Okay," the towheaded cop said suspiciously. "Where you going?"

"Captain Fogherty wants to see us," Sanchez said without a trace of anger in his voice.

"Where's your badge?" the patrolman then asked me. He knew from the way I was dressed I didn't have one but he just couldn't let us go. I noticed that policemen were standing around their cars, and up on a high curb, looking at us.

"It's at the cleaners," I said. "Gettin' a touch-up and a shine."

"What?" The cop made a motion with his shoulder. He wanted to do something but hadn't decided on what—yet.

My heart started moving blood at a fast pace. I gritted my teeth and watched the white man's light brown eyes.

Sanchez stepped between us.

"Mr. Rawlins isn't a police officer," he said. "He's here to advise the captain on the Gasteau killing."

The policeman's smile reminded me of Pharaoh. "That's what happens when we let your kind up here," he said.

I could think of five answers; only two of them involved words.

"Can we go on, Officer . . . " Sanchez looked closely at the flat badge under the officer's shield. "Peters?"

Patrolman Peters stepped sideways and we went through the pair of swinging double doors behind him. The doors opened into a long, light-lime-colored hall. It was lit by bright lights in semiopaque glass bowls that were screwed into the ceiling.

We walked the length of the hall and then turned left down another, even longer hall. There were no doors along the way, just the tunnel.

A large roach scuttled down the corridor past us. He was scared, it seemed, and was hell-bent to get away from the direction we were headed.

"How long have you been sergeant?" I asked Sanchez.

I figured that I wasn't a prisoner, or a criminal, and so I could speak freely.

But Sanchez didn't see it that way. Either that or he was deaf.

Or maybe he was concentrating. The tunnels under the jail crisscrossed often, going off at various angles.

We turned and then turned again.

Each corridor was less green and more yellow. At the end of the final passage was a large iron door with a small portal fitted with extra-thick, bulletproof glass.

Through the glass we could see another door, this one like a cell door, formed from bars. On the other side of the bars was another, older police officer. When Sanchez tapped his badge on the glass the guardian looked up slowly. Sanchez showed his ID at the window. The older man got up, rummaged around a large metal key loop. There were only four keys but he had to try every one to open the barred door. He walked across the metal chamber, to the door that we stood behind, and peered at us.

He made a movement with his hand saying that he wanted to see Sanchez's ID again. He looked at the picture for a long time and then started fumbling with the keys again.

After four attempts I heard the key slip into a lock and turn, but the door didn't come open. The elder cop went back across the chamber. It wasn't until he was safely locked away that he reached under his desk and pulled on something. A loud click went off in the door we were standing before and Sanchez pushed it open.

We entered the ironclad chamber.

"Shut it behind you," the guard/cop said.

Sanchez obliged.

"What do you want?" the guard then asked.

"I'm taking Mr. Rawlins here to see Captain Fogherty."

The cop looked hard at me. "He under arrest?"

"No."

"Why'd you come this way?"

"This is the way the captain said to come."

Another long look.

"Okay," he said, and he fumbled with the keys.

Beyond him was another metal door that had to be unlocked. And beyond that was the dim-lit room of cages. Twelve boxes of crosshatched bars with a man, or two, in every cell. When we came into the room I could see, through the grated floor, another twelve cells below. The steel latticed ceiling revealed an upper cellblock. They all wore drab green pants that had the word PRISONER stenciled on them in dark red dye, and matching T-shirts. Each man stared silently, wondering if our presence there had to do with their case. They stared from their cots, or standing at the crosshatched bars, or squatting down on the steel toilet seat. They had nothing to hide, nothing to say.

Just thirty or so men living in cages underground. Like livestock waiting for some further shame to be laid on them. Like sharecroppers or slaves living in shanty shacks on the edge of a plantation.

There was evil in that room, and on that plantation too. Because, as I knew too well, if you're punished long enough you become guilty of all charges brought against you.

"Mistah."

It was a hoarse whisper. The man who called was black. He was half crouching, half lying at the grid cell door. The white of his left eye was full of bright blood. His nose was so swollen that he was gasping open-mouthed. There was blood coming from his mouth and you could see that he was missing teeth. I couldn't tell if he had lost them in the fight or at some earlier time.

"Mistah."

I slowed.

It was hard to tell through the bruises and the blood but I didn't think that the man had reached twenty-five. Hefty but not loose, he'd taken off his shirt to mop the blood and sweat from his face.

Behind him, at the back of the cell, was another young man. This one, also black, was long and lean with his legs stretched out and crossed on the cot where he reclined. He was in repose with open eyes and the satisfied smugness of a bully in his face.

"Help me, mistah," the beaten man begged. "Tell'em t'lemme outta here."

"Come on, Rawlins," Sanchez said at my back.

"What's that?" the lanky bully said.

The beaten man cringed at the crackling sound of his tormentor's voice.

The bully sat up. He had the name Jones stitched over the left breast of his prison shirt but I doubted that that was his name.

"Get back over here, Felix," Jones said. And then, "I'ma count to three. One . . . "

Felix looked up at me.

" ... two ... "

Felix flinched and went, on his knees, to Jones's feet. Jones looked across the cell, through the grating, and smiled at me. He was also missing a few teeth.

Jones stepped out of his shoes.

"Get the fuck up in yo' motherfuckin' bed an' spit-shine my goddam motherfuckin' shoes," he said. When Felix didn't move fast enough Jones bent down and socked him on the ear.

"Don't hit me again!" Felix shouted.

"Then get up in that bed an' shine'em. An' you better not get no blood on the motherfuckers." To make the job harder Jones punched Felix in the nose, bringing blood and tears.

Jones had his back to us.

He talked to Felix but the words were meant for me.

"You think that man gonna help you? That what you think, Felix? Well, just as soon as they gone I'ma whip yo' ass good. I'ma give you such a ass-kickin' you gonna wish you had kep'it quiet. An' that man bettah hope I never catch his punk ass out in the street. He bettah hope not."

"Come on, Rawlins," Sanchez said. "We'll report it to the guard."

Through the next cell door portal we saw two guards. They stood behind yet another barred doorway. They flipped a switch and we came through the first door.

Both men were beefy and balding. One squinted while the other had rosy cheeks. They took Sanchez's badge through the bars and set it down on a table behind them.

Neither one had said a word.

"Well?" Sanchez asked.

The one on the left squinted at his partner's bright cheeks.

I was thinking about Felix, wondering if his shouts could be heard through steel.

"What are you trying to pull, son?" Squinty asked back.

There was a steel door behind me, a steel door in front of me, and for some reason I couldn't catch a deep breath.

"You better get back to your cells, boys, until we can check this out," said the red-cheeked man. "Pop the locks of seventeen and twenty-four, Ron."

A spasm went up my spine but Sanchez held still. He stared at the men. Ron finally blinked and reached for the keys. He got them as far as the lock and then stopped.

"You sure you belong here, Pancho?" he asked.

His partner snickered and then they both laughed.

Ron unlocked the door and swung it open. My breath was waiting for me across the threshold.

Applecheeks was clapping Sanchez on the back.

"Just a joke, amigo," he was saying.

"There's a fight going on in one of the cells back there," Sanchez replied. "One of them is getting beaten up pretty bad."

"Oh," the cop said. "Two niggers?"

"I think somebody could get hurt," Sanchez said with emphasis.

The policeman turned to his partner and asked, "What time is it, Bob?"

Bob had to hold his wristwatch at arm's length to read the dial. "Three-fifteen."

"Oh. I'll tell you what, amigo," the cop called Ron said to Sanchez. "It's only half an hour until the next shift comes in. If we have to charge somebody it'll take an hour at least. But we'll tell the next shift when they get here."

There was nothing left to say and so we left Felix to his fate.

We went down another long hall that actually went from one building to another. The next building was the old police station. The halls became more slender with woodwork around the doors. We took a staircase up two flights and then down another hall. In this passage sunlight shone in through open doors and illuminated the frosted windows of closed ones. At the far end was our destination. The brass plate on the door said "Captain Josiah Fogherty."

"Come in."

It was a small room, barely large enough for the junk-piled desk and folding chairs propped up next to the door. Not a captain's office at all.

Fogherty had a full mane of silver hair and drooping eyelids that were sad and smiling at the same time. His skin was darkish but not by race, or the sun. He had the look of a dusk-to-dawn drinker; whiskey without a mixer if my imagination was correct. He wore no wedding band and his white shirt was too wrinkled, even for a cop, with one too many stains poking out from underneath his brown jacket. He looked up at us with a smile that could have been a mourner's valiant attempt to console a bereaved widow.

"Sergeant," he said to Sanchez even though he was looking at me.

"Rawlins," Sanchez answered.

"Sit down, sit down." Fogherty gestured at his poor chairs.

We unfolded our seats.

"Mr. Rawlins works ... " Sanchez went right into his story.

Fogherty held up his hands to stall the speech. He picked up the receiver to his phone and pressed a big green button down under the dial. After waiting a few seconds he said, "You got four-A ready yet? Okay. Uh-huh, sure. Yes, that's right," and then hung up.

He raised his head and nodded at Sanchez to continue.

"This is Mr. Rawlins," the sergeant said. "He works out at the school where the victim's wife teaches."

"Terrible, isn't it, Mr. Rawlins?" Fogherty said to me.

"Sure is," I said with as much feeling as I could muster.

"We see it every day, you know," he added, nodding wise. "Household spat that gets out of hand is most of it. Good friends that drink too much, maybe with the other friend's wife, and then, bang—somebody's dead." When he smiled I realized that my trip through the bowels of the jailhouse had been calculated to break me down.

"You wanted something from me, captain?"

"Did you know Holland Gasteau?"

"No, sir. Idabell and I are just work friends."

"Do you know where she could be?"

"No, sir. I don't." I was as sincere as a man can get. But that didn't mean a thing to them.

An honest cop, when asked by a judge, "Did the sun set in the west that day, officer?" will answer, "I believe so, your honor," and leave the truth for the court to decide.

Fogherty smiled.

A uniformed police officer stuck his head into the room.

"Four-A is ready, sir," the officer said.

"You get all five?" Fogherty asked.

"No, sir. All we could manage was the four."

"Damn," Fogherty hissed.

It was the same word that was at the back of my mouth.

"You know, you could do me a favor, Rawlins." If you were to believe the wonder on the captain's face it was the first time he thought of what he was about to ask me.

"What?"

"We're having a lineup. It's nothing. But the guy is colored, see, and we'd like to have a good mix up there—you know, to make it fair."

"What's it for?" I asked.

"Murder," said Fogherty.

Sanchez was looking at my eyes.

They had put up a plasterboard wall to divide a small basement room. I was ushered into one side by Fogherty and Sanchez. There were three uniformed white cops and six black men, all of them dressed casually, except for the manacles that two of them wore.

Fogherty had the prisoners released from their chains. The real wall had evenly spaced vertical black lines drawn along it forming man-sized rectangles that had numbers across the top: 1—2—3—4—5—6. We were all told to stand up against the wall and under a number.

"What the fuck you got me here for?" one of the prisoners complained. "I told ya I been sick. I ain't done a damn thing."

"You want to go back down the hall?" a policemen asked in way of reply.

I noticed then that both of the men who had been manacled were bruised around their faces.

From the central vantage point of number three I looked up and down the row. No two of us bore the slightest resemblance. The shortest was five foot six while the tallest was a full three inches taller than I am, a shade over six feet. There was yellow, gray, brown, and black skin. Our faces spoke of the variety of peoples of Africa and of the white masters who raped those ancestors. The tallest man weighed maybe one eighty—so did the shortest.

It was a setup, but I still had some points on my side. We were still a row of Negroes—and white folks, on the whole, could barely tell us apart.

That old white lady hadn't gotten a clear look at me leaving Idabell's. I'd hidden my face upon leaving the house, distracted her with my keys, changed my height.

I was innocent.

"Face forward, number three."

A panel of six large floodlights flared from the ceiling; they were hot on my skin.

"What're you lookin' up for, boy?" The cop was young; his accent at home in the northeast somewhere. The derogatory words sounded odd on his tongue but the meaning was clear.

I was back, suddenly, in the deep south. All feeling drained out of my body and my face went lax. My eyes felt nothing, my mouth had no words or expression. I was empty of all past doings. I had no future. I stood up straight and presented my face toward the wall, but still, it wasn't me standing there. Easy had gone undercover and there was no bringing him out.

There were peepholes drilled into the wall opposite us. I noticed them without seeming to see. My mind was back on a hot swampland road, back in the days when I could have disappeared, in half a moment's notice, from any job or town or girlfriend. Back to a time when the rear door was the only door—and it was never locked.

A number was asked to step forward and then another. When my turn came I stood out under the hot lights and stared right into them.

In the beginning . . . The words came into my mind and I was my own master.

The floodlights cut off, leaving just the overheads. Suddenly it was darker and cool.

"You can go out now," the eastern bigot said.

I followed the line into the adjoining room. The prisoners were clapped back into chains and led off to their cages. The other men just left.

I made to leave too.

"Rawlins." It was Fogherty.

He and Sanchez approached me with serious faces.

I realized, with a scared shock, that I had forgotten my lawyer's phone number.

"Where do you think you're going?" Fogherty asked. He was no longer friendly or sad.

"Home."

"Our witness thought that he recognized you, Rawlins."

I knew when he said it that the lineup had failed; that Fogherty and Sanchez were trying to scare me, or to see how hard it was to shake my tree.

I knew that I shouldn't show too much fear or they'd think I was guilty. The best thing for an Honest John to do would be to stutter out a "Wha?" That way I could seem the innocent kind of scared.

"The hell you say," I said instead. "I didn't do anything for anybody to see."

"Maybe they saw you afterwards," Fogherty speculated.

"Bullshit," I said. "I wasn't anywhere but work or home. If somebody saw me in one'a those places I'd be glad to confess to workin' or feedin' my kids."

"I don't have to let you out of here, Rawlins," Fogherty said. "You could be down in that cellblock that you came through."

I was still defiant but his threat had numbed my tongue.

Fogherty's smile was demented. "Yeah. Sanchez told me that you saw Felix Wren down in his cell." Fogherty watched me and nodded, sage-like. "He's only in on a drunk driving charge but he resisted the arresting officers—bit one of them. Don't worry about him though, he'll be okay. We won't even charge him. Once he gets his last tooth knocked out we'll send him back home to his mother."

That was the first moment I felt murder in my fingers. It's not that I wanted to kill Fogherty particularly. I could have killed anybody.

I turned and went toward a door with a red-and-white EXIT sign above it.

"We know you're in it, Rawlins," Fogherty said to my back.

I kept going, following the EXIT signs.

Nobody stopped me or even noticed as I made my way through the station. Somewhere on the lineup I had become invisible again. I'd taken on the shadows that kept me camouflaged, and dangerous.

CHAPTER 21

Sanchez and Fogherty showed me bloody Felix, they told me that I could end up like him, but they stopped short of arresting me and throwing me in the cell with Jones.

They wanted something from me, but what was it? There was only small coverage of the murder of the two brothers in the paper; nothing about the circumstances of their deaths. That lack of coverage in itself might have been surprising if it wasn't for the fact that Roman and Holland were black men and it was early in the sixties.

You had to kill somebody white to get any kind of news splash in the sixties.

Foreign blacks made the news, however. That very day the Congolese had jailed two Russians for espionage, and five hundred Haitians had been reported dead from flooding. To the white press, and many white Americans, black people were easier to see as exotic foreigners, somebody else's people. But the lives of black Americans were treated with silence.

I didn't know when they'd identify Idabell. Los Angeles is a vast complex of unassociated towns and municipalities. The bureaucracies didn't communicate well and so Idabell's identity might take a day or two to surface.

The storm dominated the headlines. The Congolese and a political science teacher who claimed that the Russians had framed him for a spy were below that. Idabell's death was ignored by the radio and TV and newspapers.

Ignored by everyone except me—me and the little yellow dog.

But for a while I put revenge out of my mind. I rolled up my sleeves and started to get ready for dinner with my kids.

I decided to go Mexican because the kids loved it and it was a lot of preparing. I defrosted a large stack of corn tortillas that Flower kept me stocked with. Flower was a Panamanian but she learned Mexican cuisine because that was all that Primo would eat—at home.

I deseeded dried *ancho* chiles and then pan-roasted them for about fifteen minutes, to get that smoky flavor. After that I softened them with hot water and ran them and the water through the purée cycle of the blender. I filtered out the flecks of skin by passing the liquid through a metal strainer and made a roux, with wheat flour and margarine, to thicken the sauce so that it would stick to the flat tortillas.

I grated my yellow cheddar and Monterey Jack. There was the ground beef and chicken to sauté, separately of course.

When the meat started steaming, Pharaoh slinked into the room. He crouched down and growled while he sniffed. He wanted some food but I'd be damned if I ever fed a mouth that bit me. The food I cook is too good for that.

I love to cook. When I was a boy down in Louisiana, and later on in Texas, I spent many a day with no food and no prospects. So when a piece of meat or some grain passed my way I knew what to do. Preparing a meal for me was like going to church; there was a miracle and a deep satisfaction in my soul.

It wasn't until I was heating lard in a large iron skillet that I started thinking about my problems again. It hardly seemed real; two dead brothers and a woman too. I couldn't imagine my simple little working life at Sojourner Truth mixed up with murder and death.

It had to be money. I lit a Camel and watched the steady gas flame under the black pan. It had to be money. That phrase played over about twenty-five times in my mind but it didn't lead anywhere.

I dipped a stiff tortilla into the hot lard. Instantly it took on the texture of a wet sheet of paper. I immersed the flimsy bread into the sauce and then flattened it out on a plate. I put a line of chicken down the center of that one, rolled it all up, and placed it in its corner of a large ceramic baking dish.

Whoever killed Idabell wanted that croquet set; that child's toy and revenge.

She and her husband, and his brother, stole it from him. He wanted his property—and the people who stole it. Bonnie had said that she hadn't seen Idabell in months, but that was a lie. Idabell said that they had gone to Paris together and, to prove it, the killer was waiting for Bonnie to come home. Maybe Bonnie knew more than Idabell thought.

Dear Bonnie,

I just wanted to leave you a note and tell you again that I couldn't help what I did. If there was any other way I would have come to you first. But I couldn't have taken that chance.

I know that I can't make it up to you. All I can say is that I have paid dearly for the wrong they've done. I've lost my husband, my home, and my job. I'll probably never see you again and so I've also lost the best friend that I ever had.

I hope that you'll forgive me one day.

Your friend always,
Idabell

Along with the letter I had three scraps of paper from her purse. A laundry receipt, something that looked like a restaurant tab with the amounts in francs, and, finally, there was a handwritten note. The note read "William, Whitehead's." There was an address scrawled at the bottom.

I put the tray of enchiladas in the refrigerator to keep until dinnertime. Then I chopped tomatoes, Bermuda onions, and a little green pepper together with ripe avocado to make a light relish-like salad. I laced it with lime and a touch of cayenne (I couldn't make it too hot because then Feather wouldn't be able to eat it).

The rice I baked in a tomato sauce mixed with minced garlic and two hot peppers. I sprinkled in a handful of tiny dried shrimps to give my kids a treat.

The house was smelling pretty good when Jesus and Feather came bursting in the door. Pharaoh went mad, whimpering, wagging, and licking all over Feather.

"You better feed that dog," I told her.

"Can we keep him?"

"No. His mother be back the middle'a next week. She said that she'll come and get him." I still planned to take Pharaoh out to Primo.

"Come on," Feather whispered to the dog.

"What you gonna give him?" I called out into the kitchen. "I don't want him eating anything that I cooked."

"I bought him some dog food with the grocery money, Dad," Jesus said.

"You did, huh?"

Juice nodded and looked at my feet.

"Did you put any'a that money upstairs in your soldier box?"

He shook his head.

"Why the hell you take my money? Why the hell you take it?" It came out of me suddenly. I didn't want to confront him until I was out of the woods with Sanchez. I didn't want to get mad for the wrong reasons. But the words leapt out of my mouth like vomit from an unexpected stomach virus that just had to have its way.

"I was savin' it, Daddy."

"Savin'? What the hell for? Don't I give you everything you need?"

Jesus raised his head. "In case we didn't have no money and you were broke."

The damage in Juice's face stood out like an extra nose. The half-remembered nightmares of his infancy as a slave; the insecurity of living with me. All the times I'd come home bruised or bleeding came back to me; them and my deep blue moods he could never understand.

Jesus loved me but he didn't trust that I could handle the hard world. He was my backup and I didn't even know it.

He was more of a man than I was.

"Go on," I said. "Do your homework."

CHAPTER 22

The kids loved it when I cooked Mexican food. We ate and joked and told stories. Pharaoh even yipped happily from under Feather's chair.

After dinner I put on a dark blue shirt and a loose brown leisure suit.

"Juice."

"Yes, Dad?"

"I got to go out for a while. You take care around here until I get back, okay?"

He grinned and nodded, understanding that I trusted him again.

We understood each other. The money in the box upstairs was his domain.

"I might be late but you and Feather get to bed on time."

Jesus nodded.

Feather said, "Okay."

I had three stops planned for that night: Whitehead's, Jackson Blue's, and the Black Chantilly. The last one promised to be the most fruitful.

Whitehead's was a black tile building that sat on a high foundation. There were fourteen steps between the slender double doors and the street, but I could still hear the music and noise from outside.

Inside there was a lot of drinking and eating and loud talk from every table. It was like a big party. People were calling across the room between the tables. One waitress got so engrossed with what a portly man was saying to his friends that she sat down and put her elbows on the table.

"Reba," a man from another table said to the waitress.

"What you wan'?" she answered, clearly bothered about being distracted.

"Where our meat loaf?"

The man's date, who had brown skin and chalky chiffon-pink lips, looked as if she was going to abandon her man if he didn't produce some food soon.

"You know where the kitchen is, Hestor. Go an' get it yourself," Reba said to her complaining customer.

Pink lips parted indignantly but the young man scooted up behind the counter and grabbed two large platters loaded down with meat loaf, mashed potatoes, and turnip greens.

"Mister?" a woman's voice asked.

"Yeah?"

The woman standing behind me resembled a bowling ball. She was round and hard and black—not blue-black or brown-black, but black-black. There was no sheen to her eyes and her head was pulled back, making it seem as if she didn't have a neck.

Her looks would have spelled danger except for her tinkly high voice and sweet smile.

"We ain't got no free tables, mister," she sang. "But you could sit at the counter."

"This a nice place," I said easily. "You work here?"

Her smile grew large.

"I'm the owner," she said.

"Really? What's your name?"

"Arletta."

"Hi, Arletta," I said. "Idabell Turner told me that this was a nice place. She asked me to come on down here and shout at William."

Distaste flicked across Arletta's lips but the smile returned quickly. "She's a nice girl but she got to realize that William is workin' an' what she want ain't always the most important thing in the world."

"Listen, Arletta," I said, putting my hand on her bare upper arm. "You don't have to tell me. But you know I need to talk to the man for a minute."

Arletta was the kind of woman that you wanted to touch. She was older than I, maybe fifty. I wasn't trying to get over with her by caressing her skin. I wasn't trying to but I did just the same.

"Well," she said. "He's out here in the kitchen."

Arletta walked through a swinging door into the kitchen. I followed. There we found a large bald man who held a meat cleaver in his left hand. A once-white apron barely covered his large middle. The apron was stained with thick patches of pocked cow's blood. Behind him hung what was left of a whole side of beef.

"William," Arletta said a little loudly as if the cow-chopper was hard of hearing.

"Yeah?" The sharp voice came from behind the side of beef.

A small, gold-colored man came out from behind the slab of meat. He also wore an apron but he was so slim that it fit him like a wraparound dress.

When I saw his face I knew that I was in trouble deep. Up until that moment I knew that I had to be cautious; that there was trouble just waiting to rub off on me. But I had thought that it was other people's troubles—not mine. What did I know about crazy mulatto brothers or swinging math teachers? What did I know about international smuggling, extortion, or murder?

Nothing.

I didn't know a thing up until that moment. But I did know Idabell's friend's face. I'd seen it in a three-year-old Sojourner Truth yearbook. He was William the butcher at Whitehead's but he was the blackmailer Bill Bartlett to me.

William carried a small knife and had no blood on him even though there was a rough cut of meat dangling from his other hand.

"This man need to ax you sumpin'," Arletta said.

"Arletta, I cain't work wit' this shit," the big, bald, and bloody cook interrupted. "I need William if we gonna prepare this meat an' get the food out on the tables too."

I walked quickly over to William with my hand outstretched. "Brad Koogan."

William held up his knife and flesh to show that he couldn't shake.

"Pee-dro!" the bald butcher shouted.

A Mexican man with mean eyes came from somewhere in back of the kitchen.

"What?" He was as large as the butcher.

"Get over here and help me with this meat."

"I got six orders up," Pedro replied.

"Com'on," William said to me.

He turned and went through a back door. In the moment it took me to follow he'd put the knife and meat down on a plate, removed his rubber gloves, got a cigarette between his lips, and was ready to strike a match.

The speed he showed sent a chill through me.

"What you want, brother?" the little man asked.

I was noticing how large his head was in comparison to his body.

"What you said your name was again?" he asked.

"Brad Koogan."

"Sound like a white man's name."

I chuckled. "Yeah, man. Every time I send in a application for'a job, and call about it, they always say on the phone, 'Yeah, come on in, we got a openin'.' But just as soon as they see my face the position has been filled."

"Dig it," the chef's helper said.

"But the reason I'm here," I continued, "is because this woman said that she saw you here an' I need to get in touch wit' her."

"Who is that?" William spoke in short sentences and quick bursts, like a burp gun.

"Idabell Turner," I said as he inhaled the smoke from his cigarette.

He held the breath a little too long and then, instead of saying anything, he took the pack of Winstons from his pocket and shook it at me.

I took the cigarette.

I took a light.

"What you want Idabell for?" he asked.

"She send a friend'a hers over to drop her dog off with me. He said that she'd come by today to take Pharaoh back but she ain't showed an' I already had to clean up shit twice."

"How you know Ida?"

"Met her. At a party. Her an' her hus'bun. Brother-in-law too, I guess. Damn! Look like twins t'me."

I was saying one thing and thinking something similar. Did Bartlett know Roman and Holland? Was he involved in the killings? I wanted to grab the little man by the throat and choke the truth out of him but it wasn't the right time—not yet. If he was involved and knew who I was, and that I knew him, then he'd run before I could gift wrap him for the cops.

So, for the time being, the only information I could get from him was what he let slip.

"I'ont know where she is, man." His bullet words were a

warning just over my head. "Bitch owe me three hundred dollars for six months. Come by last night to pay me off."

Our eyes met in the involuntary agreement that we were both liars.

"But if I do hear from her I'll tell'er you come by," he lied. "What's your number?"

"They took out my phone," I answered. "But do you know her husband? Maybe I could call him."

"Who's husband?"

"Mrs. Turner's. Idabell's."

"Naw, man. Not me."

"Where you know her from?"

"Around," he said easily. "Listen, I got to get back on the job. Maxwell don't hold much with no coffee breaks."

I wanted to keep him talking. I wanted to break his face. Instead I said, "Yeah, man. It's a bitch."

"See ya, brother. I'll tell Ida you lookin' for her—if I see her."

CHAPTER 23

Down on Pinewood Street, somewhere on the road from Watts to Compton, was a small turquoise apartment building. Not many people knew that Jackson Blue lived there.

His door was on the ground floor. I knocked. I rang. I called out. I knocked again. I was so persistent because Jackson had become shy about public appearances ever since the white gangsters of downtown and Hollywood had gotten interested in his gambling operation.

After a long time the window to an apartment on the third floor slid open. Someone was leaning away up there, staring down while remaining hidden in shadow.

"They gone!" a woman's voice called.

"Doris?"

"Easy? Easy Rawlins, is that you?"

"Yeah."

"Well come on up here and say hey." Her words were gay but she didn't sound that happy.

She opened the door and came outside, looking both ways down the hall as she did. Doris was a deep brown woman with features that were a series of perfect circles; her nose, her nostrils, her eyes, even her mouth. Her hair had been straightened and now stood up, held by stiff hair spray, like a manicured lion's mane.

Doris pulled her robe close at the chest. She gave me a worried, searching look and then peered down the hall again.

"You alone, Easy?"

"What's goin' on, Doris?"

"Jackson gone. They after him, Easy. Them bookie men wanna kill'im. They send some colored mens down here after him."

"Where is Jackson, Doris?"

She looked up and down the hall again.

"Doris, I ain't got time for this."

"I ain't s'posed to be sayin' t'nobody."

"All right." I could live with that. I turned away.

"He's at thirteen twenty-seven and three-quarters Morton Street," she said to my back.

I kept walking.

"Did you hear me?" she asked. "Easy?"

I kept walking.

I walked down the stairs and out to the car. I saw Doris looking from the window above but I didn't acknowledge her. I was thinking that Jackson's help might not be worth its price.

Jackson and his evil friend Ortiz had been running a numbers and bookie operation to oppose the established white gangsters. Jackson had developed a tape recorder system that he could attach to the telephone lines. That way nobody could catch him at his phone center because there was no phone center. Jackson made a few connections at the telephone company and crazy Ortiz ran the collections.

They made more money in three years than an honest man could make in a lifetime.

I imagined a school bell ringing and the scuffle of children's feet down the halls of the administration building. But that was all very far away.

"Who's there?" Jackson shouted from somewhere in the room beyond the door. I figured that he was to the right, behind a corner no doubt.

"It's Easy, Jackson. Lemme in."

"Easy?"

"Yes, Jackson. Easy."

The door swung open quickly. Jackson was behind it. All he let me see was his frantically beckoning hand.

"Com'on, come'on, com'on, come on, come on!"

It was dark in the small room.

Jackson Blue, the smartest man I ever knew, was also one of the most untrustworthy. He was wearing black slacks and a long-sleeved black turtleneck shirt. They were both tight-fitting and so displayed his skinny frame.

It was hard to distinguish Jackson's skin from his clothing. He held his shoulders high and his head down as if he were continually ducking from a blow.

There was a rounded couch covered by a shaggy rug and a dark wood rocking chair in that room. To the right was a door half open on a kitchen.

The only light in the room was from a streetlamp outside that shone brightly on the drawn shade.

"Can we turn on a light, Jackson?" I asked.

"No no, brother, no light."

"You standin' over there in the kitchen when you hollered at me?" I asked.

Jackson looked from the kitchen to the front door. I didn't have to tell him how easy it would have been to shoot him through the wall.

"What you want, Easy? You here about who after me?"

"No. Who is it?"

"It's not just one. Gangsters done put a bounty out on my head. Whole bunch'a soul brothers out to make a grand on my hide."

When he swallowed it was like his whole body was the throat.

"What about Ortiz?" I asked. "He think he could take anybody."

When Jackson sat on down on the shag-covered couch a dusty odor rose in the room.

"What's wrong, Jackson?" I asked. It struck me then that I was unarmed. I had gone unarmed in the streets of L.A. for over two years but this was the first time that it made me feel light.

"It's all fucked up, man. All fucked up."

"You mean the money on your head?"

I wasn't being truthful with Jackson. I knew about his problems. That's why I had sought him out. I'd heard from Mouse that Ortiz had been arrested; I figured that would have put Jackson in a vulnerable position.

"That, yeah. But it ain't just him. It's just bad luck." Jackson shook his head and stared at the floor. "Bad luck."

"What kinda bad luck?"

Jackson had his head down with his hands clasped at the back of his neck. He raised his head without releasing that grip, looked at me for a hard moment, and then sighed.

"Ortiz in jail," he said.

"What for?"

"Two dudes got it in their heads to hijack our runners. We got hit twice. Lost twenty-six hunnert dollars near 'bout. But they got greedy and went in for number three. One'a my people recognized'em an' Ortiz went down to a bar where they hung out, down on Slauson. They saw'im comin' but they decided to fight instead'a runnin'." Jackson shook his head at their foolishness. "But you know Ortiz got some heavy fists. Heavy."

"So it was just a fight?" I asked.

"Yeah. Ortiz busted'em up pretty bad but he's in jail because them white bookies got to the judge. Cops and the prosecutor actin' like Ortiz is public enemy number one. They wanna have a big trial an' meanwhile Ortiz up in jail with no bail."

"And with him in jail your butt's in a sling," I declared.

"Yeah, they figgered it was a good time t'pick me off."

Jackson rubbed his hand over his face and turned in my direction. "Can you help me?" he asked.

Like I said, I knew that Jackson was in trouble. But I had washed my hands of trouble. When I'd heard about Jackson's dilemma I worried that my buddy might get killed but I didn't do anything to help him. I didn't do anything because he had chosen his road and I'd chosen mine. But now I saw where our paths might intersect again. I'd come looking for him knowing that he'd ask for my aid.

"Help you how?"

"I don't know, Easy. I wish I did."

"What were you plannin' to do, Jackson? You just gonna sit here till somebody come in here with guns blastin'?"

"No . . . I mean, what could I do?"

When it came to Jackson Blue, things never changed.

"I need something from you, Jackson."

"Anything, brother. 'Cause you know long as I'm helpin' you I gotta still be breathin' to do it."

CHAPTER 24

"You know a place called the Chantilly Club?" I asked Jackson Blue.

He froze like a wary bug when a man's shadow passes nearby.

"Why?"

"Why? Because what I need to know got to do with the Chantilly Club. That's why."

"What you doin' here, Easy Rawlins?" Jackson sat up in his chair and tried to look threatening.

"What's wrong, Jackson? You crazy?"

"You know Philly Stetz?"

"Never heard of'im."

Jackson had the face of a scout dog from a wild pack. He was trying to sense my danger to his brood.

"What you wanna know?" he said through nearly closed lips.

"You ever hear of Holland and Roman Gasteau?"

"Mmm-hm. Roman's a gambler. Holland's his brother."

"Roman got himself killed at the school I work at and then Holland wound up dead at his own house. Holland was married to one of the teachers at Sojourner Truth. I hear the brothers hung out at a private Negro club at the back of the Chantilly Club."

"You sure you don't know Philly?" Jackson asked again.

"Who's that?"

"He's one'a them, one'a the men could be after me. He run the Chantilly."

"That's why I come to you, Jackson. I know that you deal with gamblers. I thought you could help me. It's no surprise that I'd ask you 'bout somebody you know."

Jackson nodded and rubbed his face again. "How you gonna pay me for this help?" he asked.

"Get you outta this mess you in."

"How?"

"I got a place for ya," I said. "And who knows what after that? You get me the right information and maybe I'll find you an honest job mopping up floors."

Jackson frowned at the idea and I laughed.

I went out to the car while Jackson gathered his things. By the time he came out to meet me I had the engine going.

"Whose apartment is that, Jackson?"

"It was ours," he said. "Just a room we kept in case things got rough."

"I guess they did, huh?"

"Guess so."

Jackson was better than a library when it came to information about the criminal side of L.A.—both black and white. His head was a vault of who did it, when they did it, and how much they got paid for it. That was the way he stayed out of jail for so long; the cops would arrest him for this or that and then ask him what he knew that would make them agree to let him go. That was also why he found no sympathy from the black hoods from Watts and thereabouts. Very few people liked Jackson Blue.

But he was worth the trouble he might cause. Jackson told me about Philly Stetz, the owner of the Chantilly Club. He had been a sports promoter back east who had come to L.A. in the fifties. He did somebody a big favor in city government and then took over the mansion. Stetz dabbled in gambling, fences, prostitutes, and various other L.A. pastimes. Ice didn't melt on his tongue and he didn't know, for a fact, the color of his own blood.

Jackson was afraid to stay down in south L.A. because he thought that he was open to any black man who knew the price that the gangsters had put on his head. He was afraid of Hollywood and downtown because of the gangsters themselves.

So I took him to the Oasis Palms Motel on Lincoln in Santa Monica.

"Anything else to tell me about the Chantilly Club?" I asked.

"Naw. Just say you know Blackman. Tell'em he sent ya an' that'll get ya in back."

"You know anything else 'bout the Gasteaus?"

"No, uh-uh," he said.

"I'll come by in a few days wit' someplace for you to stay till you can try'n get outta this mess," I said.

"Easy?"

"Yeah?"

"Could you let me have a couple'a dollars? Just till you get back."

"You don't have no money?"

Jackson studied his hands.

"Jackson?"

"What?"

"How much money you and Ortiz made in this last year?"

"You mean since a year ago exact, or just since January?"

"This year."

"I'ont know. Mo'rn fifty thousand, that's sure."

"Where is it?"

"Gone."

Gone. The one-word sentence that describes so many people's lives. Jackson Blue making more money in ten months than most black people see in ten years. Where is it? Gone. Like my mother and the house I was born in. Like my wife and, with her, my first child—lost to me in the hills of Arkansas with a man who had been my friend. Gone.

I wanted to strike Jackson.

Instead I gave him one hundred dollars that I'd lifted from a dead man's pockets.

"Wait for me here, Jackson. I might have one more thing for you to do."

"I ain't got no place to go, Easy."

And that was just the way I wanted it.

CHAPTER 25

The Chantilly Club was half a mile up in the hills behind Hollywood Boulevard. The nightclub was housed in a large mansion once owned by some famous star, I was never quite sure which one. The mansion, constructed from pale stone, contained over eighty rooms and had the look of an English country home for royalty.

Young men in white shirts and black trousers ran around

the front gate getting into the cars of partygoers and taking them to the back for parking. The patrons wore gaudy clothes and bright jewelry. It's amazing how a flashy style can make even diamonds look cheap.

I watched for a while from across the road and down the street. Then I took the winding road up behind the mansion and parked my blue hot rod in a large dirt lot along with a lot of older-model Fords, Pontiacs, and Dodges.

At the edge of the lot was a field. At the end of the field was an iron gate lit by a single flaming torch. It would have seemed magical and exciting if I was out for a good time. But instead it looked like a solitary gate to hell set out to lure unsuspecting men to their dooms.

From the top of a steep stairway I could hear the weak strains of a jazz horn. Three notes and I knew who was playing. Three notes and I remembered the first night I'd heard that tune, the woman I was with, the clothes I was wearing (or wished I was wearing), and the rhythm of my stride. That horn spoke the language of my history; traveled me back to times that I could no longer remember clearly—maybe even times that were older than I; traveling, in my blood, back to some forgotten home.

The stone stairs were slippery and narrow through dense low-hanging foliage. I found myself doing a crouching crab-walk to keep my footing.

The stairway wasn't straight—it cut and turned, curved and went around things. I descended for almost five minutes before I got to another iron gate.

There I found Rupert.

I knew about Rupert Dodds from Jackson Blue. Rupert had been a wrestler, performing under the name the Black Destroyer, for local TV in Philadelphia before he broke Fabulous Fred Dunster's neck in a televised wrestling match. Rupert said that the claims that Dunster was making time with his girlfriend were just publicity talk to make it seem like their bout was a blood feud. But he left the East Coast for California and got the job as bouncer for the black part of the Chantilly Club from a fellow Philadelphian, Philly Stetz.

Rupert was taller than me and wider. The muscles on his split-sleeved arms were like half-hard bags of wet cement. His dark face looked as if it had been carved from onyx—with a ball-peen hammer.

"What you want, man?" Rupert's question said that he didn't recognize my face.

"Blackman sent me."

"He did?"

"Yeah." I tried sound tough. Why not?

"What he say?"

"He didn't say nuthin', man. Now let me in here. I'm s'posed t'say the words an' then you s'posed t'open the do'."

Rupert coughed. That was his laugh. He pulled open the gate, scraping it loudly on the stone path.

When I walked in he grabbed my upper arm, squeezing it so hard that I could feel my fingers filling up with blood.

"You doesn't has to be smart," he whispered. Then he pushed me down the path toward a large house.

It was just a guesthouse for the main mansion but it was still three stories. They took my password at the front door and I walked into that long ago I'd heard at the top of the stairs. The room I came into was large, maybe forty feet by sixty, it was most of the bottom floor.

It was a room full of black people, with a number of slumming whites.

The Black Chantilly was started to entertain these wealthy white folks, Jackson had said. They liked to feel that they had some connection with real soul.

The far wall was a big window that looked down on the nighttime vista of L.A. lights. It looked as if a galaxy had been pulled down out of the skies and laid, like a sheet, across the land.

In the center of that spectacle was a boy-sized man holding on to a silver trumpet. He was playing a high staccato riff that had temporarily dampened conversation. Behind the man was a simple wooden chair. I imagined how Lips McGee would fall back into that chair after finishing a set.

There was a big fat bass man and a beret-crowned drummer behind Lips but they had run out of ways of keeping up with the old master. Their hands were down and the only beat they kept was with barely nodding heads.

Lips brought it up as high as he could and stopped. He licked his lips and took a tight breath, then he hit a note that was somewhere west of the moon. He was a coyote calling up the dead; and we were all willing to hear his desecration.

When he finished, the bass man thumped in; the drummer decided on brushes after that fine high plateau. Lips sat down and wiped his face. The room cheered him. Cheered him for all the years he'd kept us alive in northern apartments living one on top of the other. Cheered him for remembering the pain of police sticks and low pay and no face in the mirror of the times. Cheered him for his assault on the white man's culture; his brash horn the only true heir to the European masters like Bach and Beethoven.

Or maybe they were just applauding a well-made piece of music.

"Drink, mister?" She was young and doe brown. The high I got off of Lips' music made me think that there were whispering secrets in her heart.

"Drink?" the young woman asked again.

"Yeah, I mean, no. I don't drink."

"Seventh-Day Adventist?" she asked.

"Naw. Just a man who's seen one good time too many."

She liked me. Her eyes said so. "I could get you a soda. You got to buy three drinks in here if you wanna stay. Either that or go up to the gamblin' room. You gamble?"

"Only with my life," I said. I guess it was the right answer because her shoulders bounced up and down telling me that she would have liked to laugh with me if she wasn't on duty.

"You work here long?" I asked.

"Bout a year or so."

"You know Holland and Roman Gasteau?"

"The twins?"

"Yeah."

"They dead." She did something with her lips that meant she'd been through a lot in life, that she'd learned to leave the dead where they lay.

"You know 'em?"

"Not really. I seen Roman a couple'a times after work. He used t'go out wit' some'a the guys out back after we closed up. You know we like to go out then."

"Where you go that late?"

"Place called the Hangar," she said. "Offa Avalon. They make scrambled eggs an' serve it wit' scotch if you want it."

"That Roman owed me some money," I said, speculating.

"You gonna need a shovel t'get it."

"He had some partners. If I could find out who they were maybe I could collect what's mine."

"He owe you a lot?" Her interest in me was shifting but it was no less intent.

"To some people. I mean, maybe twenty-five hundred dollars don't mean much to you but I could use it to fill out my pockets."

"You got a car?" she asked.

"Yeah."

"You could come on an' meet me up at the torch after three. I could take you on down to the Hangar. Roman's friend Tony prob'ly be there. He works here but this his night off. He usually come down to the Hangar if he workin' or not."

I touched her arm and asked, "What's your name?"

"Hannah."

"Well, Hannah, maybe I'll go see what's happenin' around here in the meanwhile."

"I still got to get you a drink," she said.

I laughed and ordered a glass of milk.

"An' if you cain't make that then melt me some ice, okay?"

Hannah liked my jokes.

The house was divided into areas of interest. On the first floor was music and dancing, drinking and sweet talk. The next floor was a series of gambling rooms. Poker, blackjack, craps, and roulette. The one pool table had no line waiting because every ball cost five dollars.

Only the best played at the Black Chantilly.

The third floor was women. At the bottom of the stairs sat a man who looked like Rupert's midget brother. He took two twenties and gave you a key ring with the number of the room attached.

I peered up the stairs, past the brawny midget, but I couldn't think of an excuse to part with forty dollars.

"Nice up there?" I asked.

"If you got the green," the little man answered.

"Easy?" Her voice came from behind me.

I turned around and said, "Hey, Gracie. What you doin' here?" I asked the question but really it seemed perfect that I'd see Grace Phillips at the Black Chantilly.

She almost smiled. The faraway look in her eye was way past alcohol.

"T'as jus' talkin' 'bout you t'Bertie," she said. Her mouth gave up on each word before it was finished. "You know he likes you. 'Spects you."

"He around here?" I asked, looking over her head down the stairs. There was a man coming up behind her but it wasn't my boss. It was a cream-colored Negro in loose brown pants, cinched tight, and a coral shirt. Between his first two fingers was a burning cigarette; between the second and third finger was a fold of green, forty dollars I'd bet.

He popped his eyes and said, "Hi, Gracie," as he went by. She turned away and looked uncomfortably at me, pretending to smile, until the fish-eyed man passed.

"Hey, Li'l Joe," the customer said to the guardian. "How's it goin'?"

Li'l Joe took the fold of green. He grimaced at the two twenties but smiled when he saw the extra two-dollar bill.

"Fine, fine, Greenwood." He handed a key over and Greenwood sauntered and whistled his way up the stairs.

"I thought you straightened out, Gracie. Don't you have a baby now?" I asked.

Grace smiled, accepting some imagined compliment. "They beautiful, huh, Easy? Babies the most beautiful thing in the worl'."

Grace had on a darkish beige dress that made it down to about three inches above her bare knees. She was the kind of woman you could look at without embarrassment.

"A couple could go up there for just twenty," she said.

"They can?"

"Uh-huh. The house only take twenty. The other twenty is for the girl." She looked down at her chest and I did too.

Grace was a good-looking woman, and I could tell, by the way she nearly smiled, that time with her would be as far from death as a workingman could get. It would be as good as or better than Idabell's soft embraces.

It was the thought of Mrs. Turner killed my ardor.

"I don't think that Bert would look on it too kindly if I was to go up those steps wit' you, Gracie," I said.

"No," she agreed. She smiled too.

"Why'ont we go downstairs," I suggested.

"Could I borrah twenty dollars, Easy?" She didn't trip on a syllable of that sentence.

"We'll see."

Hannah didn't approve of Grace. She wouldn't even look at me when I ordered the soda and scotch and soda for me and my friend.

"Grace, you should go home to your baby," I said after she'd gagged on a gulp of scotch.

"I know," she said. "I know. If you gimme twenty dollars I promise I will. . . . Bertie'd pay you back."

"What's Bert gonna do when he finds that you been out here in the streets?" I asked.

Her sneer would have dissuaded the bubonic plague.

"What he know?" she said. "Lea'me all by myself all that time. Sallie an' all'a his friends wou'n't say boo t'me an' I had t'make it on my own. On my own."

"You should go home, Grace."

Just that fast she put me out of her mind. Her gaze

swung left and then right, looking for anybody with twenty dollars in his pocket.

"You ever hear of Roman or Holland Gasteau?" I asked the back of her head.

"No."

"If I could find out about either one of them it'd be worth twenty dollars." I wasn't really hurting Bert. I figured that she could do a lot worse for that twenty dollars than just talk.

"They come around," she said, swinging back toward me. "But I heard sumpin' happened with them. I'ont know what though."

"You know 'em?"

"Not really. Roman's sweet to talk to. He's nice. Holland's kinda weird."

"You know what kinda business they're in?" I asked.

"Roman's a gambler. I don't know what Holland do."

"They do anything together?"

She swallowed—twice—and then shook her head, no.

"You know I know where you live, Gracie," I said.

"Then you should come by sometimes."

"Can you tell me anything else about the Gasteaus?"

"I could ask around." She got me with her eyes that time; almost, anyway.

But I pulled back. I hadn't fallen that far yet.

I reached in my pocket for the money but before I came out with it I had a thought.

"You seen Bill Bartlett around anywhere lately, Grace?"

"Who?" she asked and I knew that anything else she told me would be a lie—or half of one.

"Bartlett. You heard me. The man tried to blackmail your boyfriend."

"No. Like I said, Sallie'n his friends wouldn't have nuthin' to do with me after that thing wit' you an' Bertie." She was looking at my pocket.

"You hear anything about 'im?"

"You mean Bill Bartlett?"

"Yeah." I let my hand rummage around in the pocket a little bit, to keep her attention.

"They said that he got a cook's job someplace after you got him fired. I'ont know where though."

I gave Grace two tens and she was gone from my table.

I went from there back up to the gambling rooms and dropped thirty dollars at blackjack. I asked the dealer if that was Roman's game. He said that he'd never heard of any Gasteau. Sometimes a lie will tell you more than the truth. I took his lie and pondered it on the way downstairs.

A woman was crooning "I Cover the Waterfront." Lips was seated at the window behind her.

His hands were on his thighs; his eyes were on the moon.

"Hey, Lips."

"Easy." His long-drawn-out voice was the human counterpart of his horn

"How you doin', man?" I'd known Lips since I was a boy in Houston.

"Oh," he mused, "gettin' kinda slow, man. Gettin' kinda slow."

"You sure sound good."

"I did?" The orange in his brown skin was fading. His long hair had been so processed over the years that it wouldn't lay down or stand up.

He sighed. "Used t'be I liked t'play, Easy. Get high, get me a girl for the night. But that's all over now. My mouth ain't right no mo' but even if it was there ain't nuthin' new t'play. All people wanna hear is songs an' they ain't no jazz voice out there. They all wanna shout. They all wanna boogie-woogie. Shit."

I felt for him but I had my own problems that night.

"What can you tell me about the Gasteau brothers?"

"That they dead. That Roman was all right. Yeah, he was okay. But you know Holland was a crusher, man. He always want the light on him. One night he even tried to get up here with me."

"What?"

"Yeah. Got out his guitar an' come up to play next to me. Shit. I had to sit down an' wait till Rupert come."

"Could he play?"

"Maybe, if he turn the motherfucker over an' beat it wit' a stick."

I laughed so hard that tears sprouted from my eyes.

I waved at Hannah and pointed at Lips. She went to get his drink.

"Anything else about 'em?"

"Roman rode a big white horse into town."

"Really?"

"Uh-huh. He was talk' 'bout a herd."

Hannah came up with his drink. She gave me a hard look and then made to move away.

"Hannah," I said before she could go.

"Yeah?"

"You know Lips, right?"

"I don't know him," she said, slightly shy. "But I like his music all right."

"Thank ye," my old friend said.

I touched Hannah's elbow. "I'll still see you later, right?"

She smiled, forgiving me for Grace.

When Hannah left I asked Lips, "You gettin' too old for that?"

"Easy," he said with a wisdom I hope never to attain, "I ain't even int'rested in po'k chops. Food don't even mean nuthin' to me no more."

After that he got up to play a long sad number called "Alabama Midnight." He blew one sad song after another for the rest of a long set. I listened to as much as I could take and then wandered out to the torch.

I stood at the end of the field looking down over the dark trees and shrubs that gathered on the edges of L.A.

I used to live on the edge. I used to move in darkness.

I was excited about Hannah coming out and taking me to her late-night haunt. She liked my jokes and my promise of wealth. I wondered why I had ever left such a simple and honest life.

Behind me people were leaving the club. I heard them laughing and joking, kissing and slamming car doors. A young couple were making love in the backseat of an old

Buick. Her sighs pierced the night like the cries of a dying bird.

I wondered if there was a place for me that could be like this and still allow me to hear children's laughter in the morning.

The crunch of gravel seemed closer than other footsteps leading toward the lot.

Hannah, I thought, and then a heavy weight came down on the back of my head. The moon broke into several sections and my mind tried to go sideways, looking for a way to keep conscious.

CHAPTER 26

"Wake up," my mother said. It was Sunday morning and she wanted me to get ready for church. She shook my shoulder and I knew that she was smiling even though my eyes were closed. She had grits with redeye gravy on the table—I could smell it.

"Wake up!" She slapped me hard across the face and I cried out because she was so unfair to hit me in my sleep.

Rupert was standing there with Li'l Joe.

"He's comin' to, Mr. Beam," Rupert said to someone behind him.

Out from between the two ugly wrestlers came a middle-sized white man. He had a large pitted nose and eyes that only laughed at pain.

"Who are you?" he asked me.

I felt a slight swoon and decided to go with it. I let my head fall forward and Rupert slapped me again. The blow jerked my head up. My eyes opened for a moment but then I played back into the swoon.

Rupert hit me again—this time a little harder.

"Don't knock him out, Rupe," Beam said. "I need him to talk. Hold him for me."

Rupert tried to grab me by the hair but it was too short. So then he pushed his hands against my forehead. I let my eyes loll open but didn't focus them.

"Who are you?" Beam asked. He was wearing a yellow suit. The brightness of the fabric hurt my eyes. "Who are you?"

"Arlen," I said. "Arlen Coleman." I let my head fall again. I almost slipped down to the floor but Rupert grabbed me and set me straight.

At least I knew that I wasn't tied up. I was free. Free to die any way I pleased.

"Why were you asking about Roman and Holland Gasteau in my club, Mr. Coleman?"

I let my eyes settle on Beam for just one moment. I wasn't looking at him though. I wanted to see where I was.

It was a toolshed. Hoes, shovels, and spades lay up against the walls. A bare bulb hung down on a cord from the ceiling. My nostrils opened up to take in the scents of earth and fertilizer.

There was a better than even chance that I'd die in that hut.

"Roman told me he had a job for me."

"What kind of job?"

"He didn't say. Just that it might get a li'l rough. But I told him I like it like that."

"Rough how?" Beam asked.

"He didn't say." I feigned another swoon.

Beam slapped me that time. "Wake up!"

I shook my head and brought my hands to my eyes.

"Where are you from, Mr. Coleman?" Beam said loudly.

"San Diego, San Diego."

"And what did you do down there?"

"Boostin' mainly." I let my head sag down to my knees. I moaned with pain that I actually felt.

"You should have stayed down south, Mr. Coleman," Beam said. It was a final sentence. He was through asking questions.

I should have been thinking of a way to talk myself out of there. I should have told my true story, all of it. About Sojourner Truth and Mrs. Turner and Sergeant Sanchez. But I was silent—dumb. All I could think about was Mouse.

Mouse who saw everything and anything as the means to his survival. The dirt on the ground, his bodily functions. Thinking about Mouse and his drive to survive flowed through me like molten steel. I stood straight up and yelled, "What the fuck's goin' on here!" I reached for Beam, not expecting to grab him. I wilted before Rupert's fist reached me, throwing myself backwards as the punch connected. I had hoped to hit the plank wall hard enough to go through it but when that didn't happen I fell, seemingly senseless, to the ground.

Rupert kicked me once in the back but stopped after that.

"Go get the car," Beam said.

It would have been grand if I could have waited for Beam to say, "Okay, kill him now," as my cue to move. But that only happens on the TV, where they also play a musical warning before you die.

There was no time for me to get to my feet. I grabbed a straight-bladed spade by the metal end and swung it around without looking. The groan I heard satisfied me more than I can say. I rose quickly to my knees and threw the spade, handle first, like a spear at Beam's head. Li'l Joe was coming at me with one hand down at his crotch. Rising on my left foot, I drove the best right uppercut of my life under his chin.

Beam was half the way down to the floor but he was reaching for something in his pocket. Behind him was my freedom. I ran right into the yellow-clad gangster, knocking him on his back and stomping over his body as I made it to the door.

I came outside near the White Chantilly Club. Running past the young valets, I made it through the front gate. I went down the first driveway across the street and started my evasive maneuvers. I climbed over one fence after another. I landed in a swimming pool. I ran into a guard dog in one yard. He was going to do me some serious harm, or so he thought. But I tore out a dwarf palm frond and whipped it through the air yelling, "Lunatic!" as I ran at him. He tucked his tail and wailed back to whatever kennel he could find.

Lights came on in the houses I left behind but I kept moving through the dark wet leaves and silent yards ahead.

By the time I was back in civilization I was wet, with torn clothes and torn skin. I was breathing hard and the cold of evening went all the way through to my bones.

The streets were empty but I hurried along just the same. Any policeman would arrest a man like me on the street. I went down Whitley, past Los Feliz, and on to Hollywood. There I found a discreet phone booth at the side of a newspaper and magazine stand.

The number was stored in my finger, I guess, I hadn't called it in over two years.

"Hello?" He didn't sound as if he'd been asleep.

"John?"

"Easy? What's wrong?"

"You got to come get me, man," I said.

"Where are you?"

CHAPTER 27

Half an hour later John drove by with the door already open. I ducked in and he handed me a half pint of bourbon. I took a hit of it before I remembered that I'd quit drinking. I held the bottle away from my face and thought about tossing it out of the window.

Instead I took another long draft.

Then I threw it.

"What you do that for?" John asked.

. "Taste too good to me, man. Too good." I felt the heat of the whiskey doing its work on my body. So many things I had missed.

While John drove I couldn't bring myself to talk. He didn't press me.

We drove to his house and pulled up into the driveway. There was another car parked further up but I didn't give it a thought.

Even in the dark I noticed that the lawn was trim and healthy. There were large ferns on either side of his front door.

"You fixin' up around here, man?" I asked.

"Shh." He brought a finger to his lips as he turned the lock on the door.

When we came in I expected him to turn on a light but instead he whispered, "We got to go down to the back."

We went through the sitting room up front and then down the long hall that led to his "recreation room" toward the back of the house. We were halfway there when a light snapped on and a woman's voice called out, "Johnny?"

Johnny?

"It's okay, Alva. It's just a friend'a mines come by."

"At four in the morning?"

John and I both turned.

From first glance I knew that Alva was John's perfect mate.

John was an intense man. He was good-looking as looks go but if somebody asked you was he handsome you might say no because his hard stare made him seem intimidating and remote.

Alva was his complement. Tall and striking, her lips would have left their impression on bone. Even in that chiffon robe she seemed to be an ebony statue striding toward us down that hall.

"He got some trouble, Alva," John explained.

"Who?"

"Easy Rawlins, ma'am. Pleased to meet ya."

"Easy," she said, looking me up and down. "I think they named you wrong, honey."

All three of us grinned.

"Easy an' I gotta talk, Alva," John said.

"You hungry, Mr. Rawlins?" she asked me.

"Well, I better eat anyway."

"You two go on down there an' I'll come in a while."

John's recreation room was where he had friends come. There were six chairs that he'd made himself from old-time beer barrels, a bar, and a Navajo rug on the cement floor. He offered me another drink but I refused it. (But I wanted it too.)

I told him the whole story from back to front; everything except for Grace and Bill Bartlett. I hadn't seen John in a while and so he was surprised to hear that EttaMae worked for me. He was shocked to hear that Mouse had a job.

"I heard about him killin' Sweet William," John said. "You know back where I come from we woulda put that boy down."

"That's why he left outta where you come from, John. But you know he's changed. Few days ago he was talkin' about church."

"Church?"

"You know the Gasteaus?" I asked, suddenly needing to get back to my problems.

"Met'em."

"Met'em where?"

"It was Holland mostly. You know, he was tryin' t'act all flashy and cool. Come in with a tramp on each arm and spendin' all kindsa money. Big mouth too. One time he come in wit' his brother. Made a big deal over him at first but then he started tearin' him down. You get some people like that, Easy. They get a couple'a drinks in'em an' some kinda shit come out. Holland wanted to arm wrestle, that kinda shit.

"But you know Roman was cool. He just laughed it off. That niggah had some cold in him. Cold."

"You mean Roman?" I asked.

John nodded.

"I heard that Roman was sellin' heroin."

"Could be. That niggah'd do anything. Anything."

"But you don't know nuthin' else?"

"Naw, Easy. I don't wanna know. I don't like the life no mo'. That's why I'ma sell the bar."

"You are?"

"Yeah. I bought these three lots over on Rice. I'ma build me some houses over there."

"No jive?"

"I hope you like eggs, Mr. Rawlins." Alva was coming in the door. On a cork-inlaid tray she had a plate with scrambled eggs, crisp bacon, and dark buttered toast. There was a cup of coffee too.

Alva knew how to cook but that was only window dressing on a woman like her. If she had the strength of mind and spirit to pull John out of the sour funk of his life; if she could get him out of the bar business and into gardens and building houses—then she was Helen and Cleopatra in one.

I was hungrier than I knew. John and Alva sat patiently while I devoured her meal.

When I was finished John asked, "What do you need, Easy?"

"A car and five hundred dollars."

Alva cut her eyes at John. She knew that he never lent money to anyone.

Maybe that's why she looked surprised when he handed his keys over to me and said, "You can take my Ford. I got the money in the room. Come on. I think I got somethin' fit you too."

Upstairs in John's room I tried on a woolen sports coat and a pair of heavy wool slacks. The jacket was loose and I needed to punch another hole in John's leather belt to keep the pants up around my waist.

I looked like a hipster from the forties in my baggy clothes.

"Where'd you meet Alva?" I asked him after I finished with my wardrobe.

"At Omar's wedding."

Omar's father, Odell Jones, was one of my best friends. It hurt to hear that he had thrown a wedding for his son without inviting me. But I understood why. Odell was a good friend but we both knew that when he called on me it would be because of trouble. He probably thought that it would have been a bad omen for me to show up at the service.

He might have been right.

"Yeah," John was saying. "Omar met his girl down in Arkansas. He was doin' riggin' work for a oil company an' then he met Cordelia. He knew right away that he was going to get married and brought her back up here. Cordelia had Alva come to be her maid of honor.

"Odell asked me to cater an' bartend. I seen Alva once an' that was it."

John's words were so heartfelt that I hesitated to ask my next question.

I hesitated but I did not fail.

"You heard from Grace lately, John?"

All of the dark reserve flowed back into John's face. He didn't have to utter a threat for me to choose my next words with care.

"I got to know, man. Listen, you remember that man she was in trouble with? That Bill Bartlett? He's connected to this trouble I'm in. Somehow he's in it."

"How?"

"You don't wanna know."

John trusted my judgment. He knew I wasn't trying to fool him.

"I heard she was doin' smack," he said. "That she got mixed up with some bad folks after that white man put her down."

"The Gasteau brothers?"

"I don't know, Easy. And like I said, I don't wanna know."

"I might have to call on you again, John."

"You can call, brother," he said. "But we'll have to see if I come."

CHAPTER 28

I wanted another drink. Canadian Club whiskey—no ice, no chaser. Straight up and straight down. But instead I stayed in John's Ford outside of Bonnie Shay's apartment building. It was a hair past five and I figured that if I waited long enough she'd appear. I didn't want to go into any more hallways or apartment buildings. I didn't want any more surprises.

I wanted to surprise somebody else for a change.

And I wanted some whiskey.

The sun was far off somewhere. The edge of the world had begun to glow orange. I planned to be home before Jesus and Feather woke up. But if I didn't make it in time I knew that Jesus would be up to dress and feed Feather; she'd be there to hug him and kiss him good morning. I had children who were more adult than I was. Jesus didn't have an after-school job because he was always taking care of us.

A small gray bus pulled up in front of Miss Shay's apartment building. It had the words AIR FRANCE stenciled across its side in blood-colored paint.

Bonnie Shay, in a sleek little uniform, got out and put down two small bags. Somebody said something from one of the windows. Bonnie laughed and waved. When the bus drove off she bent down to pick up her bags.

"Miss Shay!" I yelled out of my window. I got out and stood across the street waiting for her reply.

"Yes?" She didn't recognize me at first.

"I was given a letter by Idabell to give to you. I wanted to ask you what this was all about, so I waited here." I held the letter up over my head.

If I was out to hurt her I could have slipped from my car and hit her over the head, she knew that. But maybe, maybe I was slick and wanted to get her in the car with me. She looked at the bags she had hanging from either hand, then put them down and waved for me to come over.

"Thank you," I said as I came up to her.

I handed her the letter and she read it. Then she read it again.

"Where is she?"

"I don't know," I said. "She said that she had to get out of town but she didn't say why. She just left her dog with me and went."

"She left Pharaoh with you?"

It was a mistake to mention the dog, I knew that as soon as it was out of my mouth. But I had to go with it once it was out.

"Yeah. Yeah, she said that she didn't know where she was going first and that she was going to go by bus. I told her that the dog wasn't gonna like his cage for weeks on end. I said that I could take him, or give him to you, until she sent for him."

"They don't allow pets in my building, Mr. Rawlins."

"Oh. Tell me, Miss Shay, what's goin' on?"

Her eyes narrowed just a bit and she said, "Do you want a cup of coffee?"

"Sure thing."

Her apartment was designed for what they call architectural efficiency. That is to say, the most rentable space with the least waste—or comfort. One big square room was the living space. Tucked off in the corner, behind half walls, was the small open kitchen. Her bedroom, I suspected, was exactly half the size of the living room so another bedroom for the apartment next door could neatly fill in the gap.

There was an Air France poster on the wall. It was a cartoonish drawing of Paris with a bright blue gendarme twirling his whiskers while ogling a pretty brunette. The Eiffel Tower was falling on them, or so it seemed to me. Along the floor were dark African carvings; all of them of women with pointed breasts and "outie" belly buttons.

She put her bags down, went in the kitchen, and flipped the on switch of her electric coffee percolator. She'd probably set it up with grounds when she left so that there

would be coffee waiting almost when she came in the door.
Her life seemed simple and elegant to me.

"Excuse me," she said. "But I have to wash up a little
before I can sit down."

She went through the door to the other room, closing it
behind her. She could have been making a call to somebody
dangerous. But there was nothing I could do about that.

The coffee smelled strong. French roast.

I heard a toilet flush and then water running. The building was constructed from the kind of cheap materials that
allowed you to hear mice sneezing through the walls and
ants tramping across the floor above.

When she came out she had changed into a one-piece
lime dress. It revealed her womanly figure without a lot of
fanfare or too much sex.

"You work for the airlines?"

"Air France. I'm a stewardess."

"You just comin' back from there now?"

"Uh-huh." She was concentrating on the coffeemaker.
"Sugar and cream?"

"Black," I said.

She gave me a smile with the cup.

"What do you want to know, Mr. Rawlins?"

"I'm a simple man, Miss Shay. I'm a head custodian for
the Board of Education and I own a few apartment buildin's here and there . . . " I stopped myself. That was the
first time in my life that I told somebody about what I
had just in conversation. Where I came from you kept
everything a secret—survival depended on keeping the
people around you in the dark. The tenants in my buildings
didn't know that I owned them. The government didn't
know where I got my money from. Nobody I worked with
knew, with the exception of Etta and Mouse. The cops knew
but I'd been on intimate, if dicey, terms with them for over
a decade.

I blamed my slip on the whiskey and I swore silently
never to take another drink.

"Mr. Rawlins?"

"Yeah?"

"You were saying?"

"Oh, yeah. Yeah. I go in to work one day and Idabell comes crying to me that her husband wants to kill her dog. The next thing I know her brother-in-law is dead—right there on the school grounds—and her husband gets shot at their house. She disappears, and then when she calls me she says that she's runnin' away."

"I read about Roman in the paper. And the police came here to question me about Idabell and Holland. They should probably have this letter?" She looked to see how I'd take that question.

It wouldn't have looked good for me if she went to the police and told them that I'd seen Idabell in the last couple of days. A cold chill ran up under my scalp. It hurt where I'd been sapped.

"What's it say?" I asked innocently.

She handed it over to me and I pretended to read.

"What's all'a this mean?"

"Why do you want to know, Mr. Rawlins? This doesn't have anything to do with you. All you have to do is go home." She was harsh but it didn't bother me. I was a fool.

"I got a history with the cops, Miss Shay," Whiskey said. "They don't like me and they know that I was talkin' to Idabell the day she left. I didn't tell'em 'bout her dog 'cause she'd lied about the dog at school, she said that he was in an accident and that's why she left that day. Now if I do say they'll lean pretty hard."

"If you didn't do anything there's nothing to worry about."

I knew right then that she wasn't a fully American Negro. A black man or woman in America, with American parents, knew that innocence was a term for white people. We were born in sin.

"I like my job, Miss Shay. I got a pension and a ladder to climb. They will fire me if the cops do something like cart me off to jail."

Bonnie Shay gave me a long look. I liked it. I hadn't lied to her, except about Idabell and that damned dog. But that was just a lie of necessity. I was sure that she wouldn't hold that against me.

"Roman," she said. "Her brother-in-law. He stole something from me. I told Ida about it. I guess she just felt bad about it."

"What did he take?"

"What?"

"What did he take from you?"

"Oh. Well, yes. A ring."

"It sure don't sound like that," I said.

"It doesn't?" she dared me. "What does it sound like then?"

I decided to go out on a limb. "It sounds like Roman was smuggling heroin from France into L.A. and using you to do it. It sounds like Holland was in on it with him. It sounds like Idabell took the heroin from Holland and killed him for playing her like a fool. It sounds like you're into it up to your neck and you'd be lucky not only to keep your job but to stay outta jail."

The hardness in her face was something to behold. I had delivered a devastating stroke and she weathered it.

"What do you want, Mr. Rawlins?"

"All I want is enough to give to the cops if they decide they want me. I wanna know who killed the twins and why they did. I wanna know why Idabell ran."

"I don't know any of it. Nothing."

It had to be the whiskey. Had to be. There I was talking about murder with someone who was obviously involved, and all I could think about was how much I liked it that I could tell when she was lying. I was feeling an intimacy with her. I would have liked to get to know her as well as I understood her.

She felt it too, I could tell. It was like we were looking over a field and catching each other's eye; our animal sides slowly overpowering our minds.

Who knows what might have happened if there hadn't come that knock on the door?

It was three hard raps and then silence. Bonnie was

about to say something but I put up one finger for her silence.

Ten seconds passed.

Three more raps. This time harder.

I stood up and went to the kitchen.

The raps turned into blows. "Bonnie Shay!" Rupert sounded as if he were in the room with us.

I put my fingers to my lips to keep Bonnie quiet and lifted an iron pan from the stove. Bonnie's eyes showed fear but she trusted me—at least more than she trusted the man banging on her door.

The door was hollow. I was surprised that Rupert hadn't broken through it with his knocks.

"Open up!" Rupert called.

I sidled up to the door and readied myself for the wrestler.

He probably used his shoulder to batter the door. On his first blow he cracked it down the middle, almost going through.

Bonnie let out a small screech.

"Who's out there?" someone shouted from down the hall.

"Hey, man," Rupert said. "Mind your own . . . Hey! Hey watch it!"

"Clear outta here or I shoot, bastid!"

"Hey, watch it!" Rupert shouted. His voice was already down the hall.

"I'm callin' the police!" our savior yelled. "I'm callin' 'em."

Then there was a brief stretch of silence.

The next knock on the door was mild.

"Miss Shay? Miss Shay, you okay in there?"

"Yes, Mr. Gillian." Bonnie went to the door and opened it.

He was an older man, smallish. But he made up for his size with the three-and-a-half-foot shotgun levered in the crook of his arm. He was black, yellow actually, with web-like soft white hair. His orange flannel robe was open at the throat. You could see the skin of his throat sagging, as if it knew that it was time to abandon the bones.

He had one foot in the room, the other one in the hall.

His eyes were on me as he asked Bonnie, "You want me to call the cops?"

"No, Mr. Gillian. Thank you for scaring him away. I don't think that he's going to come back."

"You know, you should watch the company you keep," he said, still looking at me.

I kept my hands down at my side. I didn't want to scare Mr. Gillian into shooting me.

"Thank you again, Mr. Gillian," she said.

Bonnie moved to push the door closed.

"You can come on down with me and Cheryl if you want, Miss Shay," he said.

I liked him. He was worried that I was a threat and that she was scared to run from me.

But Mr. Gillian didn't like me.

"Why'ont you come on with me, Bonnie?" he said.

He leaned forward to cut off my approach to her, balancing the gun so that he could swing it up into action with speed. The only problem he had was the length of the barrel. If he wasn't used to wielding it it might take a second too long.

Gillian knew what I was thinking. He gave me a little smile that dared, "Go on, boy. Try it."

He said, "Come on, Bonnie. Let's go."

Bonnie saw what was happening. She held the broken door by the knob and looked at me. Who was I? At least she knew Mr. Gillian. Mr. Gillian and Cheryl were safe.

They were safe but what did they know about the man pounding at the door?

"It's okay, Mr. Gillian. Mr. Rawlins was helping me."

"You sure?" There was disappointment in his voice.

"I'll come down and talk to you and Cheryl later on," she said while pushing the cracked door to usher him out.

"Okay now," he said as the door was closing. "But I'll be keepin' a ear peeled."

The moment the door was closed Bonnie gasped and brought her left hand to her breast. I moved to help but she held up the other hand to ward me off. Then she shook her whole body, head and all, making a noise with her flapping cheeks like you do when you're very cold. The shiver subsided slowly until only her head and neck quivered slightly—her eyes shut tight. Then she took a deep breath and opened her eyes to look at me.

"Do you know who that man was?" she asked.

CHAPTER 29

"Rupert works for two white men," I was saying at the Dunkin' Donuts franchise down near La Cienega and Pico. Bonnie had taken her coffee with two creams and two sugars. "Philly Stetz and a guy named Beam."

We had gone down to the back of the building and out through the laundry window. I didn't know if Rupert was outside, if he was armed, or if Li'l Joe was with him. But even if he was alone and unarmed, I doubted my ability to stop him from taking Bonnie.

We tripped and stumbled through a cluttered cement deck that offered the building's trash cans to the alley. A German shepherd growled and barked once but he backed down when I took a metal lid from the nearest can. Dogs had become my least favorite creatures over the past few days.

We caught a bus to a cab stand on Jefferson. From there we took a taxi to the doughnut shop. I was in no rush to take this woman into my home. I mean, I liked her but I loved those kids.

"You know either one of them?" I asked.

She shook her head.

"Well, what do you know?"

"I don't know much, Mr. Rawlins. For instance, I don't know if I can trust you."

"Hey." I held up my hands. "You sure in hell cain't trust Rupert."

For some reason that made her laugh. She brought her hand to her lips in an attempt to suppress the giggles.

"What's so funny?"

She tried to talk but the laugh wouldn't let her.

Bonnie put her fingers at the back of my hand to steady herself.

"You looked pretty funny there," she said.

"Where?"

"At my place. Your face got all cockeyed and you were holding that pan like it was a fly . . . " She couldn't manage to finish for laughing. "A flyswatter."

I laughed then. I was thinking that Rupert did resemble a fly. A big ugly fly who had had his wings clipped.

"You were so scared." She laughed some more. "Kinda cute though."

"More than cute," I said in a somber tone. "If you would of opened that door you'd be dead right now."

"You don't know that," she said defiantly.

"They killed Idabell, Bonnie."

She shook her head the smallest little bit and winced.

"I was comin' to leave you that note and she stayed down in the car. It was raining and she didn't want to get wet but I think that she was also afraid to see you after what her people did. While I was up at your door somebody shot her in the head."

"The police didn't say that."

"Uh-uh. The cops you talked to don't know yet. The Santa Monica police found her but she didn't have no ID."

"Why? Why would they do that?"

"Because somebody was waitin' for you. Because they saw me drive up an' leave her in the car. Because she had something they wanted."

"What could she have that would get her killed?"

"A child's croquet set."

I might as well have slapped her. Whatever words or arguments or points she had to make died in her throat. Her mouth hung open, silent.

"Come on," I said. "I'll take you over to my house. It's not too far."

*

The stewardess had on flat shoes and so the walk wasn't too bad. It was about seven. A strong wind was blowing and light filled the weak blue sky. Cars moved with purpose on the broad boulevard.

Feather was in the front room laughing with Pharaoh. She stopped dead when she saw that a woman had come into the house. Feather didn't have much experience with women in our house. Jesus brushed her hair and saw that she got dressed. I cooked the meals and wiped her nose. I answered her questions about right and wrong, good and bad.

She went from seven years old to three in a twinkling. With two fingers in her mouth and one up her nose she stared at Bonnie as if she had never seen a woman before.

Pharaoh was growling at me. Of course.

"Feather, this is Miss Shay," I said.

Feather stared.

"Hi, Feather," Bonnie said. "Are you playing with Pharaoh?" She bent down to scratch the dog behind his ears. He loved that, but not enough to stop eyeing me.

"His name is Frenchie," Feather said, sticking out her stomach and rocking on the balls of her feet.

"Frenchie. That's a nice name. Did you give him that name?"

"Uh-huh. I did because Daddy said that he was a French dog, um, Carolina."

"I like Frenchie much better."

Feather took her wet hand from her face and put her arms around Bonnie's neck. Bonnie stood up with my girl in her arms.

She looked good like that.

"Will you be my mommy sometimes?" Feather asked.

"Hi, Dad." Jesus came in from the back hall.

"This is my son, Jesus. Jesus, this is Miss Shay."

"Hi," Bonnie said. She stuck out her hand as far as she could while holding Feather. All three of them laughed at how silly it looked.

It was a regular family scene. All we had to do was to

clean up a few murders and a matter of international dope smuggling, then we could move next door to Donna Reed.

Jesus and I made breakfast. That was his Bisquick phase. We turned out pancakes and sausages while Feather sat on Bonnie's lap and Pharaoh took turns barking with them and snarling at me.

It was all over by eight-fifteen. Jesus took Feather off to school after which he was going to practice for track.

The smile faded from Bonnie's face as the two children left.

"They're beautiful," she said sadly.

"I think so."

There was an awkward moment then. We didn't know each other, there were no common friends or interests we had—at least none that we knew about. The only thing we could do was talk about murder and neither one of us had the heart for any more talk like that.

"Where you from?" I asked.

"Originally?"

"Uh-huh."

There was a tiny spot on her dress, over her left breast. It was probably a food stain. Something that she saw but then said to herself, "It's just a little spot."

Her beauty couldn't be dampened by a blemish or a wrinkle.

"I was born in Guiana," she said. "French Guiana's what they call it. But I was raised in New Jersey. That's why I can work for Air France. I'm fluent in French and American English."

"Yeah. You're the first black stewardess I ever heard of."

"There's lots of black people doing things outside of America."

"You spend mosta your time outside America?"

"We do lots of flights to Africa. Algeria, the Sudan."

"How come you live here then?" I asked.

It was an innocent question but I struck a nerve there. We were still standing at the front door so I said, "Here, have a seat." Bonnie sat on the couch. The brown one that I bought after I bled all over the old sofa.

"You want some coffee?" I asked.

"Would you?"

When I returned from the kitchen she'd calmed down a little. She tasted the brew and smiled when she saw that I put in the right amounts of sugar and milk.

"I came here because of Roman Gasteau." She said it all at once, in a hard voice. "I met him in Paris. I mean, I was introduced to him by Idabell. He was her brother-in-law. He was from Philadelphia but spent a lot of time in New York. Paris was my home base but I flew into New York twice a week. Ida told him where I stayed and he looked me up."

"So how'd you wind up here?"

"I liked Roman. He was fun and he made me miss living in the States. He'd spent a little while with me in Paris but then he was offered a job in Los Angeles. A blackjack dealer's job in Gardena." She looked at me as if to say, So. "Idabell was here. It's not too hard to change your route if you have seniority. All I had to do was wait a few months for a slot to open up."

"So you came to L.A. on a lark?" I was unconvinced.

"It wasn't like that. Not really. Roman and I had gotten close. He wanted me to come to L.A. I thought it was because he was too jealous to leave me in Paris. I was flattered. I didn't know that he was using me to make visits to Paris to set up some deal.

"Roman was wonderful to be around. He was playful and smart—he was a great dancer. And he believed that people should be responsible to their community. There's an elderly couple who live in his apartment building, the Blanders. He used to do their shopping and once or twice he even paid their rent.

"From everything I knew about him he seemed perfect. So of course I wanted to come out here, to be with him and live near Idabell."

"And then he made you his mule," I said.

"He said that he was importing French toys that he sold

on the side. He wanted me to bring them in now and then so that the tariffs wouldn't cut into his profit. It was only toys. A set of Italian boccie balls, a dollhouse."

"An' you didn't know?"

"Not until I forgot once. I left this set of wooden carpet balls on the plane. I forgot. When I got home and Roman came over he went crazy. I told him that I'd go back in the morning, that the ground crew had probably put the package in my basket. It had my name on it.

"He struck me. He knocked me down. I was afraid that he was going to kick me when he pulled me up by the hair and told me that he'd kill me if I didn't go down with him right then to get it. He dragged me down there at three in the morning. I told him that that would be suspicious but he didn't care. I had to sign all kinds of forms and I think the customs agent was suspicious but he knew me and let it go. . . . Roman took the balls to his car and left me to take a bus home."

Bonnie trembled with the memories. I didn't doubt a word that she said.

"What happened then?" I asked.

"I broke off with him. I put in for a transfer back to Europe but I'm still waiting for an open slot."

"Did he threaten you?"

She nodded.

"That why old man Gillian is ready with his shotgun?"

"I didn't know if it was drugs or something else, Mr. Rawlins. It didn't matter, because he hit me. My mother always told me that you can't let any man treat you like that." The steel in her eyes was fine by me.

"But you did talk to him again."

"Why do you say that?"

"Because of that croquet set. Because of that note Idabell wrote."

I was pushing to see how far she would trust me.

"He came to my apartment after they beat him up."

"Who?"

"The people he dealt with. He didn't say who. He told

me that they had made a deal for six deliveries but we'd only finished five—"

"So they were going to kill him," I finished the sentence.

"And me," she said. "He'd told them how he was getting the toys into the country. He said that they were going to kill me too unless I went along with it."

"And you believed it?"

"You should have seen him. He was all beaten up. Bleeding, swollen. There were bruises and lumps all over his body."

"So you told him yes."

"I told him no." Bonnie Shay reared back like a king cobra. "I told him to get out of my house. I told him to send his killers, but I wouldn't be his whore."

That phrase played over and over in my mind for the next few weeks, and years.

"So what's the problem?" I asked, trying to seem unimpressed with her heroism.

"Holland got Idabell to do it."

"How does that work?"

"Roman kept calling but I wouldn't talk to him. I was afraid to go to the police, I didn't even know what I would say. So I just waited it out. When nothing happened I thought that everything was okay.

"And then a month or so later Idabell calls and asks if we can spend a few days in Paris. She said that Holland was going out of town. I got her a ticket. It was only when we were landing in L.A. that I saw the croquet set. It had been delivered to our hotel and she got it without me knowing."

"But why would she do that? She didn't owe anything to Roman, did she?"

"It was because of Pharaoh."

"The dog."

"Roman promised to share the money with Holland if he would get Ida to do it. So Holland hid the dog and told Ida that he'd kill it if she didn't do what he said. You know Ida's crazy over that dog."

"But who killed them?"

"I guess it was the people who they were doing business with. The man who came to my house today."

It made sense. It was a simple case of a falling out among thieves.

"But maybe Idabell killed Holland," I guessed out loud.

"No," said Miss Shay. "I don't believe that."

"Maybe to save her dog?" I speculated. "That damn dog seems to be the reason for every problem we have."

"Idabell wouldn't even know how to kill a man. Where would she get a gun?"

"Out of her husband's top drawer. That's where most men keep their guns, you know. In the top drawer, next to the bed." I was just talking. "So now what do you want to do?"

"What do you mean?" She looked around, coming aware that she was in a strange man's house. After all, what did she know about me? Killers had kids too.

"You wanna go to the cops?" I offered.

"Maybe I should."

"Maybe so. I mean, if your life is in danger then maybe the cops will help; maybe they'll believe that you didn't know what was going on. But if they don't believe you you'll be alive, but you'll also be in jail."

She stood up quickly and took a step toward the door.

I stayed in my chair.

"Why are you trying to scare me, Mr. Rawlins?"

"I'm not tryin' to scare you, honey," I sighed. "I'm just tryin' to point out that we both want the same thing."

"What's that?"

"To be let alone. That's all. We both got lives and jobs and we both want a future. Police don't care about none'a that."

Bonnie stared at the floor in front of my feet the same way that Jesus had.

"You want to sleep for a while?" I asked.

"I, I don't know. I'm tired, but . . . "

"You can have my bed. I'm'onna be here for a while. You could get some sleep and then we'll figure out what you should do."

I took her into my room and she stretched out on top of the blankets. I spent the next half an hour in the kitchen going over the crimes in my mind again. Sanchez and Fogherty smelled the drugs somehow. I don't think they knew what or how, because if they did they would have either left me alone or thrown me in jail.

No, they had suspicions, that's all. They wanted to know more about the whiff of dope that stuck in their nostrils.

He didn't know it, but Sanchez wanted Bonnie. I'd never give her to him. She wasn't the kind of woman that a fool like me could give up.

When the phone started ringing I decided not to answer it. On the sixth ring I wondered who it was. On the tenth bell I picked up the receiver.

"Hello."

"Hello, Mr. Rawlins," Hiram T. Newgate bellowed. "I see that you're still at home."

"What do you want, Hiram?"

"What do you think? You've decided not to come in to work anymore. The police are investigating you for theft— maybe worse. I'm calling to ask for your resignation."

"My what? Are you crazy?"

"I have a school to run," he said. "A school. I can't have the people working for me disappearing without a word."

"Didn't Stowe call you?"

"This isn't his school. He can't just take my people. And anyway, you aren't even working. You're at home."

I moved the receiver from my ear, intent on slamming it down, but I checked myself.

"Mr. Newgate, listen to me." I breathed through the sentence so that he could hear the hiss in my throat. "I'm doin' a job for the area office. Mr. Stowe is my boss—not you. I work for him. He provides my services to you. If you have a complaint then call the grievance office—and lodge it."

"I won't have you working for me, Rawlins."

"Goodbye," I said. And we both hung up.

"Mr. Rawlins?" She was standing at the door to the kitchen.

"Yeah?" I let my eye settle on that small stain.

"I don't want you to think I'm flirting with you," she said.

"If this was you flirtin', then love would strike me dead."

She smiled and said, "Will you come lie next to me?"

"What?"

"You're right, I'm very tired, but I'm scared in the bed alone. When I get up the room starts spinning. Just lie next to me—until I fall asleep."

I sat up against the head of the bed while Bonnie lay curled toward me. We weren't touching.

"Is she really dead?" Bonnie asked.

I didn't answer her.

"I couldn't go to sleep for thinking about it. I was afraid for her. I was afraid something would happen while I was gone."

"You thought Holland or Roman would do something?" I asked.

Bonnie sat up and looked me in the eye. "Tell me what happened," she said.

I told almost all of it. Not the lovemaking, I was shy about that, but I told her about meeting Idabell and taking her to Bonnie's street. I told her what we talked about and about the man running through the rain. I told her about the park and Pharaoh's cries.

"She deserved better," Bonnie said.

"I know."

She looked at me as closely as Sanchez had. And when I said my last words she nodded and allowed her eyes to fill with tears. Her intuition told her that I was telling the truth.

I'd never felt closer to another soul.

Bonnie lay on her side, facing me, a peaceful look on her sleeping face. I wanted to touch her, to run my hand down the curve of her breast. But instead I stayed on my back with my hands behind my head.

Most people say that a man loses his rational abilities

when he gets sexually aroused. I've often found the opposite to be true. My mind is sometimes clearest when there's no doubt about how I'm feeling.

The tiles began to fall together in my mind. The characters of my little play, living and dead, picked up their parts and rehearsed their lines. I started with a happy ending and then worked backwards from there.

"Mr. Rawlins?" I was down in Louisiana again working my hoe on a row of snap beans. "Mr. Rawlins?"

Bonnie was standing over me but she wasn't looking at my face.

My hand was down over my crotch.

"It's noon, Mr. Rawlins."

"Easy."

"What?"

"That's my name. Call me Easy."

She had a nice smile. "You should get up."

CHAPTER 30

There were butter-grilled ham and cheese sandwiches and lemonade, made from the lemons in my yard, waiting on the kitchen table. A raven was stalking around outside the back window, searching the lawn for seed.

"You got someplace to go?" I asked her. "To lay low."

"I have friends in France."

"Can you get on a flight?"

"I'd rather stay in L.A. until I know what's happening. I mean, I want to be sure."

"Why would you stay here in Los Angeles if you're in trouble with gangsters *and* the police?" I asked. "You got somethin' else on your mind?"

"You can't run from trouble, Mr. Rawlins," she said.

"Yeah," I said. "I guess you're right about that. Yeah. You can stay here for a while. After that we'll see."

I picked up the phone and dialed. Mouse answered on the seventh ring.

"Hello?"

"Raymond?"

"Hey, Easy. How you doin'?" He didn't seem to care much.

"I need a ride into the school today. You wanna come and get me?"

"Now? You mean you want me to come in to work early?"

"You could do some overtime. I can give it to you. I'm the boss."

"Yeah, but for how long?"

"What's that s'posed t'mean?"

"Nuthin'. I'll talk to you later, man."

Bonnie went back to bed.

After she was asleep again I bathed and shaved. By the time Mouse got there I was ready to go. He pulled up in front of the house in his tan Ford and tapped on the horn.

It felt good running out to get in a buddy's car for a ride to work.

"What you mean about that crack about me not bein' around?" I asked while he drove.

"Newgate come 'round askin' 'bout you," Mouse said. "He wondered if you missed work a lot. Then he asked me stuff about what you used to do—before you come to work for the Board."

"That all?"

"He said that it was unusual for you to get such a high job of responsibility so fast without no college." Mouse grinned. "Then he said that somebody like me might have to work a dozen years to get that high."

"Oh," I said. Then, "You know, Raymond, I might need some help from you later on."

"Sumpin' at the school?"

"No."

Mouse cut his gray eyes at me. "You don't want me to do sumpin' wrong now, do ya?"

"If there's any doin' t'be done I'll do it," I said. "It would just be good if I had somebody to come with me."

"Hm." Mouse brought a finger to his chin. "'Cause you know I went down to Etta's preacher yesterday afternoon."

"Yeah?"

"Uh-huh. I asked him what a sinner could do to repent, an' he said to admit my sins and to accept Jesus. He said that way I could be forgave. He said if I did that then the Lord would give me a sign, just like you said.

"I tried to confess right there but he heard the first few words and told me to shut up. He said that we wasn't Catholics to hear confession. He said that my repentance was just between me an' God.

"That was my first sign, I know."

Mouse had answered my request, but I didn't understand him.

"Will you come with me tonight?" I asked again.

"Sure, Easy. Who knows where my next sign might be?"

When we got to school I found four messages for me in the administration office. They were from the boys' vice principal, the principal, Mr. Stowe down at the central office, and Sergeant Sanchez up in Mrs. Teale's room.

I went to see Mr. Langdon in his wood shop.

His classroom was a bungalow like the ones on the lower campus but it was older and placed up next to the science building. The turtlelike teacher was pawing over thin flats of wood with four of his advanced students. They were building a large chest of six drawers, each of which was designed to be a unique size. You could see the intention by the frame of the chest that was standing behind them.

"Mr. Rawlins," he said when he saw me.

His serious students looked up, and one of them even blinked like Langdon did.

"I have something to discuss with you, Mr. Langdon," I said.

"I'm sorry," he said, "but we're in the middle of a very delicate operation right now. Maybe if you came by tomorrow morning, before class . . . "

Mr. Langdon had regained his confidence and so now I was the well-dressed janitor again; a man who would have to wait no matter what he needed to know.

"Okay," I said mildly. "I just wanted to know about that special croquet set you worked on for our friend."

To see a pale man turn white is a frightening thing.

"Go on, boys," Langdon said. "We'll start over tomorrow."

"But the glue is ready, Mr.—"

"Go on now. Go, go," the great white turtle stuttered and snapped.

The boys left complaining under their breath.

I sat down on the long bench of vises and smiled.

"What, what . . . what can I . . . " Langdon was floundering on his own tongue.

"You hollowed out a set of croquet balls and mallets for Roman Gasteau, right? Some Italian carpet balls and wooden dolls too."

Now Langdon could only gasp.

"You did that," I went on. "And he used them to smuggle drugs."

"No, no, no," Langdon said.

"Yes, yes, yes," I said.

He looked around the room for help but we were alone. "It's not so bad really, Mr. Rawlins. I did make the croquet set but it was just for grass. We used to have marijuana parties." He was talking loudly. I knew then that Roman Gasteau had been a fool. Only a fool would have taken on a partner like Langdon. A child could have forced the truth out of that wood shop teacher.

"With Idabell, Roman, and Holland?"

"Lots of people would come over."

"How could you be such a fool to get involved with dope smugglin'?"

"It's not like it was real drugs," Casper said. "It was only pot. Roman used to go down to Tijuana and stuff the mallets or the dolls or the lawn balls with grass, sometimes hash."

I didn't correct Casper because I couldn't see why he

should know more than he admitted. He was scared enough to be involved with marijuana.

"It's a girl, right?" I asked.

Langdon looked down. He held out his hands in front of his face and big tears splatted down on his fingers.

"What's her name, Mr. Langdon?"

"It's not what you think," he said.

"Yes it is," I said. "Roman took you out an' got you high. Then he showed you a girl didn't need any kind of promises or flowers. I know. I know."

"She liked me." Langdon blinked his heavy lids. The droplets clung to his eyelashes.

"What's her name?"

"Grace," he said. "But I haven't seen her in two months."

Any hope that I had for innocence was gone with a name. Roman knew Grace. I knew Grace. Grace was how I came to my job. It was as if I had been looking for the criminal and came upon myself on the way.

"Grace Phillips?"

"Yes."

I don't know how long I stood there speechless, staring at his fat white cheeks.

Finally I turned away from him and went to the bungalow door.

"Mr. Rawlins?" Langdon called from across the room.

"What?"

"Are you going to tell the police or, or Mr. Newgate?"

"The cops haven't talked to you about this?"

"No. They showed me a picture of Roman and asked me if I knew him. I told them that he was Mrs. Turner's brother-in-law. That's all they wanted to know."

"Well, you better hope that they don't come back to you, Mr. Langdon. But if they do come back you better be quiet about what you know. Roman might have told you that it was all right but I don't think that Sergeant Sanchez would agree."

"Oh my God."

Sergeant Sanchez was sitting at Miss Teale's desk.

"So, you decided to come in to work at last, eh, Rawlins?"

"Well, you know, there were some things that I had to do."

He smiled. "You ready to talk to me?"

"Nuthin' t'say, officer. I don't know a thing."

"Nothing? What about heroin, Mr. Rawlins?"

"No thanks."

"This is no joke, man," Sanchez said. "We got a serious drug problem here. The Gasteau twins were selling drugs."

"Really?"

"We found traces in a wax paper bag in the hole in the garden. He had everything there he needed to cut drugs and package them."

"What difference does it make?" I asked. "Those men are dead. Unless you think they gonna be sending drugs up from hell then that case is closed."

"This is serious," he said again. Maybe he was going to say something else but I cut him off.

"Naw, man. What's serious is you got four or five dozen kids in this neighborhood climbin' up under the bushes in front'a the school ev'ry night disintegratin' their brains on airplane glue." I was mad. "Every mornin' you walk right over the rags. You see the kids stalkin' an' staggerin' around and what you do? You come in here an' try'n scare me because of somethin' that happened years ago. I don't know nuthin' 'bout no heroin. I do know about glue though. You wanna hear about that?"

"That's just penny-ante," Sanchez said. He was dead serious.

"So what you worried 'bout is how much the drugs cost, you don't care about what they do."

Sanchez probably cared about what was happening to the glue sniffers. Many of them were his own people as well as mine. But there was no budget to stop the flow of wine and glue in the ghetto streets.

"So you don't know anything about the drugs?" he asked.

"Man, I never even met either one'a them men," I proclaimed. "It's you who think I'm in it. It's you come on out

to my house and trick me down to a lineup on some lies.
I'm just doin' my job, sergeant. I'm just livin' my life."

"I got you on more than that, Rawlins," he said darkly.

I gritted down, intent on silence.

"We got a call down at the station, Ezekiel. About all
those burglaries from your school and other ones too."

"Yeah. Somebody blamed it on me, I know."

"This time they told us where you hid the loot."

I stood up. "Come on, man."

"Sit down." The steel in his voice told me that it was all
true. "I think that you better come on over to the station
with us."

Right on cue two cops came in from the hallway.

"I'm under arrest?"

"It's just questioning for the moment, but I will arrest
you if you refuse."

The Seventy-seventh Street station hadn't changed
much. The same yellow wax covered the dark-green-and-
white-tile floor. The furniture hadn't aged well.

"Down the hall past the sergeant's desk—to your left,"
Sanchez said.

I knew the way.

I knew the room.

I still remembered the corroded plaster and the mil-
dewed floorboards. I took a quick glance at the corner to
see if the mouse, crushed fifteen years ago, was still there.

It wasn't a clean room.

"Sit down," Sanchez said.

There were two wooden chairs. I took the one facing the
door.

As I sat a tall white man came in, closing the door behind
him. He wore dark gray pants and a white shirt with
sleeves rolled high above his elbows. He took his place
behind the seated Sanchez, and practiced making fists
with his left hand.

Sanchez's smile told me that he'd been waiting for this
moment. I tried to look brave but that only made him gloat
harder.

"You see, Drake?" Sanchez seemed to be talking to me.

The white shirted man nodded, clenching his fist hard enough to pop a knuckle.

"Okay," Sanchez said. I didn't know who he was saying it to. "Now we're going to have a serious talk with some serious answers."

My mouth opened—I wanted to speak—but there were no words to say.

Sanchez did a meaty drumroll against thighs with open hands.

"Just to show you that I'm an okay guy," he said, "I'll answer your question."

I hadn't asked any questions but maybe Sanchez thought that he could read my mind.

"You asked me how I got my stripes."

Actually I had asked him when he'd become a sergeant but I saw no reason to point that out.

"I had a lot of help," he continued. "People like you helped me. Negro people and my own Mexicanos—living like dogs instead of standing up and taking advantage of what's right in front of them.

"It was hard for me to get this job because the bosses downtown didn't believe that a Mexican could speak good English or work hard. They think our people are lazy, Ezekiel. They think that we're all no-good crooks. Because of people like you. And because of you I made myself perfect to get this job.

"And now I have it. And I'm not going to hold your hand and say how sorry and sad I am that you were poor or that you think it's too hard to be as good as other people. That's why you're going to talk to me now—because I know what you are and I don't give a shit about you."

There was a lot I could have said but I didn't. Sergeant Sanchez was a zealot and he couldn't hear anything unless you told him that you believed in his vision. And seeing that his vision was that I was a lazy crook—silence was my best choice.

"You can start with the little shack down on Olympic,"

he said. "How'd all those wind instruments from Locke High get down there?"

Half a minute passed; then thirty seconds more.

"I don't have all the patience in the world, Mr. Rawlins," Sanchez said.

I prayed silently and was rewarded with a knock on the door.

A uniformed officer came in.

"What?" Sanchez's lip curled as if he might damage who-ever it was that interrupted us.

The uniform, a beefy specimen with a red bristle brush for a mustache, crossed over to Sanchez and whispered something.

"What?" the sergeant barked again.

"That's what he said." The uniform hunched his shoulders.

Sanchez stood up so quickly that I flinched, thinking that he was on the attack.

"Come on, Drake," he said.

"Come on where?"

"Just come on."

Sanchez went out in long angry strides followed by the red-whiskered cop. But Drake lingered a moment, cradling his fist.

"Drake," Sanchez called from the open doorway.

Drake was pulled by his superior's voice but I could see that he wanted to hit me at least once before going.

"Drake! Let's go!"

Drake opened his fist and used his big hand to blow me a kiss.

Another goodbye kiss. He closed the door and I was back fifteen years. A long time had passed but the helplessness felt just the same. The fear was the same too.

I sat remembering that the last time I was in that room I hadn't tested the door. Maybe it wasn't locked. I wasn't under arrest. If the door was open I could walk free.

I was going to test the door this time. But I just needed a moment to steel myself.

I skipped the moment and went for the door. The knob

turned. When I pushed the door open my heart was pounding and I wondered if every time I breathed hard I would be reminded of Idabell and our moments of love. I didn't think long though. I stepped into the hall and ran into a man who was approaching my door.

"Hello, Easy," Lieutenant Arno T. Lewis said. He was almost smiling.

Long and lean, hard as ironwood, the bespectacled policeman angled his opaque lenses at me. "Looks like I just saved you from a good ass-kicking."

"I'm gettin' too old for this shit," I said.

CHAPTER 31

His door was next to the EXIT sign.

"Sit down, Rawlins." He wagged a hand over his shoulder as he went around his desk.

He was taller than I, spare as the barrel of a .22-caliber rifle. His head was shaped somewhat like a square loaf of store-bought bread. Arno was the second-most-powerful man in the hierarchy of the precinct; second only to the captain. It didn't surprise me that he had the authority to send Sanchez on an errand in the middle of an interrogation. What puzzled me was why he chose to do so.

Lieutenant Lewis didn't like me. He didn't like, or dislike, anybody. He simply sat in his office and pulled the strings of the law. He didn't play favorites and so he didn't have any friends to help. He caught the bad guys—and put them in jail. We'd brushed up against each other now and then, but there was no love lost at our partings.

He leaned back into the swivel chair and gave me another rare smile.

"In trouble again, huh, Easy?" He even showed a few teeth.

"I don't know a thing about it, officer. Not a thing."

"What about Idabell Turner? She's your friend, you've admitted that. She was at the school early on the morning that her brother-in-law was killed. She could have gotten access to keys to the gardens. Her husband was shot in her own home after she left the school. No forced entry there either.

"At that very house she hosted pot parties with people from your own school. Even one of your own janitors attended. And by the way, Miss Eng claims that you tried to get information out of her by saying that the police were looking into her relationship with Mrs. Turner—you didn't tell old Sanchez about that.

"You're the centerpiece, Easy."

"How you figure?"

"We get a call. Man says that Easy Rawlins has been stealing from schools in the South Central School District. He even gives us an address up on Olympic where you store the stuff before you sell it. It's just a shack but it's got this trapdoor cellar where the stuff is hidden. Caller knows all about that."

"And you think I hid it there?" I asked.

Arno smiled a second time. "No, I don't think it's you, Easy."

"No?"

Lewis shook his head but instead of allaying my fears he just made me more wary. His head moving from side to side was less a gesture of human kindness and more like the sway of a cobra marking distance.

"It's too easy," he said. "Man gets killed and then out of thin air we get this call on you. Somebody's trying to cover his tracks and he's using you for the broom."

"So if you think that then what am I doin' here?"

"Sanchez wants you here, that's why. He thinks he knows how to do things down here and doesn't want to listen to old fools like me."

For the first time I saw some light.

"I want to find the real crooks and put them in jail," Lewis continued. "I want to stop gangsters from running the streets. And I want my precinct to belong to me, not to some snot-nosed goody-goody from a two-year college."

"Uh-huh," I grunted. "So what could I do to help you?"

"I know that you're not moving drugs, Ezekiel. I know because I haven't seen you that you're trying to do okay. But you might have had a moment of passion. . . . " He let those words hang in the air.

"No, sir," I said. "All this is news to me. All of it. I know Mrs. Turner like I know any number of people up at the school. I asked after her when I heard that her dog got run over, but that's it. And I don't steal, man. You know that. Whoever called you just wants me to look bad, like you said."

My explanation was lame in both legs. I knew it. Lewis knew it too.

"Some people think that you know more than you've said."

"Do you?" I asked.

"Me? I don't care. I don't care if you go to work, go to jail, or go to your grave. None of that matters to me."

"What does matter, lieutenant?"

"You like my office?" he asked.

"Yeah. Sure."

"I sit here next to the back door but I make sure that things happen. I keep up with all the goings-on. All the names and places. Captain Connery never has to worry because he has me and I have my ear to the ground. I don't ever sneak over to the Hollywood division behind his back. I don't try to make a big name for myself with some spectacular arrest. I just do my job."

"I could look around," I ventured. "Ask some questions if it could help."

"You'd be doing us both a favor," Arno said. "Because you know there are some people in this building who don't feel kindly toward a man who wants to set things right in his life. Sanchez wants to see you go down, Easy. He wants you fired and he wants you in jail. Me, I don't care. You seem to be trying to do okay. I believe in live and let live."

"You want me to look around . . . " I began.

" . . . and bring what you find in through that back door right there."

"Anything you wanna know in particular?"

"That's right," the lieutenant said. "I want to know anything you find."

That got me to my feet.

"One thing, Rawlins," Arno said before I could pick up speed.

"What's that?"

"You know a woman name of Grace Phillips." It was no question so I didn't answer. "You might want to look into her a little bit."

I was out of that jailhouse in sixty seconds flat.

I don't know exactly why I returned to the school. Maybe I just felt comfortable there, heaven knows why.

Gladys Martinez told me that Vice Principal Preston had gone down to my office to wait for me.

On my way down the stairs I took the time to look out over the flat, pale asphalt streets of the neighborhood. The deep green of carob trees and the woody green of the laurel trees made rough lines in between the streets and the red- and brown-roofed houses. Every once in a while there was a wanderer out on the sidewalk making his way, or her way, slowly.

I took the stairs at a slow pace. Not because I felt lazy and calm but because I was wary. Everybody was after me, it seemed. My principal, my supervisor, and two different kinds of cops. Bill Preston had the temper to break a man's jaw in the name of what was decent and moral. Maybe he'd try to crush my skull down in the main office.

Ace and Bill were sitting at the far end of the long table. Bill wasn't surprised to see me. Ace leapt up, he always did that to make me think that he was showing me deference.

"Mr. Rawlins." Preston came to his feet too. "I have to show you something." His voice and manner were brusque and unfriendly. He seemed angry and even a little off, a little crazy.

"I have to talk to you too, Mr. Rawlins," Ace said.

"'Bout what, Ace?"

"It's a private thing, uh, but I guess it'll wait till you're finished."

"You do your classrooms yet?"

"I'll get'em."

"Okay then."

When Ace let the fire door roll shut behind him I realized that I was completely alone with the Jawbreaker.

Don't get me wrong—I wasn't afraid of Bill Preston. Actually I found myself hoping that he would start a fight with me. It would have given me no end of pleasure to inflict pain on someone who was trying to hurt me.

"I have to talk to you, Mr. Rawlins."

"Go ahead. Talk." I wandered over to a chair near a wall of hanging tools—where there was a large rubber mallet dangling in easy reach.

Preston pulled two envelopes from the breast pocket of his jacket. Then he sat down next to me, placing the envelopes on his lap.

"Newgate was talking this morning," Preston said.

"Yeah?"

"He was saying to me and Mrs. Teale that you wouldn't be on the job much longer."

"Really?"

"Yes. He also said that Sanchez would be arresting you soon."

"Arresting me for what?"

"He didn't say, but what else could it be but those murders?"

"I don't know, Mr. Preston. You know more about all of this than I do. Did you speak up?"

Preston stared straight at me. "No," he said.

I waited him out.

"As a matter of fact," he continued, "I didn't tell you all of it. You see, Ida didn't just come down to my office to tell me about Holland threatening her."

"No?" I glanced at the envelopes on his lap.

"She gave me these two letters. One of them is from her saying that Holland was crazy and that she was afraid he would kill her. The other one is a letter that Holland wrote to her."

The letters sat there on the vice principal's knee. I looked at them while he stared at me.

"You read 'em?" I asked finally.

He nodded. "The one from him is crazy."

"Uh-huh. Well? What do you want me to do about that?"

"I don't know. I haven't thought about what you could do. It's just that Idabell said that she'd call me soon. But she hasn't called."

"So? Take the letters and go to the police." It seemed simple to me.

"I can't. It would jeopardize my job and my marriage. I already told the police that I didn't know anything."

"Well," I said, "you really don't know anything. Holland's dead. He might have had something to do with her not calling you but more probably she killed him."

"I don't believe that for a moment. Idabell couldn't kill anybody."

That was the second vote for Idabell's inability to kill.

"So what do you want from me, Bill?"

"I can't handle these letters. I'd just get in trouble, I know it."

He was probably right.

"So," he said, "why don't I give them to you?"

"Why me?"

"You can tell the police, if they arrest you, that she gave you the letters and was afraid for her life. You didn't know her husband or her brother-in-law and so you didn't put the bodies together with the body in the garden. That way, later on, when they started to ask questions, you were afraid, you see, and then you finally decided that it would be best to give them the letters. That way they won't suspect you."

"I thought you said you didn't know what to do?" I asked. "Why don't you give them the letters? Or better yet— put 'em in a big envelope and send them to the police."

"Will you do it?" he blurted.

I wanted to say yes. I wanted to read those letters. But I wavered. I didn't want to be impulsive.

"What are you trying to do?" I asked.

"What do you mean?" Again, the rough innocence of the man made him hard to doubt.

But I tried anyway.

"What I mean," I said, "is that you could be using me here."

"How?"

"Somebody has already called the school, and the police, blaming me for the break-ins. Maybe if I take those letters you run to Sanchez and tell him that I know more than I'm tellin'."

"Is that what you think?" Preston was astonished. "I'm not trying to get you in trouble. These letters show that whatever trouble there is is in that family. I want the police to know the truth, but I'm trying to stay out of trouble myself."

He held the letters out to me.

I strummed my lips with my right hand and then reached.

"Thank you," Preston said.

Then he put out his hand. I shook it. Why not?

CHAPTER 32

I didn't know about Bill Preston. Maybe he was honestly too afraid to handle those letters. Maybe he thought that they might get lost in the mails or misunderstood by a self-confident Sanchez.

Maybe he killed Idabell and he knew that the postmark would be after her death.

None of that mattered though. I wanted to read those letters and so I took them.

I bolted the fire door, intending to burn the letters if anyone tried to break in on me.

Then I sat down to read. The first letter was in the lovely hand of Idabell Turner. The words were barely contained by the blue lines of the classroom essay paper. It was dated on the morning we made love.

To the Police, the Public Prosecutor, and the Criminal Courts of the state of California:

I. Idabell Turner/Gasteau, do hereby state that my husband, Holland Bonaparte Gasteau, has threatened my life and that I am in such fear of him that I am fleeing my home, my job, and any friends that know both me and my husband. I leave this letter, and a letter from him to me, in case Holland finds me and murders me without a witness to point at him.

Idabell Turner

Holland's letter was also handwritten, printed actually. The script was larger than in the note I'd found in his wallet but there was still that angry slashing slant to his words. He'd used such force with his ballpoint that the paper was torn in spots.

I am a man Idabell

Not a henpecked thing for you and your friends to mock. It's me who you have to support and stand behind. Not your girlfriends and not that damn dog.

You will do what I tell you to do. And you will be at home waiting for me even if I don't come back all night or all weekend. And if I do come back at three in the morning and you're not there then I will come out after you with my pistol. And if I find you with another man I will kill him too.

I'm writing you this letter instead of talking because I love you and I don't want to hurt you. Because you might get me mad and then I'll have to hurt you and I don't want that. So I want you to read this letter

and hear everything I have to say before you give me
any of your mouth. Because all I want to hear from
you is—Yes Holly.

I'll be home later on. You better be here.

The letter wasn't signed but I was sure that it was
genuine. I was also sure that he'd meant every word. He
loved his wife; he wanted her to happily be his slave; he
would kill her if she didn't accept her role.

Idabell had waited a month too long to run away. She
should have done it on the night she got that letter. The
minute the pistol appeared on that page it was bound to
go off.

I folded the letters and put them in my pocket. There
was no reason to give them to the police. They didn't prove
a thing that would help me.

I had completely forgotten about Ace when he caught up
with me on my way to the parking lot and Mouse's car.

"Mr. Rawlins," he called from far off. "Mr. Rawlins."

I watched the small man approach me across the blacktop. He took the baseball cap from his head when he
reached me.

"Mr. Rawlins, I have something to talk to you about."

"Is it important, Ace? I got things on my mind."

"I think so."

"What, then?"

"Newgate called me to his office yesterday. When I went
there he was with that Sergeant Sanchez fellah. They, uh,
they started asking all kinds of questions about you, Mr.
Rawlins. They wanted me to be a Benedict Arnold and give
you away. Sanchez wondered if there was anything I could
tell him about you."

"Like what?"

"If you stole something, maybe. If you broke the rules
with some of the children."

"Naw." I believed it but I didn't want to.

"Yes, sir. But I told them that I didn't know a thing

except that you were the best boss I ever had." There was passion in his voice that I'd never heard from him before.

"Well thanks, Ace, uh, thank you."

"But I mean it, Mr. Rawlins. I've worked for a lotta people down here in Los Angeles. And up until you I didn't have much use for them. The way they put a hand on your shoulder and pat you like you weren't no more than a dog. The way they tell you things like they knew it all and you were just stupid. But I like you, Mr. Rawlins, because you make it a good place and when people get harsh you don't come down on me even if I did something wrong. Like that time I left the window in the electric shop open. All you told Mr. Sutton was that it was a mistake. You told him that you allow for mistakes."

I had forgotten the incident. I had misjudged Ace. What else had I lost or missed?

"So I'm gonna tell you something, Mr. Rawlins," Ace said. "You know I don't talk to the cops much. I mean, they're okay for traffic and like that but if you start testifying the police will find some reason to turn it around on you."

I had never heard him say as much in the whole time he'd worked for me.

"I won't tell the cops, but I'll tell you just in case it means something to ya."

"What's that, Ace?"

"That man who was killed in the garden. He had a key to the fence. I seen'im go into the garden four or five weeks ago. It was that week I was opening up early for you. You know I came in a whole two hours early because I was so nervous that I'd get something wrong. I didn't dare do the boiler without going through all the steps of bleeding it out first. Anyway, that's when I saw him."

"Why didn't you say something?"

"If something happened I would have, but I didn't know. I didn't want to get into any trouble if nothing was wrong."

All the times I distrusted Ace, all the times I saw his respect as guile—now all I saw was a kindred spirit; a man trod on by his history, his poverty. A man who knew that the people in power wouldn't notice his broken bones, or if they did, they would blame him for his own misery.

I put out my hand and said, "Thanks, man."

CHAPTER 33

Grace Phillips lived on Pinewood Terrace down below Adams. When John was helping her to look for a place I told him about a woman I knew, Mrs. Grant, who'd been looking for a long-term tenant. Grace took the little cottage huddled behind Mrs. Grant's house. You had to walk through the driveway to get there.

"Easy Rawlins, is that you?" The voice came from behind the opaque sheen of her front-door screen.

"Hello, Mrs. Grant," I said, squinting at the doorway.

"She givin' a party back there?" the screen door asked.

"Not that I know of," I said. "I just come by to shout at her."

"You might have to raise your voice pretty high," Clara Grant said. She pushed the screen door open with the rubber tip of her cane. The light on her face revealed why she hid behind that door. She'd been laid low by stroke. Her pear-shaped, walnut-brown face was cut in two by the broken vessel. Half made of warm brown wax that was flowing down from the skull; half left to wonder why she couldn't do what she used to do.

"Why's that?" I asked.

"She always got a pack'a yowlin' dogs back there yappin' an' carryin' on."

"Somebody back there now?" I asked.

She made a gesture that would pass as a nod. "I don't exactly know who but I heard footsteps a while ago. You know I nap when the sun come in."

"Okay now, Mrs. Grant. See ya later."

At another time I would have offered to come by and see after her now and then. But my working life kept me away from the everyday country kind of living that I had known in Texas and Louisiana. It bothered me that I couldn't be of more help, but I had chosen my path—and I followed it down to Grace Phillips.

The door to the cottage was open. There was a baby crying somewhere in another room. I rapped lightly on the doorjamb.

"Anybody home?" I called.

A woman's scream was cut short, punctuated by a blow.

I rushed into the house through a room of cheap imported wicker furniture. I heard another wail and went through the door, into a bedroom that was almost all bed.

She was on the floor, arms around his knees and begging, "Please, I got a cough," pretending to hack a little. Bertrand Stowe was holding a medicine bottle high over his head; his sternest face looking down upon her.

In the middle of the jumbled-up bed was a naked brown baby, howling and waving both hands and feet.

Stowe caught me out of the corner of his eye and turned, fearful of who I might be. At that moment Grace yelled and leapt at the bottle in Stowe's hand.

"Stop it!" he shouted. He unleashed a clubbing slap that knocked her down on the bed, almost on top of the child.

He raised his hand but I moved in and pushed him down. He rose up to fight me but I pushed him down again. When Grace went to go after the bottle in his hand I grabbed her around the waist and yelled, over her screams, "Pour it down the drain! Pour it down the drain!"

It took him a moment but then he knew what I was saying. He went into the small bathroom that was next to the bedroom and poured the green fluid into the commode.

"Nooooooo," Grace cried, just like the dying witch in *The Wizard of Oz*.

She fell to the floor, weeping. Bertrand slumped down beside her.

I picked up the baby. He was a powerful boychild with

strong legs and arms. He struck me again and again
with his fists and feet. I rubbed the top of his head and
made deep sounds in the pit of my throat; all the time
aware of my supervisor and his junkie girlfriend.

The baby needed a quiet moment, so did the adults. Bert
and Grace stayed on the floor, dumb and drained.

After a while the baby stopped his crying and gave me
the kind of stunned look that babies get when they receive
pleasure from an unfamiliar source. I sat down on the bed,
putting him across my lap, and rubbed his back. After a
while his eyes stuttered shut.

I laid him in the center of the bed and we three adults
then went into the other room.

Grace moaned, "My baby, my baby."

Stowe and I sat down on a dilapidated wicker couch and
Grace lay crying at our feet. Her eyes were bloodshot
and watery. Her skin had taken on a blue hue. Her chapped
lips were blood-flecked from Stowe's slaps. And her mouth
never stopped moving, though very few intelligible words
came out.

"What's happenin' here, Bert?" I asked my boss.

"She wanted to quit, Easy. She wanted it. I thought that
she had quit months ago but then I found out that, that she
had been getting it from a friend but now that was cut off.
I came over to help her quit."

Grace raised up and said, "Please, Easy. Tell'im t'lemme
go. Please. Please."

"You shouldn't hit her," I said as if she wasn't there.

"I had to stop her."

"You should just hold her back. You should just hold
her an' tell'er that you're tryin' t'help. Hittin' ain't gonna
help a thing."

"I know," he said. "I just, I just . . ."

Grace's moan turned from general despair to a kind of
painful retching. She crawled, then staggered to her feet
and made it to a door behind the couch. We could hear her
vomiting into the kitchen sink and then the sound of the
tap running.

Bertrand got up. "I better go see about her," he said.

The baby started whimpering after a while. Grace cried along with him from the other room. That was as close as she could come to being a mother right then.

We undressed Grace. I could tell that Bertrand was still crazy for her because he kept trying to shield her breasts and pubic hair from my sight. I wanted to tell him that he could have all of that junkie—I didn't want any.

She didn't actually fall asleep but closed her eyes lying there next to her blood child. In that darkness she writhed with the pains of withdrawal.

"How long you been here?" I asked Stowe.

"All day."

"How long you plan to stay?"

"I don't know."

"You gonna stay here till your wife leave you?" I asked. "You tryin' to get rid of her?"

"No."

"But you gonna spend the night here?"

"I, I . . . I hadn't thought."

There was a phone next to the bed. I dialed the number and Alva answered, "Hello."

"Hey, Alva."

"Who's this?"

"It's Easy."

"Okay, Easy," she said. "I'll go get him."

There was a moment's hesitation in her voice. That little gap of silence told me everything Alva thought about me. I was a menace, a threat, a violent piece of John's past that she hadn't been able to cut out—yet.

"Yeah?" John said when he got on the line.

"I got a problem, John."

"My car?"

"No, man. Your car was okay the last time I saw it. No. It's Grace."

John didn't want to hear about an old girlfriend. Alva wanted to hear about it even less. But he was the only one I knew who would sit with Grace through the worst of it.

"A friend'a hers is coming," I told Bertrand Stowe. "The man who told me about your problems before."

Stowe nodded, yielding to the necessity of the situation.

"Who was her connection?" I asked.

He shook his head.

"Don't lie to me now, Bert. It's not the time to lie."

"I don't know," he said.

"Yes you do too."

He wanted to keep his secret but the pressure of all that pain in someone he loved had worn away his resolve. "It was the man who got killed at your school."

"Roman Gasteau?"

"Yes," he sighed. "He was . . . Lonnie's father."

"Who?"

"The baby. Roman was his father. I made a deal with Roman when Grace left him. I gave him a job."

"A job?"

"Yes. Nighttime building consultant. I gave him the master keys to the district and a salary of eight hundred dollars a month. He promised to leave Grace alone."

"That man had the keys to my school?"

"He had keys to all the schools."

"So he's the one been stealin'?"

All Stowe could do was to steal glances at my eyes.

"That why you killed him?" I asked.

"I didn't kill anybody. All I did was to give him a job in return for his promise that he'd leave Grace and Lonnie to me."

"Are you crazy? All the cops got to do is read his name in the records and you're busted."

"They won't find his name in the files."

"Oh? And why not?"

"Because I hired him under another name. Landis Defarge. He used the name Landis Defarge."

"You hired a man who had your girlfriend on heroin for a job under an alias—but you know his real name. And now that man is dead at one of your schools." With each word Stowe wilted more.

"I didn't know that she was back on drugs until after he was dead," Bert said. "Ask her if you don't believe me."

I didn't mean to laugh.

"What possessed you to do all that, Bert?"

"It was the child," he said earnestly. "I couldn't let Lonnie be brought up in that kind of life. I know I was wrong. I know it but it would have been worse any other way."

"Except now they might look at you for murder."

"Well," he said, "I didn't kill him."

"How about her?"

"No."

"You know that for a fact? Cop was askin' me was there anybody at the school at four or five in the morning. Where were you?"

Bertrand's mouth started to tremble.

"Honey," Grace said.

"Yeah, babe," he answered. Yeah, babe.

"Could you hold me please?"

Bertrand ignored me and my questions to mold his body around the woman who gave his life its spark.

John and Alva came together. I think Stowe was relieved that he didn't have to leave his woman with a solitary man.

Alva took the baby in her arms and John sat down next to Grace on the bed. When she started acting up he said, "Lay down and be quiet, Grace. Ain't nobody got time for your noise."

She did what she was told. John had a powerful presence about him. Not many a man, or woman, would tell him no.

When I was leaving, John came to the door and asked, "Where's my car, Easy?"

"I got it parked somewhere, John. Don't worry, I'll have it back to you by day after tomorrow."

Out on the street Stowe asked me, "What are you going to do, Easy?"

"Save my ass."

"What do you have to do with it?"

"More than I want. I'll tell ya that. You go on home, Bert. Go on home and I'll call ya about Grace. Don't worry, John'll take care of her."

"Thank you," he said.

I left him trying to start his car.

CHAPTER 34

Bonnie was in the kitchen when I got there. She was talking to Jesus while Feather fooled around with Pharaoh. There was a pile of freshly made chocolate chip cookies on the table.

"What's goin' on here?" I asked from the doorway.

They were all smiles and giggles.

"Hi, Daddy," Feather said. "We made cookies."

Bonnie looked proudly down on my girl.

Something good had happened while I was gone. I tried to remember the last time in my life that someone, other than Jesus, took care of something for me, without me having to ask; the last time that I could lay back and relax, sure that someone else was at the wheel. I thought all the way back to my childhood but I couldn't remember it still.

Don't look too close, a voice said in my head. I shuddered and blinked and turned away from Bonnie Shay.

"What's wrong, Easy?" she asked.

"Nuthin'," I said.

"Huh," Feather said, voicing the question for everyone in the room.

"Nuthin'," I said again. "Here, let me throw some dinner together."

"That's okay, Easy," Bonnie said. "You just sit with the kids."

Bonnie had been preparing dinner while the kids ate cook-

ies. We had thin string beans made with slivered almonds
sautéed in butter and drop biscuits that were very short.
The main course was omelets made with fine herbs and
white cheese. Feather made herself a can of tomato soup
too.

After dinner Jesus went to bed while the rest of us
watched TV; *Rawhide*, half of *The Jimmy Dean Show,* and
then *Hazel*. Feather loved *Hazel* but she fell asleep before
Jimmy Dean.

Then Bonnie cleaned up in the kitchen and I bundled
Feather off to bed. When I came back Bonnie was sitting
on the sofa looking sad. Pharaoh was nuzzling her thigh
with the side of his snout.

Maybe that dog and I hated each other because we were
so much alike.

"Hi," I said.

Bonnie looked up at me and smiled. She extended her
hand to draw me down next to her.

"You have a beautiful family, Mr. Rawlins."

"They look even better wit' you."

That's where the conversation stopped. We sat there
listening to Pharaoh move his nose on her leg. I felt so
comfortable right then that I had the urge to pet the dog.

"I've got to get my clothes, Easy," Bonnie said. "Do you
think it's safe?"

"That depends," I said.

"Depends on what?"

"On how deep you've gotten yourself into this mess."

I believe that Bonnie would have talked to me before
then—if she could have gotten the words up to her mouth.
She needed to be primed.

"What did Idabell do with those croquet sticks when she
got off your plane, Bonnie?"

"Roman was waiting for her. He was in his red Mustang
convertible out front. I remember Ida was all slumped over
because she was so embarrassed. But Roman waved just
like he was happy to see me."

"Did she leave with Roman?"

"No. She threw the sticks in the backseat and then I

waited with her until a taxi came. They won't take non-employees on the Air France shuttle bus."

"But I don't understand," I said. "She told you that it was Holland who took the dog."

"Yes."

"Then why wouldn't Holland . . . "

"They were always competing," Bonnie said. "One was always trying to outdo the other one. Holland used to come up to see me when Roman was out of town. He wanted to kiss me but it was just because I was with Roman."

"You kissed him?" I asked, but she didn't answer.

I wanted to kiss her.

She wanted to kiss me.

But there had been too much kissing lately and none of it had come to any good. That voice in my head, a voice that I rarely heard, was trying to protect me from any more pain.

I must've been looking pretty hard at Bonnie. She bowed a little and said, "I'll sleep on the couch, Easy."

I didn't argue.

She leaned over and kissed me on the lips, lingering for a moment. She moved away and then back to kiss me again. I touched her hair.

I felt very close to her at that moment; and then the doubt flooded back in.

"What are you doing here, Bonnie?"

"What do you mean?" she asked softly.

"I mean, why would you trust me? Why would you come to my house here when you don't know a thing about me?"

"But I do know about you. I knew who you were when you came to my apartment the first time."

"How?" I asked, but I already knew the answer.

"Idabell told me. She called after she ran from the school. She told me what happened between you in the classroom and she said that you took Pharaoh. So when you came over asking about her I knew that you could be trusted."

"How's that?"

"Because you were trying to protect her."

I leaned over, not necessarily for another kiss, but she moved away.

"We have time," she whispered.

"You take the bed," I answered. "I got some stuff to think about out here."

She rose and went back to my room.

The phone rang an hour later. When I put the receiver to my ear the first thing I heard was a blaring horn. Then:

"Easy!"

"Yeah?"

"It's me, Jackson!"

"I can hear ya, Jackson. I know who you are."

"I'm in trouble, man."

"What kinda trouble? Are you at the motel?"

"Naw, I'm outside'a this pool hall down in Venice."

"Pool hall?"

"I didn't hear from you, man. I was goin' crazy in that room. I didn't even have no book or nuthin'."

"So why'nt you go to a bookstore?"

"Shit, man. You know," Jackson said. "I wanted a drink and some music, that's all."

"Somebody see you?"

"Yeah. Guy named Paul Dunne. He's a pool hustler down on Jefferson. I never knew he made out this far west."

"Paul gonna turn you over?"

"They got money on my head, Easy. Anybody turn me over for cash."

"Get back to the motel, Jackson," I said. "An' keep your nose inside too. I'll be there tomorrow at the latest. Okay?"

"Okay, man. Okay." He sounded scared. I liked that, because the only time Jackson ever did what he was told was when he was scared.

After I got off the phone with Jackson I went back to thinking. Thinking about Idabell making love to me on that early-morning desk; about Roman lying dead in the garden while we did; about the dog and the croquet set;

about Holland laid up dead; and then about Idabell dead in my car.

It all came down to Bonnie Shay. The killer waiting in front of her house and then even coming back. Yes, coming back. I was sure that it had been Rupert who killed Ida. And he was coming back for Bonnie.

I didn't want to think about how good Bonnie was because thinking about her sooner or later would lead me back to thinking about her role in Idabell's plight.

"Bonnie." I shook her bare shoulder. "Bonnie."

There was a peaceful look on her waking face. A trusting, good-morning kind of look.

"What time is it?" she asked.

"What you do with the heroin?" I asked.

"Huh?"

"Come on now, Bonnie. Tell me."

She sat straight up. "What are you trying to say?"

"The only reason Beam would send his killer after you is because you stole from him. And the only thing you could have stolen is the heroin."

For the first time I noticed that she was bare-chested. There was a small blemish over her left breast about the size and temper of an inflamed pimple. She saw my eyes and pulled the sheet to cover up.

"I . . . I threw it away," she said.

"Come on now, Bonnie. You could do better than that."

"I'm not lying, Mr. Rawlins," she said with dignity that was barely forced.

"Naw."

"Yes. I threw it away. Ida had unscrewed the mallets and balls and taken out the heroin."

"How'd she know about the heroin? You said you didn't know when Roman was movin' it. Why'd him or Holland even take a chance on tellin' her?"

Bonnie's face relaxed and she sighed. I could tell that all the lying had gone out of her.

"Roman didn't want her to know," she said. "But Holland did. He gave her a sachet of potpourri and an empty can of baby powder. He wanted her to open up the hammers and balls and put the heroin in the can. He gave her the glue and said that she could refill the balls with flour and then seal them."

"So if Holland was supposed to get the drugs, how'd you end up with 'em?"

"He never got them."

"How's that?"

"Ida put flour and the potpourri in the empty can. She had the heroin in a hot-water bottle in my travel bag."

"A hot-water bottle?"

"I didn't know about it until the plane was almost landing, Easy. That's the truth. She'd done everything on her own. She was keeping the drugs as insurance that Pharaoh would be safe."

"She put her life on the line, and yours, for a dog?"

"That was her heart."

I could have cried. Pharaoh definitely had to leave from my house.

"And so you threw it away?"

"It was an evil thing and I wouldn't trade my life for my soul."

I was trying to understand; trying to believe. But I couldn't.

"Where'd you throw it?"

"In the trash," she said as if I were some kind of simpleton.

"You mean in one of those cans behind your building?"

"Yes."

"When?"

"The morning after we got back from France. Right after Idabell called and said that she had Pharaoh."

"And when's garbage pickup?"

The question startled her. "Oh. I . . . Today, I mean . . . tomorrow . . . this morning coming up."

I looked at my watch. It was still a while until Mouse got off of work. Even if I was late he would wait for me, because I had his car.

*

I was going through the fourteenth trash can and wondering at what a fool I was. If any of the neighbors heard me the cops would come. If Rupert was still waiting out front, which he probably was, I was dead from his hand.

And there I was sifting through soggy newspapers and greasy brown paper bags. One can held a half-eaten ham that was alive again with a thriving colony of leaping maggots. Ants crawled along my ankles. A dog barked out of a corridor that led to the main body of the building.

I was there because I wanted to believe in something—in Bonnie Shay. I wanted her to be what she said she was; a good woman with a strong mind who did what she knew was right. I couldn't live in the streets, and the workaday world wasn't enough—not without some kind of faith.

Maybe I was more like Mouse than I thought. Maybe somebody looking at me would have thought that I was insane. Maybe that was what Sanchez thought.

In the fifteenth can there was a bag of greasy bones and coffee grounds. Under that were various newspapers, beer cans, and a broken green glass. Finally there was a large red rubber water bottle. It was heavy, maybe three pounds. The white powder it contained wasn't flour.

CHAPTER 35

Sojourner Truth was getting to be like a fond memory, like an old house that I had once lived in but now it was inhabited by strangers. I felt like an intruder even though I used my key.

There was a light on on the top floor of the administration building. Mouse was there with his cloth push broom. He'd sprinkled the hall with oil-treated sawdust and was pushing the greenish shavings in an even back-

and-forth pattern, sucking up the dirt out of the corners and cracks of the floor.

"Hey, Raymond."

He nodded and set his long-handled broom against the wall.

Walking down that long hall toward me, Mouse looked like all the black men I'd known working late hours. His casual gait graceful like that of a woodland beast, each careful step testing the ground.

"Where you got me goin' t'night, man?" he asked.

"I just need t'talk to some people, Raymond. An' I don't wanna go it alone."

"I don't got no gun, man."

"That's fine by me, brother."

I helped him to get everything squared away. And then we left.

"I thought we was going someplace in Compton?" Raymond asked when we were almost in Santa Monica.

"Got to get Jackson Blue first."

"Jackson." Mouse grinned. He always grinned when it came to Jackson Blue.

I parked in the motel lot and knocked on the door.

"Who is it?" This time he was standing straight back from the door.

"Come on, Jackson, open up."

We settled his bill with the woman who ran the place and then headed north. Mouse took the backseat and Jackson sat next to me.

"How much you know about a guy named Beam?" I asked Jackson.

"Joey Beam? He's a bad cat. Really bad."

"He work for Stetz?"

"Not really. Philly run the place an' Beam hang out there. They both gamblers mainly. But Philly owns the numbers. At least all the numbers he could get ahold of. Philly's the top dog. He the one says what's what. But Beam don't answer to Philly. He might do a job fo'im but Beam's his own man."

"They friends?"

"T'ont know, man. They know each other. But you know those kinda men like each other just as much as their money is green."

Mouse laughed in the backseat.

"What if I went to Philly an' told him that I had a friend in trouble with Beam?" I asked. "What if I said that this friend had taken something didn't belong to him but now he wanted to give it back?"

"Who's that?"

"We'll get to that later," I said. "But this thing I got to give him he's gonna really want. Then let's say that you gonna drop the numbers and the bets. Then maybe he could get this price off your head."

"What's that?" Mouse asked.

"Somebody put out a price on my head," Jackson said. "Now all kindsa brothers wanna hunt me down. Could you believe that?"

Mouse didn't answer.

"What you got for Beam?" Jackson asked me.

"Aitch."

Jackson's eyes widened. "How much?"

"Don't you worry about that, Jackson. That don't matter to you. All you got to care about is helpin' me with Stetz."

"I ain't dealin' wit' Stetz. Nooo, no. That man wants to see me dead."

"I'll be the one to go to'im, Jackson. All I need for you to do is to help me."

Jackson didn't reply.

We were headed up Sunset for the hills above West Hollywood. Just before we got to Laurel Canyon we took a left up a smaller road. That wound around until we reached a long dirt driveway that led to a small house on a precipice overlooking L.A.

Jewelle met us at the door.

"Hi, Mr. Rawlins, Mr. Alexander," she said. She looked at Jackson, waiting for an introduction.

"This is Jackson Blue," I told her. "He needs a place to stay for a couple'a nights, JJ. I know it might be trouble—"

"That don't matter," she said, cutting me off. "We don't mind helpin' you, Mr. Rawlins."

"Thank you," Jackson said. The spark in Jackson's eye was starting to worry me when I heard Mofass coming toward the door.

His normal breathing sounded like a severe asthma attack. He struggled up the three stairs to the entrance and then stopped, leaning against the wall like a man who had just raced five miles.

"Mr. Rawlins," the gravel-toned real estate agent said. "Mr. Alexander."

He had on the ratty Scotch-plaid housecoat that he almost always wore. Mofass rarely went out. Jewelle took care of the apartments and the real estate business that they'd taken from her aunt. She took care of him too.

"Uncle Willy, you shouldn't be up here in this breeze," she said. "Come on, let's get back down to the couch."

With that the slender girl tugged and supported the two-hundred-and-fifty-pound man. She didn't ask for any help and didn't seem to want any. Her labor was a labor of love.

We followed them down the stairs to a large room that was carpeted with thick, real animal-skin rugs. There was a large fireplace roaring and a picture window that had the same view that was behind Lips McGee at the casino.

"This is nice," Jackson said, falling down into a plush settee. "Real nice. Like a little country house for a Roman senator."

"The Romans had emperors," Jewelle corrected.

"Yeah," Jackson said. "But they had senators too. You know, the Greeks started democracy but the Romans made law. They had elected officials too. Ain't that right, Easy?"

"Yeah, just like America was. They had senators and they had slaves."

"Where'd you learn that?" she asked.

"Mr. Rawlins," Mofass complained, "why you bringin' these people into my house?"

"It's just a couple'a days. Jackson and I got some business to handle, and while we do he got to lay low. You know what that's like, William."

"Yeah, I guess," he wheezed.

Mouse and I didn't stay long. I sat with Mofass for ten minutes pretending that he ran the business. He barked out some orders to Jewelle and she answered, "Yes, Uncle Willy," every time. She ran the business better than he ever could, but she loved him and respected him. She would have thrown away all that money and all that land just to be there. Her love was a jagged scar, it hurt me to see it.

CHAPTER 36

"Where we goin' now?" Mouse wanted to know.

"A place called the Hangar. It's an after-hours place where all kinds of night-shift workers go after the whistle."

"Oh, yeah," Mouse said sadly. "I know that place. I used to go there a while back."

"Yeah? What's it like?" I was just making conversation.

Mouse concentrated on my question for quite a while. The way his eyes squinted and how he nodded his head now and then it seemed as if there was a whole dialogue going on in his head.

"I'ont think it's wrong to kill somebody, Easy," he said at last. "I mean, that's what life is all about—killin', killin' to survive. You see it in bugs and animals—hell, even plants kill to survive. It couldn't be a sin because I been hearin' stories out the Bible my whole life; ev'rybody in there's killin' an' gettin' killed. An' you know it ain't really against the law, 'cause we both know a cop'll snuff yo' ass as easy as he could sneeze. Shit. Government kill more people than a murderin' man could count an' ain't nobody takin' no general to court. Uh-uh. No. It ain't wrong."

"So what you sayin', Ray?" Most times I would have

simply listened to Mouse and nodded where it seemed right; it doesn't pay to get yourself too far into the logic of a killer. But seeing that we were going into a tough situation I wanted to know what I could expect out of my friend.

"I don't know, man. I don't have a gun on me but that's just because I don't wanna kill nobody right now. I mean, if I had to do it I could get me a firearm. But right now I just wanna see what it's like to live wit' your family an' work at a job. But I ain't scared. I'm lookin' for a new way—that's all."

I didn't know what he was talking about. The only facts that registered with me were that he didn't have a gun on him and that he preferred not to kill—right then.

It looked like an empty lot from the street. If it wasn't for the cars parked along the curb and in the lot you might have thought that you were on a country lane.

Behind the sycamores at the back of the lot was a small abandoned airplane hangar. It was a big room with a concrete floor and a wire-laced glass ceiling thirty feet above. It was dark and cool in the late evening.

But at the far end of the hangar was a door that led to what must have been the mechanics' offices. That was where the new Hangar was.

That was a smaller room, about the size of a diner. Behind the counter there was a whiskey bar and a fry stove. It was early yet, only about one in the morning, and so there were only a few people around.

"Hey, Raymond," a woman said. She got up off the seat at the counter and swayed over to us.

"Hey, Mattine," Raymond answered. "How you been?"

"Fine," she said, looking me up and down. "Where you been?"

"Got me a job," he answered.

"You?" Mattine guffawed.

"What you-all drinkin'?" she asked me.

"Just some soda," I said.

"And I'll take a beer, honey," Mouse added.

Mattine sucked her tooth, smiled, and then went to fill our orders. Mouse ushered me over to a small round table with two chrome-and-vinyl chairs. A pair of men sitting a few tables away waved at us. The man behind the bar saluted.

"They know you here, huh?" I asked my friend.

"Used to come here wit' Sweet William," he said.

I didn't ask him any more about it.

Every now and then someone would drop by and say a few words but Mouse wasn't very friendly and not many knew me.

"That was drugs you was talkin' 'bout in the car, right, Easy?" Mouse asked after his second beer.

"Yeah."

He waited a while and then said, "One time half'a that woulda been mines."

"What you mean?"

"You know what I mean," he told me. "I woulda said half'a what happens from now on is mines. And I woulda backed that up with my forty-four. No lie."

I knew the chance I was taking bringing Mouse back into the street. That was his element.

"But you ain't sayin' that now, huh?"

"I'm th'ough wit' it," he said, disgusted. "Sick of it. All that street shit. I won't touch it."

"But you don't wanna stop me?" I was curious.

"Stop you what?"

"Stop me from givin' dope to a gangster."

"Why I care about that?" he asked.

"Because it's wrong."

"But it ain't my wrong, man. It ain't mine. That's yo' wrong an' yo' problem."

"But you still sittin' here with me," I said.

"But I ain't you, Easy. I sit here and you sit over there. That's all there is to it."

He might have changed but Mouse would always be different.

"Hey, man," a crackling voice commanded. He could have been talking to me, so I looked up.

"Yeah?"

"What the fuck you doin' here, dude?" the lanky, long-armed man said. There was a large man standing behind him; a sweaty fat man who looked to be formed from a pile of wet mud.

"I'm looking for a woman named—"

The man grabbed my collar but just as fast Mouse's hand was on the man's wrist.

"We don't want no problem now, brother," Mouse said.

The lanky man turned to Mouse. When he focused on Raymond's face his eyes actually fluttered. The man behind him garbled, "Mr. Alexander."

"Hey, Puddin'," Mouse said to the glob of a man. "Ask your friend here to let go on Easy."

"We didn't know it was you, Mr. Alexander," the lanky man said. He pulled his hand from me quickly as if he had gotten a shock.

"You boys don't have to push on people. No need to do that. What's your name, man?" Mouse smiled.

"Tony," the lanky man said in a voice quite a bit higher than the one he used on me.

"Sit down, boys," Mouse said. "Sit'own an' we talk out our problem."

The men got chairs and sat. I gestured to Mattine and she brought the newcomers beer.

"Now what's your problem wit' Easy?" Mouse asked.

"We, uh, well," Puddin' said. "We heard he was after our friend."

"What friend?" I asked.

"Hannah Torres," Tony said.

"I ain't after her," I said in the language I knew they'd understand. "Shit, she had her boss wop me upside the head and then he beat me. All I wanna know is why."

"That don't sound unreasonable," Mouse said, holding up his beer in a gestured toast.

"Where is she?" I asked.

Our guests balked.

"Come on, men," Mouse said. "Easy done said he ain't mad."

"She's outside," Puddin' admitted. "Waitin' in the car. We seen this man here when we come in the do' an' she pulled us out an' told us that he was after her."

"Just a guilty conscience," I said.

"Go ask her in, boys," Mouse advised. "We have us a few drinks an' ev'rything be okay."

Puddin' and Tony reluctantly got up. They drifted back toward the door. I was sure that they were wondering if they could just get in their car and drive away. But I also knew that the fear of Mouse would make them stay.

"See that, Easy?" Mouse was jubilant.

"What?"

"Ain't no need to be all mad an' surly. All you got to do is talk. People will listen. You know Etta been tellin' me that for years an' I jus' ain't never paid her no mind."

A few minutes later Puddin' and Tony returned with Hannah between them. She didn't seem to want to be coming. Tony had his hand around her upper arm.

"Here we are, Mr. Alexander," Puddin' warbled. "Here, tell Hannah it's okay."

"Have a seat, Hannah," I said.

Mouse smiled, revealing his gold-encrusted teeth with joy at his newfound diplomacy.

This time we ordered whiskey—a pint of Canadian Club with a pail of chipped ice.

When they were half a drink down I asked, "Why you set me up like that, Hannah?"

She gulped and moved slightly as if she were going to rise. But then she settled down.

"I couldn't help it," she complained. "Mr. Beam asked me who you was an' what you was askin'."

"Why?"

"I'ont know. At first I just said that you was flirtin' wit' me. But then he grabbed me and said did I know you. I said no an' that you was up here lookin' for some money that Roman owed you."

"But why would he care about me out of all the people come up there?" I asked.

"He knew you or sumpin'," Hannah said. "Cause the minute you walked away from me he was right there."

"An' then you told him about our date?"

"I really did like you," was all Hannah had to say.

"Was it him hit me?" I asked.

"Naw," she said and then she wavered. "Listen, Mr. Alexander, I don't want no trouble. If you go back to Mr. Beam an' tell'im I told you all this then he gonna get me."

"Ain't nobody gonna say nuthin', sugar," the new, beneficent Mouse said. "Easy just wanna know. Ain't that right, Easy?"

"I won't tell'im, Hannah. That is, if you don't lie to me I won't."

"It was Rupert hit you. Rupert and Li'l Joe."

"You with'em?"

"I didn't know they was gonna hit you," she cried. "They just said that they wanted to talk to you alone."

I turned to Tony and his fat wadded friend. "Give us a minute, boys."

"We ain't goin'—" Tony started saying.

But he didn't finish his sentence because I grabbed him by his throat and pulled him across the table.

"Move your ass or I'll do it for you," I said in a voice so hoarse and deep that it surprised me.

Mouse jumped up and put his hands between us, saying, "Hey, boys! Hold up! Stop it now!"

A few more people had come into the Hangar. They gawked while the bartender watched us closely.

Tony was trying to catch his breath. Puddin' didn't know what to do with his hands.

"Go on now, boys," Mouse said. "We ain't gonna hurt your girl. No no no no no no, Hannah. You stay here with us."

It was almost funny. Me the one threatening violence and Mouse calmly trying to find solutions.

Tony and Puddin' went to another table. Mattine came up to them and started asking questions, looking up at us now and then.

"Okay, Hannah," I said. "Let's get this over with."

"What?"

"You know Philly Stetz?"

"Uh-huh," she mumbled. "I work for him when you get down to it."

"What does Stetz have to do with Beam?"

"Nuthin' really, not that I know of anyway. Beam gambles an' stuff. He up at the Black Chantilly a lot."

"Did Roman work with Beam?"

"I don't know if he worked with'im. I don't know that. But they talked a lot."

"And how about Rupert?"

"What about'im?"

"Who Rupert work for?" I was discovering my destination by asking directions.

"He work for Mr. Stetz, just like me."

I stared at her, wanting something more but not knowing what it was. Beam knew me. He knew me before I walked into the club. There was only one way I knew of that he could have known; it had to be him, not Rupert, walking down Bonnie's street away from my car.

It had to be him.

"You got any more questions?" Hannah asked.

When I didn't answer she got up and went over to Tony and Puddin'.

I sat there thinking for a while, I don't know how long. But when I looked up again the room was full of people.

I got up and walked over to Hannah and her friends. Mouse was there with them. I guess he was holding them for me.

"Hey, Tony," I said as if I had forgotten to say something before.

"What?"

"You wanna talk to me a minute?"

"Talk," he said coolly.

"Why'ont you come over wit' me to the bar? I'll get'em to freshen up that whiskey."

It was the promise of liquor that drew Tony. When the bartender asked him his pleasure he answered, "Manhattan." It was a sophisticated drink at that time. Tony ordered with a sneer of superior satisfaction.

I waited for him to finish his drink before I said, "Sorry 'bout before, man, but you know Hannah's boss liked to kill me."

"Uh-huh," he grunted, not really accepting the apology.

Mouse was across the room gesturing at Puddin' and Hannah like a schoolteacher, or a cop.

"Hannah says that you knew Roman Gasteau pretty well," I said in way of a question.

"Him'n Holly too. So what?"

"What could you tell me about them?"

"Why should I tell you anything?" Tony was still petulant. The whiskey had cooled him down some though.

"Twenty dollars for anything you got to say and another twenty if it sound good t'me." It was a sentence that I'd said many times in my life.

"What you wanna know?" he asked.

I handed over the first twenty dollars. "What business was Roman into?"

Tony rubbed his hand over his mouth and mumbled something.

"What you said?" I asked.

"White pow-ter."

"Holland in it with him?"

"He wanted t'be."

"What's that mean?"

"Holland come 'round an' talk like he was workin' wit' Romny but it weren't true. Roman used to just laugh when people would talk about it."

"You worked wit' Roman though, right?" I asked.

Tony winced and stuck a finger in his ear. He rubbed his nose and then pulled up his loose trousers by the front belt loops.

He glowered at my chest and I asked my question again.

"I did some little errands," he whispered. "You know Romny liked people t'do things for'im. But I wasn't in his business. I only ever saw'im when he'd be at the Black Chantilly an' I happened t'be 'round. You know usually I'm out back washin' or carryin' or sumpin'."

"What kinda things you do?"

"Just get cigarettes an' shit. Nuthin' heavy. Nuthin' could put me in jail."

"Anybody know more about his powder business?"

Tony glowered again.

I took two twenties from my pocket.

His eyes almost closed. "A guy named Billy B," he mumbled. "Billy B and Sallie Monroe."

"Oh," I said. The last piece of the puzzle was a soft lead bullet aimed at my gut. I thought about the dapper little butcher and craved his blood.

"That enough to get you up offa that forty dollars?" Tony wanted to know.

"This Billy B," I asked. "He a little dude with a big head, gold-colored kinda Negro?"

"Yeah," Tony said. "All'a that. Light, little, an' big-headed. That's Billy B."

CHAPTER 37

Mouse was high on whiskey and so I drove him home. He let me take his car, saying that he could work out rides with Etta.

Bonnie and the kids were asleep when I got home. Pharaoh growled in the shadows.

I pulled out the drawer next to the kitchen sink and put it on the floor. I reached in under the ledge and came out with my .38 and a box of shells.

The gun needed cleaning but all I had was time. I wasn't going to sleep. There were gangsters out there in the shadows whispering my name. There were cops hoping that my body broke before my spirit did. My life had gone to pieces and none of it was my fault.

It was the dog's fault. That's what I told myself.

But by then I knew that it wasn't true. I'd dug this hole

two years before. It was just a little unfinished business that I had to clean up.

"Easy." Bonnie Shay was standing at the kitchen door. If she saw the gun on the table she didn't act like it.

"What?"

"Was I telling the truth?"

"Huh?"

"Did you find the hot-water bottle?"

"Oh. Yeah." I smiled. "Yeah, I did."

"Did you leave it there?"

"No, Bonnie. I'ma need it to get them gangsters an' cops offa us."

Bonnie's face smiled. It wasn't just her mouth but also her eyes and cheeks and the angle of her head to her shoulder.

"Come to bed," she said.

"Come again?"

Her smile was a long-ago memory of good things.

"Not that," she said. "But you need some sleep. Come lie down with me. Let me hold you."

"Bonnie," I said.

"Yes?"

"Do you know a man called Bill Bartlett?"

"William. Yes. He used to work at Sojourner Truth. I met him after that, though, at a party that Idabell gave. By that time he was working on the supply truck that brought Holland his daily papers."

"He still work a paper route?"

"No, I don't think so. He quit about the same time that Holland did. Ida told me that he became a cook."

She helped me off with my clothes and almost guided me into the bed. She pressed her warm body against me from behind and placed her hand on my bare chest—over my heart.

"Your heart's beating," she whispered.

"An' yours isn't?"

"Shh."

The warmth of her body through that thin slip was what was missing in my life. A woman who took charge of herself and her needs. A woman who could hold my desire without fear or anger.

"You know," I said.

"Hm?"

"I'd like to turn around here."

"We've got time, Easy. Let's just get some sleep tonight."

I was running hard with wild dogs on my trail. I hit the forest under a moonlit, cloudless sky and ran deeper and deeper into the thickening gloom of branches. My progress was slowed by the trees but the hacking breath of dogs seemed to be further behind. Soon I was crawling through pitch black, pushing hard against the wall of snapping sticks. Finally I was flat on my stomach.

I heard a whisper, "Shh," and then I was asleep.

I woke up alone in the bed, fully rested. It was early but Bonnie and the kids were already gone. I remembered Feather's laugh, a growl too near my ear, and a "shush," and then a kiss on my cheek.

The note, resting in hard sun on the kitchen table, said:

Easy,

Feather and Jesus are off to school. I'm going down to the airline to pick up my check and cash it. I'm really looking forward to getting to know you.

Yours,
Bonnie

There was a big kiss at the bottom of the page. I looked at the note wondering at how wrong I could be and still survive.

Jewelle was happy with Jackson Blue.

"He knows so much," she said to me over the phone.

"I don't know about that, JJ," I said.

"What you mean?" she asked. "He knows math and electronics and all about the history of the world."

"But he don't know how to survive, honey," I said. "If you put him outta that house he'd be dead 'fore the sun went down."

Jewelle didn't have anything to say to that. She was a smart girl. Smart in every subject but men.

"What time is it?" Jackson asked me when he got on the line.

"'Bout eight-thirty."

"Shit."

"Jackson," I said, "you remember what we talked about?"

"Bout Stetz?"

"Yeah."

"Go on."

"I want you to find out where he is and how I can get in touch with him."

"What for?"

"I'm going to tell him that I know how to get my hands on the final shipment of aitch that Roman Gasteau was supposed to have for Joey Beam."

"How much?"

"I already told you, three pounds," I said.

"Naw, man," Jackson complained. "How much we gonna charge?"

"Ain't no how, Jackson. I'ma tell'im that you gonna quit bein' his competition and that I'll give him the drugs back for his friend."

"But don't you think we better ask for some money, man? I mean he ain't gonna believe that you in it for your health."

"You want money, Jackson?" I asked.

"I need it, man."

"Well then," I said. "Think about your life like it was a wad'a cash. An' try not and spend it all in one place next time."

"You passin' up a golden opportunity right here, Easy."

"All I want from you is to find out how I can get in touch with Philly Stetz."

"Shit, man, I already know where that motherfucker is hid." Jackson was beginning to sound like his old self. The presence of a woman will do that to a man—for better or worse.

"How you know that?"

"Well, you know."

"No. I don't know at all, Jackson."

"Ortiz. Ortiz found out but . . . but well, you know."

"Ortiz was going to shoot Stetz," I declared.

"It was just insurance, Easy. Best to be prepared."

"Prepared," I repeated. "Jackson, you ain't prepared for shit."

When he didn't say anything I added, "One mo' thing, Jackson."

"Yeah?"

"JJ got enough trouble wit' her fam'ly an' Mofass. Keep yo' fingers outta the pie. You hear me?"

"I hear ya, man."

He gave me the address of the gangster and I wrote it down. I felt good taking steps that would lead me somewhere. I wasn't thinking of what might happen when I arrived.

The information I needed wasn't in the phone book this time.

"Bertrand Stowe's office," Stephanie Cordero said in my ear.

"May I speak to him, please? This is Mr. Rawlins."

I was put on hold for about ten seconds and then the phone rang again.

Stowe answered on the half ring. "Easy?"

"Yeah." I was about to say more when he cut in.

"Where is she? Have you talked to her? I called but nobody answered. I went by there this morning but there was nobody there. Mrs. Grant said that she'd left but she didn't even ask them where they were going." It all came out at once.

"What you talkin' 'bout, Bert?"

"Gracie, man. Gracie. She's gone."

"John an' Alva prob'ly took her over to their place. You know they got lives and there's no space for three full-grown adults and a baby at Gracie's."

"Give me his number." I heard sounds over the phone of him searching for something to write on or with.

"I can't do that."

"Why not?"

"John don't want no junkie's boyfriend callin' at all hours. I'll call him and find out what's happenin' with Grace."

"What's John's last name?" Stowe asked with every ounce of authority he could muster.

"Naw, Bert. You gotta trust me on this one."

"I need that number, Easy."

"No." I let that hang in the air and then said, "But you got to do somethin' for me. I want William Bartlett's address. Gimme that and I'll call you about Grace tonight."

The little butcher had been living on Rondolet Street while he worked for the Board of Education. He'd moved but the landlord, who also lived in that building, knew his forwarding address. That was on Courlene, a residential street not far from downtown. It was a small house with peeling white paint and bare brown dirt for a lawn. There was an overflowing trash can right there on the porch. The front door didn't belong to that house. It was an unfinished plyboard door meant for a temporary bungalow out on some construction site.

I hated that house.

I hated the disrespect it showed for the neighborhood and for itself.

I played the front door like a kettledrum.

"Bartlett!"

When I'd pounded a dent in the cheap wood I remembered Rupert. The next thing I knew my shoulder was making kindling from the door. I stumbled into the house stunned by my own violence.

Billy Bartlett was stunned too. He stood toward the back

of the surprisingly neat and sunny room wearing boxer shorts. He had a long and slender knife in his fist.

Remembering the little butcher's speed I took a large piece of the door and threw it hard; I came right behind it. I hit the confused cook in the nose and he went down.

No one was shouting from outside so I disarmed him and dragged him through the doorway he'd been standing in.

It was a neat little bedroom. Bartlett struggled to his feet and staggered around to get his balance. Blood was coming from his nose and front lip.

I unplugged a long extension cord from the wall and disconnected it from a lamp and an electric clock.

"Com'ere!" I grabbed Bartlett and made him put his hands behind his back. After I'd tied his hands I kicked the crook of his knees to make him fall on the bed. I tied his hands together with his feet, making him a bony bow on the trim single mattress.

It was then that I noticed that my vision was cloudy, dark. My fingers were numb and restless. That was murder in my blood.

I realized suddenly that I had to relieve myself.

I collided with the doorjamb going into the toilet off Bartlett's room.

The crash of water as I urinated jangled my nerves.

"Hey!" the butcher called out.

"Shut up," I said. "Or I'ma come in there and shut you up."

Silence saved his life.

I washed my hands in cold water and then doused my face.

'What you want, man?" Bartlett asked me. I was sitting in a chair next to his bed.

"My hands hurt," he said. "I cain't breathe through my nose."

"You ain't gonna be breathin' at all you don't talk to me," I said softly.

"Talk about what?"

"You know who I am?" I asked. "My name is Easy Rawlins."

"I thought you said your name was Koogan?"

"You know who I am?" I asked again.

"Yeah, yeah."

"Then talk to me."

"What you wanna know?"

I just slapped him—that's all. Knocking him around, tying him up. That wasn't much considering what he had done to me.

"Hey, man!" he cried. "Lemme up."

"Talk to me, Billy," I said. "Talk to me."

"You wanna know 'bout the schools? Is that what you want?"

I didn't reply.

"It was Sallie Monroe, not me. It was Sallie. I met Roman at Idabell's house, at a party they had. We got friendly and I introduced him to Sallie. Next thing I know Roman's with Grace an' she's on junk. Roman got the job and then Sallie got me to go in to help him 'cause I knew the school setups and how things worked. You know, alarms and electric systems, where stuff might be stored."

"What about Holland?"

"What about him?"

"How was he in it?"

"Roman cut him in 'cause we could use his paper shack to hold stuff sometimes."

"What did Idabell want wit' you that night she came to Whitehead's?"

"She wanted some money. She knew I was in it with Holly and she wanted three hunnert dollars."

"What did she say to you?"

"Nuthin'. Just that she was goin' outta town."

"Is that all?"

"No. I mean I asked if she needed a place to stay but she said that she was going to stay with a girlfriend."

"Who'd you tell?" I asked the flesh and bones.

He saw my face and realized what Joey Beam must have done.

"I didn't know, man," he pleaded. "I swear I didn't know."

"That ain't gonna save your life, Billy." I didn't even know if I intended to kill him, but I certainly was on the edge.

"I'll turn myself in, man. It was Sallie wanted to call cop on you. Roman was dead and he thought you could take the fall. It was Sallie."

"No," I said.

"What you mean—no!"

"I mean no, Billy. I mean whoever called knew Roman was dead before the cops or anybody else did. The man who called the cops called the principal at Sojourner Truth first. That man already knew that Roman was dead and he wanted them to be lookin' at me for his killer. You sayin' that Sallie killed Roman?"

For a moment there I thought that Billy had died. His eyes were opened wide and his mouth was too. Then I heard the high-pitched whine of his breathing.

"I don't know nuthin' about that," he said. "I don't know a thing."

"Who killed'im, Billy? I ain't gonna ask you twice."

At first I thought he was coughing; that the blood from his nose had gone down his throat. But then I saw the tears. His lips were pushing in and out and his head bobbed in a steady beat with the barks.

"That does it!" I shouted.

I ran into the living room and looked around until I found the long knife on the floor. Then I stalked back to the coffin-shaped bed. I'd run out intending to kill Billy. But standing up and going from one room to the other, bending down to get the knife, made me remember the jailhouse bully whose name wasn't Jones and Felix Wren. By the time I got back to Bartlett I had lost my desire for his blood.

But Billy didn't know that.

"It was his brother, man. His brother. His brother. His brother . . . " He kept saying that with his big eyes on the knife in my hand. He was a butcher, after all, he knew what that knife could do to his meat.

"Holland?" I asked.

"Yeah. It was Holland. Roman come an' got me to go out to the garden. He wanted to cut his drug for Joey Beam. Beam was gonna kill'im if he didn't get his aitch. Roman was gonna cut it down at the garden class."

"You dealin' wit'im?"

"Uh-uh. No. I only ever helped stealin' stuff. But Roman was in trouble wit' Sallie an' Beam. He wanted to turn the drug over an' call it square."

"But?"

"It was Holland. He come right outta the dark wit' a shovel in his hand. He was shoutin' an' I run. I went right up to the fence an' over."

"An' so how you know Holland killed his brother?" I asked.

"He killed him, man. Who else coulda killed'im?"

"Roman had keys to my school?"

"Yeah."

"They didn't find no keys on him. That's why they was lookin' at me."

"I got the keys. They in that top drawer, in the dresser. I was carryin' the keys for Roman and I still had 'em when I ran." He looked at my knife. "Look in the drawer if you don't believe me."

I looked. There was a giant key ring with over thirty master keys on it. I pocketed the keys and went back to the butcher.

"And then you called the principal about me?"

"That was Sallie. I went to him to tell'im what happened. I didn't tell'im nuthin' 'bout no drug though. I just told'im that he was outta the school-robbin' business."

A feeling of calm came over me. The story sounded right. Yes. Holland killed Roman. Now at least I knew the truth.

I was half the way through the living room when Billy cried out, "Hey! You ain't gonna leave me tied up!"

I dropped the knife and walked out the front door. Outside there was a man standing on the dirt lawn. He wore green work pants and a blue shirt, I remember. His face was shaped like a crescent and his eyes were small. His eyes darted from me to the front door.

Maybe he freed Billy after I'd gone. Maybe he robbed him.

CHAPTER 38

Philly Stetz's secret office was in a small medical building on Olympic near Vine.

Walking down the midmorning street on my way to face one of the most dangerous men on the West Coast didn't scare me. My gait was nonchalant and there wasn't a thought in my head. It wasn't that I was particularly brave. The fact was that I found it hard to imagine that I had come so far over the line in just a few days. Never in my many years of street life had I gone up against somebody like Stetz.

Never in my life had I taken such a chance for somebody else. I'd risked my life before but that was always because of my pride—or stupidity. But here I was working for a dead woman to save a woman who I hardly even knew.

Those shots of whiskey in John's car had gone right to my brain and stayed there.

The office building was really a walled-in courtyard. The path between the cottage-offices was wet brick. The offices were made of brick too. Old crumbling brick that was dark from the dust of years and not pigment. The cold those walls threw off was clammy and unhealthy.

If there was a valley of death I had stumbled upon it.

Dr. Green's office wasn't even in the court, it was through a redwood door at the back and across an alley. There stood a turquoise stucco building with potted succulents on either side of the oak entrance.

I knocked and awaited my fate.

The man who opened the door wore a green suit. Maybe, I thought, that was his joke. There was no Dr. Green. Jackson had discovered that Stetz rented the office as a partial cover to his gambling activities.

"Mr. Stetz?" I asked the dark-skinned white man. He had a bad complexion, rough caves instead of cheeks. His hair was thick and black. He wasn't a big man but you could tell by his dark stare that if he got mad you'd have to kill him just to slow him down.

"Who're you?" He jutted his head at me.

"My name is Rawlins. I've come to speak with Mr. Stetz."

"How'd you know to come here?"

I saw no reason to lie so I said, "Jackson Blue."

The ugly man froze for a second and then he moved backwards, making room for me to enter the sham office.

He led me through a dwarf foyer into a waiting room, or parlor. There, seated around a squat maple table, were five white men. All of them smoking and all of them hard. Each one was figuring how he'd have to go about killing me, if he got the chance.

"Wait here," the man in the green suit told me.

He went through a door. The men peered at me from their seats.

I was remembering the wet heat of the Louisiana summers of my boyhood. Old folks used to say that it was so hot that even God was sweating.

"What's the skinny, shine?" a roly-poly man in a dark suit asked. His slight accent was eastern European but he'd been down among my people once or twice; the twist on his words told me that.

His tone also told me that my mortal troubles might soon be over. But I was pacific. I had a .38 strapped to my thigh and a slit cut into my pants so that I could get to it fast. I could kill the moonfaced talker and maybe one or two of his friends before I went down.

It was that thought that saved me. I didn't lose my cool. I gave that man a look that said, "Don't mess, mother-fucker, don't mess." If I had gotten mad or scared he would have been on me in a second. This way he had to consider first. He had to wonder what it was that I had.

The other men started to laugh. They liked a good stand-off. The man I was looking at had probably killed a dozen men, and every one of them begged for life. But not this time.

"Hey, Aaron," a slappy-looking guy dressed in clashing browns said. "Looks like you met your match there."

All the men laughed.

Moonface tried to grin, but failed.

I took a deep breath and he measured it. He tried another smile and I lowered my shoulder to go for the gun. I was a fool but I didn't mind.

"Hey you." The man in the green suit was standing in the doorway to the doctor's office.

I looked at him, feeling unconcerned. I was in no hurry.

"Yeah?" I asked.

"Come on."

Aaron smoothed back the little hair he had as I walked by. I felt a sort of comradeship with him. For a moment the violence that we both wanted seemed okay, like it was just an expression between men—rough humor, healthy competition, survival of the fittest.

As I passed into the big man's office I shed the feelings of impending violence I had with Aaron. Now I had to be ready for a new game. I didn't know what to expect, but that's what street life is all about—you get thrown in the mix and see if you can get your bearings before your head's caved in.

"This is him, Mr. Stetz," the green suit said.

"Thanks, Arnie. You frisk him?" Stetz asked.

Arnie and I looked at each other.

Stetz shook his head.

"Get outta here, Arnie."

Arnie wanted to say something but Stetz said, "Just go."

Something about the way Stetz sent Arnie away made me like the man. In those two words he said, "You're hope-less, Arnie, but I've got to keep you around because we've known each other so long and because I can still squeeze an ounce of worth out of you now and then." It reminded me of my job at Sojourner Truth.

Stetz was a good-looking white man. Tall and comfortable with the elevation, he had a good tan and light brown hair. His eyes wavered between brown and yellow and his shoulders had seen their days of labor.

His suit was dark blue.

"Sit down," he told me. I heard the door close on Arnie at my back.

"Jackson Blue sent you?" Stetz asked. His eyes looked bored. I had the feeling that he'd asked me in because he didn't have anything else to do.

He waited for me to sit first.

"Not exactly," I replied. I didn't give much because I was still trying to figure the right approach with him. Stetz had kept the doctor's office exactly as he had found it. There were medical books on the shelves; big oak filing cabinets along the opposite walls. The meandering vine that grew in the window behind him looked as if it had been growing there for over a decade. The central stalk had gone woody.

The desk in front of him was empty except for a Modern Library edition of *Meditations* by Marcus Aurelius.

"You read?" His question startled me.

"Yeah. Some."

"You read this?" He held the volume up.

I shook my head no. "But that was his journal, right? He was waging a campaign against the Germans or somebody and wrote down his thoughts about bein' a right man."

"What do you want, Mr. Rawlins?"

"I got a problem, and so does Jackson. As I see it your waters might be gettin' a little rough too. One thing I learned down home was that sometimes men can trade off their losses and come out with a profit."

"You're losing me, friend," Stetz said.

Friend.

"Jackson's partner's in jail. There's half a dozen big-time

gamblin' men in L.A. wanna see Jackson dead, an' without Ortiz he knows he's meat. I come to him with my own problem and he sent me to you for a deal."

"What kinda deal could a nigger have for me?" Stetz said.

He drew the line between us with one word.

"The reason you can't catch Jackson is 'cause of his system. He tapped onto the phone company with an invention. A machine that records the bets. He got eighteen hundred customers layin' down bets an' playin' numbers with a tape recorder that you couldn't never find. Jackson got the edge on all you boys, an' the one that get in on it will be the top dog on bettin'.'"

It flowed out easy. One word after the other. Stetz was a smart man, I'd've known that without his book, and so he listened.

"And so what would this top dog eat?"

"Jackson's twelve bookie boxes, the recorders I mean, a paper tellin' you how to use'em, the phone numbers he got for his customers t'call, and the phone numbers of those customers."

"And what do I give?"

"You put out the word that Jackson's outta business. That way nobody got a reason to wanna see him dead. That and one other thing."

"Money."

I shook my head. Everything up until that moment had been window dressing. It was all bells and whistles to get the gangster's attention. Sure, I was trying to save Jackson Blue. But he would either survive the transaction or he wouldn't; my real business was to save my job, my life, and Bonnie Shay. "I got a friend. She's in trouble with one'a your friends. She's willin' to make up but we got to know that your friend is too."

"What friend?" Stetz asked. His voice had gotten softer.

"Beam. Joseph Beam."

Stetz winced. "And your friend?"

"Her name don't matter. All that matters is that Beam think that she stole from him, but she didn't. She got somethin' but it was by mistake. She wanna give him back his property, that's all."

Stetz ran the four tips of the fingers of his left hand around his cheek; an insincere smile was on his lips. Maybe he was scared of Beam. Maybe he wanted to stay out of his friend's business. I had tossed out the bait; it tasted good, but now Stetz had to wonder if it was worth it to swim away from the school.

"What is it?" he asked.

"You know who Roman Gasteau is?"

"Yeah."

"Him an' Beam was movin' aitch. Somehow the last shipment they was movin' got lost. Beam thinks my friend stole it."

"Why come to me?" Stetz asked. But his eyes were saying tell me more. "Why don't you go to Joey?"

"I went to him. At least I tried. But he put his boys on me. Guys named Rupert an' Li'l Joe. They sapped me up at the Black Chantilly an' was about to kill me 'fore I run."

It was all I wanted to say. I knew that Stetz would be interested in any business that his people were doing. If he knew about it, then it was a sweet deal to get his drug back. If he didn't know, it meant that he'd have to do some house-cleaning. Either way I had a chance to get what I wanted.

"You say this was up at the club?" he asked me.

"In a toolshed around the side of the main house. I had to run right through the front driveway. Somebody musta told you about it."

"How much heroin?"

"Three pounds about. I don't know but it looks pretty pure."

"And you say they were selling it at the club?"

"I don't know about that. All I know is that Beam and Roman was in business wit' Rupert an' Li'l Joe."

Stetz played his cheek with his fingers some more and then asked, "What's in it for you?"

"They already killed Roman. They probably killed Roman's brother. My friend is still alive and I'd like to keep her that way. And if I can save Jackson, well, I'd like that too."

Stetz was a cat in the window, frozen before his leap. I was a bird on the ledge, praying for glass.

"When can you get me these telephone boxes?"

"Today. I could give you the aitch too."

"I don't like drugs, Mr. Rawlins. Not too much. You keep it for Joey, that is, if Joey still wants it."

I read a volume in his words but all I said was, "When and where?"

"We use a warehouse on Alameda sometimes."

"This afternoon?"

Stetz nodded. He was thinking about something.

"So it's a deal?" I asked.

"What?"

"You gonna lay off Jackson and let me give what I got over to Beam?"

"I'm going to talk to Joey. And I'll send somebody over to the warehouse at four to pick up your recorders."

He gave me the address and I moved to go from the room.

"Rawlins," he said to my back.

"Yeah?"

"How'd you know about the guy who wrote this book?"

"Rome is closer to Africa than it is to here, Mr. Stetz," I said.

CHAPTER 39

I called Raymond from a phone booth five blocks down from Philly Stetz's hideaway.

"Could you come meet me up at Mofass's place?" I asked the onetime gangster.

"What you askin', Easy?"

"I just need some company, Ray. It's tough men I'm dealin' with, but it's them makin' money. I just need a friend to stand by me."

"I ain't totin' no gun, Ease. I won't do that. Not yet."

"That's good," I said. "No need for trouble."

We met at Mofass's house and picked up Jackson. Mouse was driving a neighbor's car that he'd borrowed.

"Good-bye," Jackson said to Jewelle at the front door.

"Bye," she said. "You gonna call?"

"Come on, Jackson," I said.

"She sure is sweet," Jackson was saying in the car.

"You got better things to think about, Jackson," I said.

"What's that?"

I reached over and opened the glove compartment in front of him. Inside was a wax-paper bag. We all knew what it held.

"We gonna sell it?" he asked.

"We ain't gonna do a thing. All I need for you to do is to tell me where you got them bookie boxes hid."

"What?"

"We cain't cut you no slack without somethin' to trade, Jackson. Those bookie boxes are worth your life."

"They worth a lot more'n that."

I don't think he realized what he was saying.

Mouse, who was sitting in the backseat, put his hand on Jackson's shoulder. "Let up on it, Blue. It's time to move on."

Mouse had a persuasive hand.

Jackson's directed us to a Bekins storage warehouse on Pico where he had hidden his boxes. There were fourteen of them. Small black wooden cases, each one about double the size of a table humidor for cigars. Along with them he had a notebook full of the numbers of his clients.

"How do these things work, man?" Mouse asked Jackson. He had one of the boxes opened up across his lap, revealing a small transistor tape recorder and a large dry-cell battery.

"It's just a circuit switch," Jackson answered, a little

distracted. "After it rings, the switch go off an' the recorder go on. Then the one who call give their number and the bet."

When Mouse smiled the blue jewel on his front tooth sparkled.

We all went back to my house to wait. Jackson didn't want to go with us to meet Stetz, and we had an hour to kill.

"What the hell is this?" There was a dog turd in the middle of my neatly made bed.

I ran that dog all over the house. He scuttled under the couch and I yanked the thing away from the wall.

"He headed out t'the kitchen!" Mouse yelled out.

I ran right into the kitchen table and banged my thigh pretty bad. Jackson and Mouse tried to help me corner him but Pharaoh was too quick and they were mostly laughing anyway.

He finally took a bad turn into Feather's room and I got him in a corner. He started yowling like Death had gotten hold of him—he wasn't too far from wrong. The running had tired me and cut my anger a hair; if I had caught him a second sooner he would have had something to scream about. As it was I brought him out to the car and threw him in the trunk.

"Easy, you shouldn't let that dog get under yo' skin like that, man. He just a dumb dog," Mouse said. "He don't know what he doin'."

I would have hit anyone but Mouse. I might have been angry but I hadn't yet gone mad.

I cleaned up my bed and sulked on the couch. Jackson sat across from me, writing out his instructions on how to use the bookie boxes.

Mouse was squatting down next to the door—reading a book!

"You read?" I asked him.

"Li'l bit, brother. Li'l bit. EttaMae make me an' LaMarque sit'own sometimes an' go through his readin' lessons. I picked up a little."

"What's that you readin'?"

Mouse showed me his gold-encrusted teeth and said, *Treasure Island*."

I could feel the world turning under my feet. At any minute I could have gone spinning off into space. My children were changing every day. The headlines spoke of every kind of tragedy. You couldn't just live life anymore— that's how it seemed to me; you had to take notes and study charts just to know how to take the same road to the same place you'd always gone. And even when you got there, it was no longer the same.

The morning edition of the paper was still on the front porch. It said that the Bird Man of Alcatraz was dead. The man who had become a scientist in his cell. He was a hero down among my people because he was one white man who understood the odds that we faced. The prison officials interviewed said that he was just a criminal and that the public, and the movies, were mistaken in thinking that he was a good man.

They had no idea of goodness or honesty. They had power and that's what they thought was good.

I would have mourned the passing of Robert Stroud, but there was no time to grieve.

"All right, boys," I said. "Let's hit it."

Mouse slammed the book shut and put it on the floor. He stood up and smiled at me like he had done so many times since we were children in the Houston slums.

Mouse stood up but Jackson stayed in his chair.

"Come on, Jackson," I said. "You could wait for us in the car."

"I cain't, man. I cain't go."

I didn't press him. I didn't care. Jackson wasn't going to be of any help. And I was happy that he played the coward; at least that way the world made a little sense.

"Mouse," I called out.

"Yeah, Easy. I'm out here in the kitchen."

I heard a drawer close shut and then Mouse appeared. He met my eye with a somber face. I shuddered but I wasn't quite sure why.

CHAPTER 40

"Easy," Mouse said when we got out to his car, "what you plan to do with that dog?"

"Take him out to Primo. Primo could find some old lady like a dog like that."

"Gimme the keys."

"Naw, man," I said. "Leave him in the trunk."

"Gimme the keys."

"What for?"

"Dog could suffocate in there, Easy. Don't worry, I'll watch him. You drive an' I'll hold the dog."

Pharaoh was calm in Mouse's lap. We went downtown to Phyllo Place off Alameda. We made good time because the traffic was unusually light.

The address Stetz had given me was on the side of an alley that fed out onto the street. There was an arrow that pointed back into the alley for the number we wanted.

I parked the car and looked.

"Don't look good," I said to Raymond.

"But it's a business deal, right?" Mouse said, the soul of logic.

"Yeah, but it's a little close back there."

"They ain't after you, Easy. They just want them tape recorders. You ain't chargin', so why they wanna hurt you?"

The world had surely changed if I was going to listen to Mouse about what was safe and what wasn't. But he made sense. All I was doing was handing over a fortune to Stetz. And I was going to help Beam too. At least until I could tell Lieutenant Lewis about who had the aitch he was moving.

I took the turn into the alley and drove down the red brick path until I came to another turn that led to large garage door.

Mouse and I got out of the car, leaving Pharaoh whining inside.

We were in a deep hole of gray cement walls. It was a bright day, but there wasn't much sun that found its way to that gangster's door. The walls went up about nine floors but there was only one slender slit of a window.

I was happy that I'd remembered to bring my pistol—just in case Mouse was wrong.

"Watch it, Easy!" my friend yelled.

I turned and saw two men and then Mouse rammed me with his shoulder. Two shots sounded and echoed in the chamber of walls. The side window of the car exploded. Mouse pulled a meat cleaver from his belt and sent it twirling at the man who had taken the shots. It was Joey Beam. He was taking aim at me when the spinning blade hacked into the side of his neck.

The next two shots caught Mouse. He grunted each time he was hit and sank to his knees.

Sallie Monroe was swinging to shoot me when I leapt up on top of the roof of Mouse's car and landed on top of the fat gangster. He dropped his gun. I threw a left hook a little wide of his head.

Sallie jumped on me when I missed and bore me down to the ground with his weight. He was good with his girth. He'd let his stomach fall against my ribs and then, when I was stunned, he'd ball his fist and hit me in the head.

Sallie grabbed me around the throat and started to squeeze. Out of one side of my sight I saw Mouse trying to rise, but he failed. On the other side Joey Beam was doing his last dance lying flat on his back, yellow jacket sopping up his own blood.

Suddenly the little yellow dog came into view. He was snarling and snapping. I waited for his attack on Sallie to throw the big man off. I had remembered my pistol by then and only needed a little room to lay my hands on it. All I needed was Pharaoh's distraction.

That's when the yellow dog launched his attack on me.

I could hear the skin of my own ear ripping as Pharaoh lent his jaws to Sallie's cause.

Hatred surged in my blood. I boxed Sallie's right ear and then his left; I did it again and kneed him. Then I grabbed his neck like it was a fat eggplant and dug my fingers in and twisted with a frenzy that no sexual act has ever equaled in my life.

I watched Sallie's eyes go from life to death. And then I was up trying to stomp the life out of Pharaoh. But the dog was too quick and made it under the car.

"Easy." It was Mouse. He'd made it halfway to his feet and was leaning up against the wall. He had both hands over his chest. "Get the gun, man," he rasped. "Get the knife."

I got Sallie's gun, which was lying at his side, and the meat cleaver that had come from my own kitchen drawer. I took them to the car and helped Mouse into the seat.

Once behind the wheel I was flying backwards.

"Take me home, Easy."

"We better get you to a hospital, Ray."

"Naw, man. I'm okay. We don't wanna get tied up in no killin's." He was smiling. Smiling.

"How bad you hit?"

"Shoulder," he whispered. "Just in the arm."

"Man, I thought you said you were unarmed!" I shouted. I didn't know why. I wanted to say that I was sorry, I guess.

"I just said that I didn't have no gun, Easy. I got the knife at your house. You know a knife don't hardly even count." He laughed weakly and coughed hard.

I drove surface streets down to Compton, mainly to keep away from red lights. I wanted to keep moving. With the window busted out I didn't want people looking to see what we were up to.

When we were about half the way there I said, "Ray. Ray?" But he didn't answer. I looked over and saw him slumped almost exactly the way Idabell had been.

I wanted to go to the hospital, and I didn't want to. Raymond had told me that it was an arm shot. He wasn't bleeding that badly that I could see.

Maybe he'd just passed out.

*

I drove on.

Etta was there when I drove up on the lawn. She'd heard the car coming and came out to the door. She saw something in the way that I was driving and started to run.

"LaMarque, stay in the house!" she shouted.

I was letting Raymond out onto the lawn by the time she reached us.

His left eye was half open. The right one was closed. The shots were to his chest. Two wicked holes in his right breast.

"Lord, no," was the only wasted breath that Etta had. "LaMarque! Call the emergency number. Tell'em a white man's been shot here at the house."

She bent down to Raymond and lifted his head. With her ear to his mouth she checked his breathing. Then she stared hard into his face as if she were willing her life into his.

She turned to me and said, "You better git, Easy."

"Etta, let me explain."

"Go on, Easy."

It was a hard dismissal. I wanted her to forgive me, to tell me that it was okay. But she had turned her attentions to her man's deep wounds.

"Daddy!" LaMarque screamed as he came running up to the scene.

When he yelled again Etta stood up and pointed her finger in his face. "Hush!" she commanded. He wilted and she asked, "Did you call emergency?"

"Yes, ma'am."

"They sendin' a ambulance?"

"Uh-huh."

"Good. Now run get me the first-aid box."

LaMarque took off, avoiding looking at his father's still body.

"Etta," I said.

"Go on from me now, Easy," she warned.

"Etta, let me take him to the hospital."

"You done taken him enough now, Easy. Ain't today bad enough wit'out you killin' my husband too?"

"What do you mean?"

"Get away from me, Easy Rawlins. Get outta here."

CHAPTER 41

I left in Mouse's car. I had to leave, to hide the weapons.

Along the streets the traffic was light, but there were lots of folks out in front of their houses and stores. People were talking to each other with rapt attention on every corner. I saw more than one woman crying. Children walked listlessly, on the whole, not playing or laughing out loud.

The world was in sorrow, it seemed. Was Mouse's death so powerful? Did everybody feel it when a brave gangster died?

Maybe it was that I hadn't looked around me lately. Maybe a deep sadness had entered my community but I had been too busy being a workingman; a company man.

On the corner of Pico and Genesee there were three white men and one white woman standing at the bus stop, listening to a transistor radio that one of them held up.

I took the heroin from the glove compartment and went up to my house.

The front door to my house was open.

Inside, Feather was crying in Bonnie's arms. Jesus stood next to them holding one of Feather's favorite dolls.

"Easy." Bonnie had looked up. There was no smile on her face for me.

"Daddy, Daddy," Feather cried. She limped over to me and I lifted her into my arms.

"Jackson here?" I asked my son.

He shook his head to say no. His voice lost again. Lost again. Everything was lost.

"What's wrong?" I asked out loud.

"Haven't you heard?" Bonnie asked me.

I was as mute as my son.

"Kennedy. He's been shot. He's dead."

"What?"

I staggered across the floor with Feather and slumped down on the couch. I buried my head in Feather's chest too sad even to cry. Bonnie came to hold us and so did my son. My lungs were burning and my throat was sore from choked tears.

I lifted my head and noticed that there was blood on my little daughter's dress.

"What's this?" I said. "What's wrong with you, baby?" My voice was high from the strain.

"It's from your ear, Daddy," she said. "Wha' happened?"

As if on cue Pharaoh yelped down at our feet.

"Frenchie!" Feather cried. "Frenchie." She pulled away from my arms and hugged the dog on the floor.

I was too sad to be angry at the damn dog. I sat there thinking that he must have jumped into the car while I was helping Mouse. He'd probably hidden under the seat where I had put the gun and knife.

Gun and knife.

"Bonnie?"

"Yes, Easy?"

"Can you drive?"

"Yes."

I gave her the keys and Primo's address. I told her about the gun and knife under the seat.

"Take the kids out to his house. He'll know what to do."

"What about you, Easy?"

"I'm tired," I said. I still had unfinished business with Philly Stetz. I didn't know if he had sent Beam to kill me or not. I didn't know if he wanted the heroin or if he knew my address. I did know that I didn't want my children in the crossfire and so I sent them to Primo.

"Daddy." Feather had tears in her eyes. "Can't you come with us?"

"Later, honey."

"Can't I keep Frenchie, though?"

Being so weak themselves I think that children understand weakness better than adults. I couldn't say no to her then.

"Okay. Yeah, okay."

At the door Jesus was the last to leave.

"Did you take the money out of my closet, Dad?"

"No."

"It's gone." He looked at me with his solemn eyes.

Jackson Blue.

I turned on the radio and the TV. Both of them droned on and on about the assassination. I didn't understand a word of it but the sad sounds of grief resonated in my heart. My best friend was wounded somewhere, maybe he was dead. It was my fault and I couldn't even go to him and tell him that I was sorry.

I don't know how much later it was when the doorbell rang. I took the pistol from my pocket and went to the moth hole in the drapes next to the window. Then I went to the door and flung it open quickly. I jammed my cocked .38 into Rupert's nose and said, "You get killed comin' around here, fool."

Rupert wasn't a fool. He wasn't afraid either.

"I got sixty-seven hundred thirty-five dollars in this here briefcase," he said.

"You cain't spend it where you goin', brother."

"It's yours," Rupert said. "Mr. Stetz sent it."

I noticed then that Rupert's face had been battered, broken, and bruised. It was lopsided and swollen.

"Could I come in?" the big wrestler asked.

"No." I stepped back and held the gun lower.

Rupert handed the briefcase to me but I shook my head and then gestured at the ground.

"Put it down," I said. And, when he complied, "What's it for?"

"It's a'cause'a Mr. Beam."

"What about him?"

"Mr. Stetz send Mr. Beam with this here money to give you. But then when he tried to kill you—"

"How do you know that?"

"I was in the warehouse. Mr. Beam didn't know that. I was there for Mr. Stetz." Rupert rubbed his hand over his ruined face and I knew that the beating he got was for working with Beam.

"You saw what happened?" I asked.

Rupert's nod was cautious.

"An' you didn't do anything?"

"I was there to watch. That's all. Mr. Stetz didn't tell me to do nuthin' else."

Now I understood why Rupert showed no fear of me and my pistol: he was already filled to the brim with the fear of his boss.

I wanted to kill him. I really did. Behind me Walter Cronkite was almost ready to cry. Mouse was dying somewhere.

"Come on in," I said to Rupert. "Come on."

I turned off the TV. I would have poured a stiff drink if there was one in the house.

I waved at a seat with my gun. Rupert sat.

I laid the gun down next to me on the couch with my hand nearby.

"How'd you find my house, man?"

"Mr. Stetz made a call to the police. He axed a man down there t'get it. You know." Rupert winked and cocked his head to the side.

It was that easy. One call and Stetz could get information that I'd have to sweat blood for. I'd gone way over to the deep end of the pool.

But I didn't care.

"You know why Sallie and Beam tried to kill me?" I asked, feeling the superiority of my close-at-hand gun.

"Not exactly," the ex-wrestler said. He looked dumb and

ugly but Rupert was not a stupid man. "Mr. Beam called me to come with him but I told him no."

"What'd he say?"

"He said that he had the man that killed Roman and stole his drug. He said that he wanted me to throw in with 'im but I said that I worked for Mr. Stetz. He said that Mr. Stetz might not be on top forever but I told him that I had made up my mind and that was that." Rupert's resolve made him resemble a stone sculpture even more.

"But you worked for Beam before, right?"

"Yeah."

"Him and Roman and Sallie all worked together, didn't they?"

"Roman started comin' 'round the Black Chantilly a couple'a year ago. He was lookin' for a way in. He showed up with this girl, Grace Phillips, an' then Sallie Monroe got in on it. Sallie and Roman went to Mr. Beam after Roman got this job at the schools through Grace's boyfriend."

"What did they want with Beam?"

"They wanted to have a meeting with Mr. Stetz, but Mr. Beam said that he could fence whatever they stole through some people he knew downtown. Then Mr. Beam asked me to go with'em so he'd have a finger in the soup."

"And you went around stealin' from school to school?"

Rupert actually smiled. "Yeah. We'd get us a truck from the Board of Education garage and go out 'bout once a month on the average. It wasn't a lotta money, but it was somethin'. And then Roman hooked up this drug thing and the money got to be big."

"Which one of you killed Holland Gasteau?" I already knew the answer but it didn't hurt to ask.

"I don't know who killed him, or Roman neither. Holland wasn't in on the drugs. Sometimes we'd use his paper shack to hide what we took out the schools, but that was it."

Rupert gave me a hard stare and I put my hand on my gun.

He said, "I wished I wasn't never in it neither."

"What were you doing at Bonnie Shay's place?" I asked.

"Mr. Beam sent me. He said that he'd already killed somebody on that street and he didn't want to be seen."

"He tell you why he was after her?"

"Yeah. She stoled his drug. He wanted it back."

"And were you going to kill her?"

I guess Rupert had told so much truth that he couldn't switch over to lying too quickly; instead he just blinked and said, "She don't have a thing to fear from me no more."

"Yeah," I said. "I'll be sure to tell her that. So what's that money all about?" Somewhere the only president I ever loved was lying dead. Somewhere my closest friend was dying because of me. I wanted to despair but as long as I could keep asking questions I could keep on going.

"It's for you. Mr. Stetz told Mr. Beam to do right. He told him to make it up wit' you. He said that he wanted to see Mr. Beam throw the drugs down the toilet. He was givin' him a chance to do right. Mr. Beam was supposed to give you that money and then Mr. Stetz told me on the phone to bring it to you."

"An' how come the odd number?"

"I dunno, brother," Rupert said. "That's what he wanted me t'give you an' that's what I'm doin'."

"What's going to happen when they find those bodies in front of your boss's warehouse?"

"They won't find them."

"Why not?" I asked.

"They're right out there."

We had left the door open. The briefcase that Rupert brought was sitting outside. Beyond that was a big '57 Cadillac. I priced a car just like it when they were new; I remembered commenting on how roomy the trunk was.

"You can go on, Rupert," I said.

He stood and looked down on me.

"Yeah?" I asked him.

"Mr. Stetz said to tell you that he respects a man that stands up."

I considered telling him to take the money back to his boss. But sixty-seven hundred and thirty-five dollars was exactly one year's salary for my grade. Stetz was telling me that he knew my price and that he could afford it. That cash could help to pay for Feather's college. And besides, I had earned it. Paid for it with the most precious things in my life.

"You tell him that I still got his recorders. I'll bring 'em up to the Chantilly in a couple'a days."

I watched Rupert drive away in his makeshift hearse, then I went to the toilet and flushed away the drug.

CHAPTER 42

Mouse was at Temple Hospital. He was in a coma and fading out. Etta wouldn't come to the phone.

"Momma said that you should stay away from here, Uncle Easy," LaMarque told me over the phone.

"How are you, LaMarque?" I asked him.

"Is my daddy gonna die?" he cried.

I watched the news all evening. All about our president and his last days; his last moments. The whole world had turned on that tabletop with Idabell.

Bonnie called and I told her that she could come back in the morning.

"The kids need to be with you, Easy," she said. Her voice was so soft and caring. It had the promise of daylight and love; it was like the lie of peace and brotherhood that had hoodwinked so many of my kind.

She brought them home at just past midnight. She was driving my car, which Primo had fixed. Jesus went right up to his bed and Feather fell asleep on Bonnie's lap. She wanted to see the TV.

"I wanna see if he's still alive," she kept saying.

Somehow she didn't hear it when we told her that he'd stay dead.

"Why'd you kill Holland?" It was past three. Bonnie and I were lying together in the bed, fully dressed.

She sat up and asked, "What?"

I didn't have the strength to sit; I couldn't even repeat the question.

"What?" she asked again.

"It's okay, Bonnie. Nobody else knows. And I don't plan to tell anyone."

"Tell them about what? What are you saying?"

"It was when I saw that lipstick kiss you left on the note for me," I said. "That's when I knew for sure."

She shook her head, and I got up on one elbow to face her. I was tired.

"Holland had a big kiss, that same dark color, on his face."

If I wasn't sure before I was then. Bonnie's look of dismay gave her away.

"That's not enough, I know, but I was already half sure when I saw that broken green glass in your trash. You might have had the same kinda glasses as your friends, but probably not. All I wanna know is if you kissed Holland before or after you shot'im."

Bonnie put her hand over her mouth.

"He . . . " she said.

"Holland?"

"Yes. Yes. He called me after he got home. When he found Ida gone he called me looking for her. I told him that she was gone; that she had left the state. I thought that that would send him off looking for her. But instead he said that he wanted me to come over to his house right then."

"Why?" I felt sorry for her in spite of myself.

"He said that he had the forms I'd filled out the night I went back to the airport, the night I forgot those damned carpet balls. Roman kept the copies that the customs official gave me. He said that he had the balls too. They had official seals glued to them. He said that if I didn't come over right then he'd give it all to the police."

"And you went?"

"He was excited when I got there. He told me that he wanted sex and for that he'd give me back the things he had."

"Did you do it?"

She didn't want to nod. "I didn't . . . he raped me. He took me to the bedroom and made me. . . . He had this big black knife."

I remembered the pillows piled high in the center of the bed, the blood on the sheets, and the cut that I thought was a pimple above her breast.

"It was over in just a minute. Holland was laughing kind of crazy. He was all sweaty and his eyes were shiny, like he had a fever. He put on his clothes and then when I asked him for the carpet balls he laughed and told me that I was going to work for him. He said that I owed him because of what Ida did."

"And so you killed him?"

"He said that I was going to be his new wife now that Roman was dead and Ida was gone. He made me get dressed. He made me sit on his lap and kiss him. It was like you said. I got the gun from his drawer while he was in the bathroom. I shot him. I did."

"He told you that Roman was dead?" I asked.

"Yes."

"And then you called Idabell at the school and told her, right?"

"I told her to come over but I didn't say that Holly was dead. We packed her things. I took my carpet balls and she took the croquet set. I took the glass because I just didn't know what to do with it." She looked me in the eye as if to say that she couldn't help it; that she'd had to kill him.

I was in no place to pass judgment.

I slept on the sofa that night. In the morning I drove her back home while the country mourned JFK.

I went to Arno T. Lewis from Bonnie's house and told

him that I couldn't find Idabell. He told me that they'd identified Idabell's corpse the night before.

I had found, I said, that Bill Bartlett was Holland's partner in the little paper route business that worked out of the shack that held the stolen goods. A few days later there was an account in the paper of how Roman and Holland and Bartlett were in business stealing from the schools. Roman, who had obtained his job under an alias with forged references, had abused his power as a night-time building consultant. In a falling-out among thieves, the article speculated, Bartlett had killed Roman and then Holland. Later on, after meeting with Bartlett at White-head's restaurant, Idabell Turner was found dead.

Traces of heroin had been found and Bartlett was being sought for questioning. However, his house had been broken into and a goodly quantity of blood had been found. Foul play had not been ruled out in his case.

Jackson Blue disappeared with Jesus's life savings.

For a week the nation mourned the passing of JFK. Everybody wondered would things ever get set straight again; they never did.

I wanted to call Bonnie, but Holland Gasteau's lip-branded corpse came to mind whenever I thought of her. Holland and also Sallie Monroe. Sallie's death had settled into my finger bones. I found myself rubbing my hands together with the strange feeling that my fingers had gone numb.

After the week was out I got the courage to go down to Temple Hospital. EttaMae hadn't shown up for work at all, nor had she answered her phone.

I had friends at the front desk. They sent me to the intensive care unit to talk to a woman named Norva Long. I asked her about Mouse.

"Dead," she told me.

"What?"

"Doctor told Mrs. Alexander five days ago that it was only a matter of a day or two. She said no and that she was gonna take him home. But the doctor wouldn't release him." Norva's tone took the doctor's side.

"An' he died?" I asked.

"I was on duty with an orderly named James Pope. There was supposed to be another man but he came down with flu and stayed home. Maybe if he was with us we could have stopped her, but..." Norva twisted her lips and shook her head. "But I doubt it."

"What happened?"

"EttaMae come about two in the morning. I told her that visitin' time was over and that's the last thing I remember, except her ham fist."

EttaMae had a strong arm.

"James said that he tried to grab her," Norva said. "But she threw him up against a wall and laid him low with a metal tray. James was two floors down with a concussion for forty-eight hours. His momma say they gonna sue."

"What happened to Raymond?" I asked.

"Front desk said that she carried him out the front door in her arms. The security guard was gonna take her but then she come out with his gun. He said he wasn't gonna get in no shoot-out with a woman."

"Why wasn't any of this in the paper?"

"They kep' it pretty quiet, I guess. James prob'ly get some money out of it, after all."

"Then you don't know that Raymond's dead," I said. "He could be alive."

When Norva shook her head it broke my heart. She was sorry to tell me that Mouse had been in a coma and that he had been steadily fading over the days. Their house was abandoned. There were still dirty dishes in the sink.

I was in the maintenance office a few days later waiting to interview the replacements for Etta and Mouse. When the door slid open I was surprised, and not very happy, to see Sergeant Sanchez. He'd come alone.

"Mr. Rawlins," he said from the door.

He wanted for me to say come in, and I did.

He came up to my desk, did not offer to shake hands, and sat down.

"I don't like you, Mr. Rawlins," he said straight out. "I just came from your principal's office and he doesn't like you either."

"You come all the way down here to tell me that?"

"No. Lewis has me looking for evidence about Bill Bartlett. I told him that he's wrong about that but I guess you have more friends than I knew about."

Our eyes met and we were equals at last.

"Were you here when Bartlett was?" he asked.

"No," I said truthfully. "I replaced the man but we never met."

"I know that you were in it, Ezekiel. And when we find Bartlett I'm going to prove it."

I didn't think that he'd ever locate Bartlett. If I'd read the man right he was too smart to stay in L.A. He was a black man who was implicated in the murder of other black people. There wouldn't be any national manhunt. They'd wait for him to be arrested on some other charge and then hope that fingerprint checks would do their job. But Bartlett wasn't the kind of crook who was arrested often, if ever. And even if he did get caught, he didn't have anything on me. I was innocent of everything except the murders of Sallie Monroe and Raymond Alexander. One I regretted and the other haunted me.

The phone rang as Sanchez was leaving.

"Where's my car, Easy?" John asked in my ear.

We drove around L.A. that evening picking up cars. We went up to the hill behind the Black Chantilly to retrieve Primo's wild roadster. I paid Primo by letting him sell Mouse's car off for parts. I retrieved the bookie boxes and dropped them off at the Chantilly. To Philly Stetz, but Rupert took them.

It was when we were headed over to Bonnie Shay's block that John got serious with me.

"Easy, I thought you had got yourself out the street," he said.

"Yeah, me too."

"You know you can't be livin' like this, man. You too old for this shit. Things gettin' serious in this town, Easy. People turnin' mean. Even Mouse got hisself killed."

"I know, John." I said it so softly he might not have heard.

"Easy, you need a woman," John said. "A woman who wants a home an' ain't gonna take no shit."

Bonnie Shay came to my mind. She smiled and carried no weapons.

We picked up John's car and drove back to his house, me in Alva's Buick and him behind his own wheel. I knew that Alva had made some headway against me, because John didn't invite me in.

"I'll drive you home, Easy," he said.

On the way I asked him about Grace.

"I did what I could, Easy. After a day and a half she called that white man and he came and got her. She said she was gonna try'n go straight."

We drove almost the whole distance in silence.

Two blocks from my house he said, "You can't be out here actin' like you can do anything an' get away wit' it, Easy. You ain't drinkin', but you might as well be, the kinda life you live."

Pharaoh greeted me with a snarl at the front door. The children were already asleep. I sat down in a chair with a glass of lemonade. The little yellow dog curled down, just out of reach, and bared his fangs. He'd tasted my blood and was hungry for more.

As the days passed I began to accept him as a part of my life; the dark, dangerous part that always threatened. As long as Pharaoh was around snarling and cursing I'd remember the kind of trouble that a man like me could find.

I only had two choices. One was straight whiskey. Instead, after nine days, I dialed a number.

"Yes?"

"Hey, Bonnie. It's Easy."

There was a long silence and then a cough.

"Hello."

"I wanted to say hey," I said. "I mean . . . I wanted to see you."

"I'm sorry, Easy, but I'm leaving for Paris tonight."

"For good?"

"No. Just for a few days. But I'm changing my home city back to Paris at the end of the month. I'll still be working this route but I'll be staying there."

"Oh."

"Well," she said. "I've got to get ready."

"Uh, yeah, but . . . "

"But what, Easy?"

"But I need to see you, Bonnie. I mean, I really do. I can talk to you and I need that, I mean I really need it." I could only hope that she understood how hard it was for me to beg.

"Can you hold it for a few days?" Her voice was gentle.

"Yeah. I been holdin' it seems like forever. A few more days won't mean a thing."

"I'll be back Friday morning. You could call me then," she said.

"What time?"

"Any time, Easy."

"An' we could talk?"

"Sure. If you think you can. I mean seeing everything you know about me."

"None of that matters, Bonnie. I trust you. I know you did what you had to do."

Neither of us said a word for the next five minutes.

"I'd like to talk, Easy."

"An' we could get together too," I said.

"Maybe."

When I hung up I felt as if I was an astronaut who had completed his orbit of the earth and now I was pulled by some new gravity into a cold clean darkness.